THE

NIGHTBIRD'S

SONG

JOSEPHINE DEFALCO

Flint Hills Publishing
www.flinthillspublishing.com

Author's Note: This book is based on actual historical events but is a work of fiction and does not depict any actual persons, deceased or alive.

ISBN 10: 1517174074
ISBN 13: 9781517174071

Dedication

For those who survived, that the rest of us may follow.
And of course, to Jenna Rose.

Prologue

The Sonora Desert finds its beginnings in central Mexico, reaching upward into the southern United States. Some look upon it and see nothing but a colorless expanse of emptiness. Others see beyond the glaring sun and recognize the life that springs from the land.

The spiny lizard that spends his spring afternoons resting on a slab of smooth, gray slate, finds comfort in the sun's warmth. The line that parts his mouth turns upward in a mocking, contented smirk. His brown and green scales glimmer in the glowing rays; his eyes gently close, parting only now and then to assess his surroundings. He is comfortable in his home, but on a summer day you will not find him foolish enough to scorch his belly on the burning stone. He watches daylight pass until the white-hot sun cools to an orange glow. It fades behind the purple mountains, casting pink rays across the parched soil. If he is lucky, monsoon rains will pass from the Gulf of Mexico, washing away the painful dryness, refreshing the air with the earthen fragrance of the creosote bush. It is then that he leaves his shelter to seek insects stirred by the cooling rains. The lizard fills his belly, rests by the damp dirt of a running wash and crawls into his hole, satisfied that another day has passed. He and his ancestors have come to know that the desert pays homage to no one. They are there because they have survived.

In the Arizona Territory, the Mule Mountains rise from the desert floor, providing reprieve from the unforgiving land. Within the canyon walls a different life stirs. Oak and sycamore trees tremble with the slightest breeze, making a pattern of lacy light on the amber canyon walls. Here and there a projection of light struggles between the leaves, highlighting a winged creature that bursts through its path. At the bottom lies a narrow trough that could be called a creek if it carried water in all seasons. Instead it serves to collect the

1

precious fluid, filling for a moment's time with the moisture from a sudden rain storm.

It is here that the desert natives wander out of their environment to mingle with the greenery. A prickly pear cactus can be found hiding in feathery ferns and lavender clover. Sleek antelope with their caramel coats, and bristled, mud-colored javelina are drawn to this canyon, seeking relief from the desert heat. At a distance, a Gambel's quail calls, "ca-hoo-hoo" to her chicks, scampering through a thicket of trees. Two worlds have collided, but they choose to blend.

When copper was discovered seeping from the mountain walls, men flocked to Mule Canyon. Filled with lust for wealth and the power it would yield, they took chances in this hostile, unsettled land. Beyond their dreams, they hoped fate would lead them to the bonanza.

In neighboring Tombstone, the seed of silver brought thousands to its door. Small mining communities named Contention City, Charleston, Gleeson and Total Wreck sprung up like orange poppies on the heels of spring rains. Everywhere the territory filled with an anxiety that someone from somewhere would get someplace first, claiming the precious metal for himself. Exploiting the land was not a concern.

Hills swelling with miners and fortune seekers were challenged by the Apache people. Their cruelty in dealing with the invaders failed to extinguish the white man's hunger for riches. Anglos convinced themselves that it was not greed that drove them, but their American obligation to manipulate uncharted land for optimal productivity. In response to the warring Apaches, Camp Detachment, later known as Fort Huachuca, was settled to exterminate the threat of remaining Indians. As the settlers saw it, all Indians were murdering heathens, and the only good Indian was a dead one—or at the very least, one corralled on a reservation.

Chapter 1

Bisbee, Arizona Territory, Summer 1905

The birthing room was thick with the damp summer air making breathing difficult. Occasionally a breeze from an open window would reach into the room, offering intermittent comfort.

"Oh no. Oh God, it's starting again." Brenna was gasping in shallow pants, getting little relief for her efforts.

"Marita, come here, come to my back so I can push."

"But *Señora,*" Marita argued, "I cannot be at both the front and the back at the same time. Who will catch the baby?"

Brenna's jaw tightened, followed by a deep breath. "There won't be any baby if I can't push it out. Come here now!"

Marita scurried, perching herself behind Brenna, helping the laboring woman by supporting her back. She had chosen a good day to wear a black skirt. Blood stains would not show after wash day. One side of her red peasant blouse slipped off her plump, brown shoulder. Her warm, strong hands were comforting to Brenna's aching back.

Brenna turned to the side of the bed, averting the mahogany footboard. A gripping urge to bear down overwhelmed her. She released a low, groaning moan that sounded anything but human, and then, holding her breath, legs spread wide and trembling, she summoned all her energy to expel the baby. Her knees flopped to the side while she took a deep recovery breath and filled her lungs with fresh oxygen.

She peered between her legs to check on her progress, but a towering belly hindered the view. Still panting, she struggled to speak. "Look, look, Marita. Tell me if you see the head."

3

"*Si, si,* it is here. Come on, push again." Marita grabbed a sheet, preparing to receive the baby. Again the ritual began. Inching its way into the world, a wet head, covered in sticky red hair, finally emerged. "Wait, wait," Marita commanded. "I must check for the cord." She carefully probed around the baby's neck, unable to locate the umbilical cord. "You are good, push again." And then the baby shot out like a bar of soap through wet hands. Brenna smiled, sighed and dropped back on the bed.

"Ah, a little girl, and she is a fat one too." The baby's cry failed to distract Marita from her mission. The blue cord stopped pulsing. In two places, four inches apart, she tied string around the cord, marking the place to be cut. Soon mother was severed from child. The infant was bundled in a clean tattered sheet. Brenna pushed herself back toward the headboard, her black, wavy hair clinging to the sides of her face. Marita walked to the window to get a better look at the new infant that was fussing at her. The baby immediately calmed with the swaying of the Mexican woman's body.

"Manuel will be surprised, no?"

So will James, thought Brenna. It was a fine thing to be birthing a child with the hired help. Why did he have to go running off to Tombstone with her so close to her time?

A door slammed downstairs and the sound of rapid footsteps and raspy breathing made their way to the bedroom.

"Mrs. McEvoy? Mrs. McEvoy?" In staggered the obese midwife, red-faced and ill fit to be climbing the steep staircases of the mountain community. Her white hair was slicked back with body oil that had collected for several weeks. It was molded in a bun at the nape of her neck. The paisley dress she was wearing was splattered with tell-tale food stains indicating she had left in the middle of cooking. To Brenna's relief she tied on a clean, white bib apron.

Brenna suspected it was not for her benefit, but so Mrs. Blake could protect what was left of her dress.

The midwife scanned the room, resting her gaze on Marita, still cradling the new baby. "Well, I'll be. Honestly, dear, you're gonna have to give me more time to get here." Brenna was still in a nasty disposition.

"I would be pleased to give you more warnin', Mrs. Blake, but it wasn't as if I had a day's notice." Marita raised an eyebrow to the midwife as a weak apology for her employer's bad manners.

"Well, a course you didn't dear. Least I can do is help with the afterbirth. Why don't you let me have a look?" Brenna fell back into the soft pillows while the pudgy hands of the big woman massaged Brenna's abdomen. Shortly, the bloody sponge emerged, and Mrs. Blake deposited the placenta in a white porcelain bowl. As she inspected, she immediately reported her findings. "Looks good and I'm satisfied. Now give me that little one, and I'll clean her up."

Mrs. Blake went about her business, talking gently to the newborn. "Yes, ma'am," she continued, "fit as can be." She handed the freshly washed bundle to her mother. Her cooing voice halted and was replaced by a serious tone like a grandmother about to recite a lecture. She wagged her fat finger at Brenna. "Now you be sure to get some rest. Will Marita be stayin' with you for the night?"

"She'll be staying through the week," Brenna replied.

"That's good. A woman needs her rest and God knows men are no help. Takes a woman to help with a woman's needs."

Marita butted in. "*Si*, you rest now. We will go pick up Michael and Eric. Later we can show the baby to Manuel. He will be anxious to see her."

Brenna herself was anxious to hear what Manuel would say about the baby. She liked Manuel. He was a hard worker and had a kind heart. Since he was Marita's baby brother, she knew Marita would keep him in line. They were lucky to have found such a responsible Mexican.

For the first time Brenna got a good look at her newborn, bundled in a yellow flannel sheet. There were wisps of strawberry blonde hair crowning her head. Her eyes were very blue and likely to stay that way. Clumps of white, waxy coating still clung to the creases of her bright, pink skin. Mrs. Blake had dusted her with talcum powder, giving her that wonderful baby smell associated with new beginnings. She inspected fingers and toes, amazed by each perfect digit. Her little feet could be no longer than two inches, curling to her mother's touch.

"I think we will name you Sara, young lady." Finally, she had a daughter. What changes would she know in her lifetime? She would grow up in this bustling mining town, and hopefully both child and town would thrive. Bisbee was like a newborn itself, with the entire future ahead. It was funny how the birth of a child could reaffirm one's reason for living. The baby seemed uninterested in her mother or their brief conversation. Brenna arranged herself close to the infant. In no time at all both fell into a deep, dreamless sleep.

Several hours passed before Sara's wail startled Brenna into wakefulness. At first Brenna thought it was the cry of a cat, the piercing human-like strains she'd heard in the alleys during spring mating. Then she remembered the newborn that had entered her life earlier that day. The sun was setting, filling the room with a warm, lemony glow.

There was an impatient knock on the door and Marita entered. "We heard a cry. Did you get some rest? Can I bring in some visitors?" Before Brenna could sit up and straighten her cotton bed dress, Eric and Michael bound into the room.

No one would have suspected they were brothers. Eric, the oldest son, was stout and thick with dishwater brown hair that fell into a haphazard part to the left. His steel-gray eyes were almost lost in his white but freckled face, and his narrow nose seemed to draw his features inward. Michael stood a head shorter than his brother with hair as black as the bottom of a well. His warm complexion was splashed with a spray of freckles across his round nose, and his eyes mirrored melted chocolate drops.

Manuel politely hung back, too timid to enter his employer's sleeping quarters.

"Manuel, where are you?" Brenna called. "Come meet Sara." Manuel entered the room, his straw hat in hand. His black hair was covered with dust from the garden. A red bandanna around his forehead absorbed the moisture from his brow. Sweat left dark stains on the back of his blue work shirt, indicating it had been a warm day filled with hard work. "Tell me what you think of my new baby girl."

Manuel stood next to the bed, peering over the heads of the two boys eyeing their new sister. He held out his index finger to the tender newborn that instinctively held on tight.

"*Que bonita*, Mrs. McEvoy, she is beautiful. She has her father's coloring, doesn't she?"

"Yes, little Michael seems to be the only one with any hint of my dark Irish ancestry." Michael was gently stroking the baby's head when her face tightened into a frown. She opened her mouth and nothing came out. There was a pause and suddenly she was screaming. "Michael, what did you do to her?"

"Nothin' Mama. I was just petting her."

"It is that one," Marita said, pointing to Eric. Eric cast Marita an angry stare, knowing she had seen him pull back the baby's toes.

"Eric, you must be gentle," Brenna warned. "A baby is fragile. Will you please remember that?" Eric nodded in agreement, pretending to heed his mother's request. His eyes narrowed as he contemplated how he would get even with Marita. Brenna sensed his dislike for the Mexican woman, but she could never ask her to leave.

"*Señora,* are you hungry? I made your favorite lamb stew, nice and thick with lots of carrots and potatoes."

Brenna could almost smell the rich broth. "I'm starving, Marita."

"Good. I will change the baby and bring back a dinner tray. Come *niños*." They started to leave the room.

"Has anyone seen James?" Brenna asked. Both Mexicans gestured that they hadn't. "I suppose he'll be back sometime tomorrow. It's too late for another train to be coming from Tombstone."

They started to leave again when Manuel turned to face her. "Mrs. McEvoy, I'm so sorry I didn't make it back in time for Mrs. Blake to help you." Brenna gave him an appreciative smile. "We don't have much choice in these matters, Manuel." She turned her gaze to Sara. "Sometimes we have to step aside and let someone else take charge, and I think Sara did a fine job today."

* * * *

James's pallid hand ran across Rose's buttock, skimming the powder blue satin robe. He drew her close, kissing her hard and rough, oblivious to how it displeased her. His unshaven beard grated on her tender skin. She stiffened and turned her face, easing away from his grasp. "You leavin' now, honey? Why it isn't even one."

His answer was abrupt and to the point. "If I stay the night, I'll never make the morning train. I'll be back soon." "Oh sure," Rose retorted. "Another kid on the way and a sweet little woman at home. It will be a long time before you come to warm my bed again." She started to turn away when James grabbed her by the arm, seating her on a bare wood chair.

"Listen to me and understand," he demanded. He leaned over, close to the side of her face until his hot breath grazed her ear. "I go where I want and do what I want regardless of what is going on around me." His hand wandered to the inside of her thigh, tracing an imaginary line upward. His hand stopped and his voice softened. "You should have figured that out by now. I thought you were a bright girl, Rose." James stood, reaching into his wallet. "Maybe this will keep you from missing me while I am gone." He wadded up the money and placed it in her hand, giving her a quick kiss on the cheek.

When he opened the door to exit the crib, the noise and saloon smoke wandered in like a rambling spirit. She watched him descend the stairs as he disappeared into the crowd of drunks, miners and gamblers. James looked back at her one more time. Not wanting to disappoint him, Rose blew him a kiss, waving his money in the air. How much more convenient could this be? He gets his way; she gets his money.

Back in his respectable hotel, he washed. After inspecting his clothes for blonde hairs, he sniffed for perfume or other clues that might reveal his infidelity. It was a game to him. He didn't define it as something that would hurt Brenna; it was just an indulgence that he allowed himself. Still, it would cause a mountain of trouble if she discovered his other life. Exposing this situation would set him back financially and interfere with his standing in the community. There was no time for that kind of horse-play. After Brenna had the baby, he had to wait a respectable amount of time before returning to Tombstone.

* * * *

8

Early the next morning, James entered the bank to make his usual deposit before leaving town. He bought a copy of the *Epitaph,* appropriately named as the Tombstone newspaper. James settled down for a smoke while waiting for the train. Near as he could tell, Tombstone was in trouble. Hard as they tried, they couldn't keep water out of the mines. Any silver deposits were going to drown there before the miners and investors would get to them. No, he had to focus his interests on Bisbee. Somewhere in those hills there was more copper to discover and he was going to make it his copper.

James's imagination continued. He would be a wealthy man with his own copper claim. The community would come to him for advice and loans. Maybe he would start his own bank. He'd have loads of employees to direct, and he'd build a bigger house. He would move the family to Warren, the city with planned home sites, sewers, utilities, a park and a private club. Like a child anticipating Christmas, the urge to go copper hunting rose up inside of him, and he promised himself he would do just that when he returned home.

The house was very quiet when he entered the front door. On the way home from the station he had collected the mail from the post office in town. It was apparent that it had not been picked up for several days. At times Brenna seemed so helpless, and he felt like things would fall apart if he wasn't there to follow up on her. He started reading the envelopes, but changed his mind. He tossed the mail on his desk, deciding that it was best to stay on schedule and have some lunch first. The breakfast from the hotel had given him indigestion. Hopefully there was something besides Marita's spicy Mexican food to fill his stomach. As he made his way toward the kitchen, the swinging door flew open, nearly smacking James in the face.

"*Señor* McEvoy, you are home!" The Mexican woman seemed delighted to see him, something unfamiliar to James. She was always respectful but this was out of character. He became suspicious.

He replied in a monotonous tone. "Yes Marita. I just got in. I thought I would have a bite to eat before attending to business. What are you preparing for lunch?"

"I was heating leftover stew. *Señora* McEvoy, she had—"

"Ah, stew. Good. I don't think I could tolerate any chilies today." He rubbed his chest as if that would help ease his distress. "Bring me a bowl and some bread when the stew is hot." He turned to leave when again the swinging door flew open, this time catching the tip of his nose. He let out a yelp, like a pup that had been stepped on. In wobbled Brenna.

"James! I thought I heard you. When did you arrive?"

"Damn it, Brenna. Can't you be more careful?" He was so busy rubbing his nose he failed to notice his wife's waistline had shrunk. Marita gave him a dirty look as he left. Brenna stayed behind in the kitchen.

"I'll fix him good," Brenna told Marita. She lowered her voice. "Let him discover his new daughter on his own. That'll give him a start."

Sara was peacefully sleeping but due to awake within the hour. Brenna took advantage of the quiet and helped herself to lunch. She ate with Marita in the kitchen, and the two of them were soon joined by Manuel. Waiting for Sara to cry was like anticipating a cave-in.

There was a shocked look on the women's faces when James walked into the kitchen carrying the infant. Once in the conversation, they never heard the baby cry. Manuel, knowing the two women had been cooking up trouble, wanted to laugh.

"You didn't tell me," James said. Brenna, pretending not to care, returned to finishing her stew.

"You didn't give me a chance," she replied. James forgot his position and sat with the hired help to admire his latest achievement.

"I've named her Sara Marie," Brenna said. "Do you approve?"

"Sara Marie. Sara Marie McEvoy." He repeated the name, rolling it over in his mouth as if tasting a new wine. "Yes, I like the sound of that name. It's sensible. She was early, wasn't she? I mean, I never would have accepted the assignment in Tombstone if I knew your time was near."

"I had another week or two, but it all turned out just as well. Thank the Lord for Marita and Manuel. I'll be changin' her now."

She took the baby from James' arms and left the kitchen. Manuel and Marita rose from the table, collected their dishes and returned to work. James remained seated, still a bit off balance. Call it women's intuition, but that whore had been right. It would be quite some time before he returned to Tombstone.

Chapter 2

The lightning took control of the storm sending a flaming spear into the petrified ground. In response, the ground shuddered with pain, releasing a roar of thunder that scattered across the canyon. The angry storm woke Brenna, greeting her weary eyes with a flash of light. The mantle clock on James' nightstand read one-thirty a.m. It was close to Sara's feeding time, and it made no sense to return to sleep.

James had moved to the guest room to avoid the baby's night time disruptions. How had he put it? *"A man can't support his family and earn a paycheck without a proper night's sleep."*

"Unless it is to wake me for my wifely duties," Brenna mumbled out loud. There'd be none of that for a while, and it was clear to her that James had no use for her in her present condition.

Brenna stumbled out of bed, positioning the wooden rocker to face the window. While nursing the baby, she could enjoy the summer lightening breaking in the distant mountains. Lightning didn't frighten her. She was enchanted by its power and strength and knew to respect it. As a child, she had heard a story about a rancher that was struck by lightning. The electricity entered his shoulder and passed through his body, blowing off all ten toes. Brenna pictured the man's toes exploding like a string of firecrackers. Miraculously, the man lived. But still she wondered how odd it would be to go through life without any toes.

Brenna continued to stare out the window, looking over the small cottages below. From her mountainside home she could nearly see Brewery Gulch. The saloons were quiet for a Friday night. On payday one could expect the eager miners to gallop to the Gulch, anxious to part with their hard earned money. When the winds stood still and shapeless, the lively piano music escaped the saloons mingling with the laughter and shouting that spilled into the powdery dirt street. It was another side of life in Bisbee that Brenna did not know or understand.

Tonight the air was not still. Lacy curtains dressing the windows danced with each gust of wind. The atmosphere stirred like a witch's caldron, bringing with it the unforgettable smell of the desert rains. Some called it greasewood, others the creosote, but when it was drenched with a desert down-pour, the humble plant filled the static space with a cleansing fragrance that a person could never forget, no matter how far they wandered from the desert.

Sara tossed in the bassinet, alerting Brenna to her discomforts. Brenna diapered the baby with such efficiency that Sara hardly knew she was being disturbed. A gentle, sweeping motion settled Brenna and the child into the comforts of the cherry wood rocker. The polished wood conformed to her body's curves and like many family heirlooms, gave her a sense of past to present.

How she wished her mother was here to see the children, especially her new granddaughter. So many things would be different if Mum hadn't up and died. It would be her mother taking care of her now and not the hired help. Maybe she wouldn't have had to marry James. Maybe her Pa would have loved her more. So much to think about but no way to change the past. Life would be lived just as it was presented, yet one thing was certain. She was better off than many others in Bisbee. If she had to find some good in James' obsession with money, there was no doubt that he provided well for his family.

The storm was progressing with urgency and began to expel large drops of water from they sky. Rain was badly needed, and the thirsty ground sucked it up without hesitation. It began collecting in the gullies and low spots of the streets, rushing to any path it could take. Anxious to meet up with its own kind, the water gathered momentum on its quest to unite with the San Pedro River.

How many times had the rain defeated this struggling town? The fury of the monsoons was a force that only God himself could control. Brenna recalled her childhood and how the floods had brought suffering and destruction to Bisbee. She must have been six, seven at most, when the worst one struck.

"Warning shots are comin' up the canyon, John. What are we to do?" Brenna watched her mother, Clare, standing in the middle of their tiny adobe home. She was paralyzed except for the wringing of her hands. Brenna had always thought of her mother as being so pretty and petite with her auburn hair and milky complexion. But in the light of the flickering kerosene lamps, she saw a stranger's face, carved with worry lines and reddened from the sun's abuse. The desert had withdrawn its share of her youth, and this time the stress seemed more than she could bear. Brenna raced to her side, hoping a daughter's touch would distract her mother from her terror. Instead she felt the woman shaking like a cornered animal.

"The wind is screamin' at the door like a Banshee. It wasn't like this in Ireland or even Caleefornia. God is angry with us," she rambled, "indeed, he is angry."

"Hush now, Clare." Brenna's father tried to reassure his wife. "We've but a few leaks in the roof, and we're safe enough from the flooding waters. The shots are to warn the folks in the low lands. Now tend to those buckets before the entire house melts away. We'll put up fresh mud soon as the rains stop."

But the rains refused to stop. The roar of the water could be heard thrashing through the dry gullies, tearing at the gap in the crumbling desert ground. When a wall of water came crashing through town, it took with it the lives of a few unfortunate souls and the hearts of those left behind. How quickly the land could reclaim its own. Homes splintered like shattered glass, washing the contents with mud and debris, blending cherished possessions back into the earth. At one point the hats from Mr. Schwartz's gentlemen's store could be seen bobbing on the water like ducks on a swim. One man stood on a corner shooting the drowning livestock and pets, destined to perish in the raging waters.

The rains spared their home, but not without undercutting a corner of the house. It was then that Pa had enough and moved his family to a home made of bricks. High on a hill they would be protected from harm's way. But Mum would never live long enough to enjoy her life there.

That was the summer mother died of the pox. Smallpox, typhoid and dysentery made expected visits during the hot months when disease flourished in the shallow community wells. The flooding waters inoculated the community, and infection spread as deadly as wildfire in the desert brush. One house after another was marked with the yellow quarantine flag. One day the flag came to rest on the Shannon home.

Mum was never very strong. Recovering from Ginny's birth was never complete, like a fracture that wouldn't heal.

Neighbors came to help neighbors, first assisting those devastated by the flood, later tending to the sick and burying the dead. Mrs. Brown and Mrs. Whelan helped prepare Clare's body for the funeral.

"But, Pa," Brenna protested, "why do we have to go stay at Mrs. Whelan's house?"

"Because a child's got no place bein' here now. When they're done preparing your Mum, you can come back home. Now go on, Brenna. They got lotsa kids there for you to play with."

That idea sounded appealing to Brenna, so she grabbed Ginny's hand and trotted down the hill. But the oldest Whelan daughter wanted nothing to do with entertaining the grieving youngsters, so after a time, Brenna returned home dragging Ginny behind her.

"Shhh. You be quiet now. I gotta make sure those ladies are gone, or we're gonna get a whippin'. Keep your head down." Brenna peeked over the window sill and saw the women working on her mother. White handkerchiefs covered their nose and mouth. She stole a glance to the right, then the left. Pa was nowhere to be seen, so she continued to watch.

Mum lay on a board, naked as a new day. They were washing her with a cloth. Mrs. Browne left for a moment and returned with one of Ma's black dresses. They finished dressing her and laid her down again. By now Ginny was tired of being quiet and ran off behind the house. Brenna should have chased after her, but she continued to watch.

They tied a white rag under Ma's chin and over the top of her head to close her mouth. Then they closed her eyes and weighted the lids with two big coins.

"Where's her rosary?" Mrs. Browne asked.

"I believe it's on that chair, yonder," Mrs. Whelan responded while nodding to a corner of the room. She had taken Mum's arms and folded them across her abdomen. "I can't get her fingers to bend," she complained.

"Ah, no matter. Just put her rosary in her hand and she'll be fine, God rest her soul. She struggled so hard to die."

"Did Mr. Shannon get the saltpeter?" Mrs. Brown asked.

"I believe he's bringing some from the apothecary when he comes back from town."

"Good, good. We'll need to keep bathing her face or it's going to turn in this burning heat. The family will never be able to lay eyes on her." Just then Ginny banged on the back door, demanding to be let in. "Oh goodness, we got done just in time. I hear the girls coming home. Quick, cover her with that sheet." Brenna ran for the back door and sat in a chair like she'd been there the whole time.

By day or night, neighbors took turns sitting with the body. There were stories of people rising from death or hungry animals wandering into the house to maul the dead, so the body was carefully guarded. The next day a river of town folk flowed in and out of the home, expressing their sympathy for the motherless family. Mum was laid out in a pine box lined with white satin. Candles glowed atop tables and sills, casting an eerie light. Visitors entered, kneeled by the coffin in prayer, and usually headed for the food table unless intercepted by Pa. If the girls were nearby, they received the expected pat to their heads. Others would stroke their cheeks and ask how they were doing. Brenna didn't know half the people parading through the house. Ginny barely knew what was going on. When no one was watching, Ginny and a Whelan boy lifted the top of the coffin.

"That don't look like Mum," Ginny remarked, peering into the coffin. Brenna came over to inspect.

"That ain't Mum," Brenna replied. "Our Mum's dead." When she spoke those words, a pain welled up inside her chest, creeping into her throat. She began wailing, uncontrollably, and the more women that tried to comfort her, the more people started grieving. Finally the priest decided it was time to start The Rosary and with that, the room settled down.

After Mum was laid to rest in the graveyard, Pa seemed more distant than ever. Sometimes Brenna felt like a shadow and nothing more. Ginny had those feelings too, but she was different from Brenna, almost glad to be left to herself. Pa kept a strict rule on them, making sure they were kept busy with chores. Somehow, Ginny always managed to get out of most of hers and slip off into the night.

"Ginny, where are you off to?" Brenna whispered from her bed.
"You mind your own, Bren," she threatened. One leg hung out the window as she prepared to leave their room.

"At least tell me where you're goin'."

"Off to the theater, and not a word to Pa. There's a new troupe in town. Me and Billy Parson are going to try and sneak in."

"Pa don't like Billy. Says he'll lead you down the road to trouble."

"I don't care what Pa thinks. All he worries about is how much work he can find for us. You'd think with Marita we'd have some time for ourselves. We'll I'm taking my time now. Mind you, not a word to Pa or I'll take it out of you later."
Brenna knew Ginny would make good on her promise to whip her, but Ginny needn't worry. Brenna wasn't one to squeal. Although she felt a need to protect her younger sister, she kept her words to herself.

* * * *

It was a couple years later when Ginny disappeared. Pa had gone mad trying to find her and had all but given up when a note was left on the doorstep addressed to John Shannon.

"What is it, Pa? What is it?" Brenna had watched her father's face while he opened the envelope, hoping for some sign of its content. His thick hands shook with anticipation. The note was in Ginny's hand, so they assumed she was all right.

At first his complexion blanched. He dropped into the closest chair, still clutching the note in one hand. The other he ran over his face, again and again, trying to wipe away the words he'd just read. His face got redder and redder until Brenna was sure the blood under his skin would rupture like a raised blister.

"Is she all right, Pa? Is she?"

"She's gone," he replied. "She won't be coming back." In fear, Brenna dared not ask any more. Weeks passed before a letter came addressed to Miss Brenna Shannon, posted from San Francisco. Brenna ran to Marita.

"Marita, she's married! She's Mrs. Levy now. Why isn't that a Jewish name? Ran off with some manager from the theater troupe that was passing through town. He promised to make an actress of her. She always did have a thing for shows and carnivals."

Marita laid a soapy dish in the basin and wiped her hands on her muslin apron. Approaching the impressionable young girl, she cupped her hands to Brenna's cheeks.

"*Mija,* I know. I have known for some time. Manuel was out drinking the night your sister ran off. He saw her leaving the back of the show house. She held a suitcase and walked with a strange man. Your sister was not happy here. Sometimes it is better this way."

"But why didn't you tell Pa?"

"It was not our place to tell *Señor* Shannon. Some things must be done for themselves. Your sister, she knew your Papa would not tell you, so she wrote to you. She still needs you, Brenna. That is good. But you must go on with your own life, *mija.* You are getting older now and must think of making a home for yourself."

That night, Brenna couldn't sleep. She was only seventeen, well, almost eighteen, and terrified at the thought of getting married. Why, she hadn't even courted yet. Who'd marry her anyway? Couldn't she stay on and live with her father? For months she held it inside her like someone withholding bad news.

On uneasy evenings when her thoughts would wander, the fear would creep back into her heart, like a vine weed choking a flower garden. She wanted to be special to Pa, like a precious jewel. What would she sacrifice to hold his hand, to share a worry or even a happy thought? It hadn't been that way with Mum. She could share anything with Mum. A faint smile crept across her face as she recalled the day she had been looking for rainbows. Brenna had returned home, soaking wet. Her mother had spied her sneaking into the house and demanded an explanation.

"Brenna, what have you done to yourself? You're wet to the bone like an old alley cat and your boots are all mucked up. What have you to say for yourself, child?"

Quickly Brenna tried to think up excuses, but opted for the truth, just like Sister Catherine's ruler had drilled into her head…and her knuckles. She looked at her muddy shoes and mumbled she'd been looking for rainbows.

Brenna's mother seemed astonished. "Lookin' for what?" Brenna was afraid she'd start crying, but turned her gaze up into her mother's face to continue her tale.

"Grandma Devine, from Ireland, she told me that if it rains and the sun dare poke his head through the storm clouds, well, if you shake your fist at him and then turn your back to him, then he'll show you a rainbow for your trouble." Brenna's face brightened. "And you know what, Mum? It works! It really works. I held my fist to the sky and kept my arm up good and straight. I turned around and there it was, a beautiful rainbow with every color I've ever seen." Brenna extended her tiny hands as far as she could, demonstrating its size. "Mum, it reached across the whole sky."

Clare stood still a moment, hands on hips, blinking in amazement at the wisdom of her young daughter. Then her face broke into a smile. She dropped to her knees, brushing wet strands of hair from her youngster's face.

"It was a grand rainbow, was it? And why didn't you call me out to see it, you little devil?"

For the rest of the afternoon Clare put her hard desert life aside. She stoked the fire to heat the small adobe room. She removed Brenna's wet clothing, wrapping her in a soft rag quilt, patched with every scrap of cloth the young family had ever worn. Together they had tea by the winter's fire until the thunderous clouds had passed. It was one of the last happy moments Brenna could recall because by the end of the next summer, Mum was dead.

* * * *

Mrs. O'Meara buried her husband about the same time Mum died. She was a young widow woman with two small boys. When Brenna discovered Pa was courting her, she would have been no more surprised to see snow in the desert. Marita had caught Brenna crying, and only then had she shared her fears.

"Do not worry," Marita had told her. "Your father has cared for you all of your life. Why would he hurt you now?"

Brenna did not explain how he'd hurt her already. She felt hollow inside, like a fruit without a seed. Days passed into months, and then her father announced there would be a guest for dinner. He was inviting a young Irishman that worked with him at the Copper Queen Mining Company.

"Make sure you dress nice," her father advised. "Tie up your black mane and look tidy." Brenna realized her fate. This was to be her match if her Pa was to have his way. It was then that she gave up the fight. What would be would be.

He was a nice enough man, Mr. James McEvoy, but not one to make your blood run hot. He was pale, so very pale that it hurt her eyes to look at him for any length of time. His fire-red hair was a startling contrast. It was doubtful he had lived in the Arizona Territory very long with his tender, white skin.

She could feel him sizing her up while they held polite dinner conversation. When he took a forkful of beef, his blue eyes would dart to the side to look at her, almost as if he was stealing something from her soul. Perhaps he was attracted to her dark color. Maybe he was repelled by her strong chin. He watched her speak, pretending that what she said was important. But Brenna knew he was tallying his conclusions as to her prospects of being a suitable wife.

When they moved to the sitting room for dessert, he held back to watch her cross the room, like a coyote stalking a rabbit. But she wouldn't run anymore, and if she must be captured, she'd play the game on her grounds.

"I'll help with the coffee," she said, casting James an inviting smile. Even her father caught the flirtation. Under different circumstances, she would have been inviting her father's wrath, but tonight she could get away with it.

"So what do you think?" Marita asked while collecting the coffee spoons.

Think about what?" Brenna replied.

"Your young man."

"My young man?" Brenna fumbled with the cream pitcher, nearly dropping it.

"You are nervous, no?"

"A little. He talks an awful lot about money."

"Maybe he has lots of it," Marita suggested. She placed the silver coffeepot on the matching tray. "Maybe you should get to know your young man a little better."

* * * *

It was the next week before James asked to see Brenna again. Her father seemed pleased when she requested permission. Most of the white, Catholic community was at the picnic that day, including her father and Mrs. O'Meara. She was clinging to his arm like sap stuck to a tree trunk. Brenna wondered when Mrs. Katherine O'Meara would become Mrs. Shannon.

"What's the matter, Brenna?" James noticed that she was no longer directing all her attention to him.

"It's my father. I think he's going to ask Mrs. O'Meara to marry him." James was quick to defend him.

"Your father is the kind of man that needs a woman by his side. He's waited a long time to court again." James grabbed Brenna's hand, taking her by surprise. "This town can be lonely for a man without a companion. I know that feeling well." James looked deep into her eyes, casting a piercing look that frightened her. Had she been able to move, she would have run for her very life.

Her heart began a rampage in her chest. She was certain he'd hear it or see it throbbing under her cotton bodice. For the first time in her life a man was showing interest in her. For once, she felt like she was part of something. Was this what love felt like?

The next day Brenna went into the kitchen to discuss her theory with Marita. Here was a woman married at fourteen with seven children and a loyal husband. Surely she could define love.

"What does love feel like?" Marita repeated. She paused from chopping her onions, gazing out the window as she pondered the question. "It is happiness, it is sadness, and it is life and also death." She paused to take a deep breath. "It is desire too, no?" She let out a giggle and a high-pitched squeal while Brenna's face turned scarlet. Embarrassed, Brenna backed out of the kitchen, still wondering whether she was in love.

As it turned out, there wasn't much time to wonder. The next week James asked her to marry him. When still another week had passed, her father wedded Mrs. O'Meara. Two nights before Brenna's wedding, a quiet knock came to her bedroom door. It was an unfamiliar knock that Brenna did not recognize.

"May I come in, Brenna?" her Pa asked. He sat on her bed and proceeded to fidget with the lacy fabric on the bed cover. Then, he cleared his throat. "I've been offered a job in San Diego. Your stepmother, Katherine is anxious to leave Bisbee, so I've accepted the position. We'll be leaving with the boys in a few days."

"But, Pa, my wedding!"

He held up his hands in protest. "No, no, no. I'll be here to give you away and see that you're properly married in a Catholic church, unlike your pagan sister, Ginny."

That was the first time Brenna heard him speak of Ginny since she left. Now she was sure that marrying James was what her father had wanted. Like Marita had said, he made sure she was taken care of. "You know, Brenna, I built this house for your Mum, but she never got to enjoy it. I want you and James to have the house as a wedding gift."

Spontaneously, she reached forward, enveloping her father in her arms. If either of them had to think about it, it wouldn't have happened. She was to have her very own home and her very own husband. Her future was laid out before her, sure as summer followed spring.

* * * *

Sara's strong sucking suddenly shot an arrow of pain through Brenna's breast. An hour had passed and Sara had nursed her dry. Her breasts were still tender and one of her nipples was cracked and bleeding. Although she was in pain, she reminded herself to be thankful that Sara had a good appetite. A youngster wasn't likely to make it through childhood if she couldn't eat her way out of sickness.

Chapter 3

"Aiieee, Maneulito! Come get this pet of demons!" Marita backed up to the opposite wall of the dining room, armed with a broom. Her gaze held fast to a creature on the other side, blending in nicely with the dark wood floors and baseboard. Brenna cowered nearby waiting for Marita to make the first move.

"Where is James?" Brenna asked. "Can't he come help us?"

"I haven't seen him, *Señora*. Maybe he is out riding."

"Blast it. When isn't he out riding? Can you see what kind it is?"

"Manuelito!"

"Manuel, hurry."

They could hear Manuel on the back porch stomping the dirt off his boots. He entered, annoyed at being interrupted.

"*Hijola*, what do you want, woman?" He was glaring at his sister.

"Do not disrespect me, Manuel. It is a snake. A big snake. He is under the table." Marita pointed toward a small corner table holding a delicate pink porcelain vase. Manuel carefully moved the vase to the large dining room table. Pushing aside the furniture, a small brown snake with mottled patches lay writhing in the corner.

"Woman, it is just a little gopher snake." He bent over to pick up the snake. Dangling it in front of the women, he took relish in their discomfort.

"Kill it. Kill it!" Marita demanded.

"Why should I kill it?" Manuel asked. "He is harmless and eats the mice that wander into the garden and hen house. If he is a she, maybe she has babies to take care of." By now Brenna was smiling, enjoying the banter between the two siblings. Manuel made a wide, sweeping gesture with his one empty hand. "If I kill him, his blood will come back for revenge and there will be snakes everywhere."

One could imagine snakes crawling in every corner of the house. "Let him go in peace." The snake had wrapped itself around Manuel's hand and wrist, content with his new surroundings.

Brenna's curiosity peaked.

"What does it feel like?" she asked. "Slimy?"

"No, no. Touch him. He is smooth and soft, like a fresh tortilla." Brenna took a long look at the reptile so she could recognize him on any future encounters. She reached out to touch him. Marita had enough.

"When you two are through playing with that devil, I will finish cleaning in the dining room." She took her broom and marched out of the room, insulted by their lack of fear.

Manuel nodded and drew close to Brenna, touching his fingers to hers. While the snake slithered from Manuel's hand to hers, she noted the rough ridges in his fingers and the thick skin that had formed from years of hard but earnest work. For a moment she was gripped with fear, but looked into his eyes for reassurance. They were still holding hands when the snake made its way toward Brenna's shoulder. Manuel saw goose bumps running up Brenna's arm while the soft, down hair stood on end.

"Does he frighten you?" Manuel asked, protectively reaching for the snake.

"No, but he tickles something terrible." She brushed her shoulder attempting to dust off the shivers that the reptile had instigated.

Manuel addressed the snake. "I think, *Señor*, it is time to return you to your home." Brenna followed Manuel outside where the snake was released into the garden. No longer afraid, he slipped beneath the folds of flowers and leaves and disappeared.

* * * *

Darkness crept into the summer night, and still James was not home. Michael and Eric reported that they had seen him in town at the livery stable saddling Chauncey, but that had been early in the day. It wasn't like James to be late for a meal, or anything for that matter. That evening Brenna was in the sitting room mending clothes when Michael drifted in.

"Can I sit on your lap, Mommy?" Not waiting for an answer he began to climb up. Poor Michael. There had been little time for him since Sara's birth. She was still a little sore from the birth, but her heart ached in answer to his request for attention.

"You've got your nightshirt on?"

"Marita helped me before she left."

"Well, let's give this a try. Maybe I can rock you to sleep." She set her sewing aside and took hold of his petalsoft hand, while leading him to the staircase.

"Where's Papa?" Michael asked.

"I don't know, love, but I'm sure he'll be home soon."

"I miss Papa. He promised he'd play ball with me after we see God tomorrow."

"See God?"

"That man you say hello to after church. He wears the black dress." Brenna realized he was talking about Father Lawrence.

"That's a priest, Michael. Father Lawrence teaches us about God. God is up in Heaven."

"God isn't in church?"

"No, he isn't...well, yes he is..." Brenna was getting frustrated. She frowned and took a deep breath to clear her thoughts. How was she supposed to explain God to a four-year-old when she wasn't even sure who God was? "Let's sit down in the rocker, Michael. Why don't you close your eyes and go to sleep now?" Michael rested his head against his mother's bosom and they began to rock. With a jerk, he lifted his head again.

"Mama, your pillows are bigger."

Her voice became insistent. "For heaven's sake, Michael, go to sleep." She nudged his head, all the while amused by his innocence. In the softness of the shadows his shiny dark brown hair reflected shafts of light from the electric lamp in the hall. Lengthy lashes fringed his translucent lids, and his skin was so smooth and velvety, it was hard to keep from touching it. How she loved this child. God forgive her, but she did favor this son over the other. Tomorrow she would see to it that James would keep his promise to play ball with him after church.

It was very early when Brenna heard the door chimes ring. She couldn't understand why James hadn't answered the door, being it was Sunday and Marita's day off. When she opened the front door the summer sun was so bright that for a moment, she could not recognize the figure standing before her. Like a revelation, it suddenly became clear. She saw the face and she understood, but the words melted into gibberish. It was as if the sheriff was standing at the end of a long tunnel, speaking to her from miles and miles away. He began to fade from sight, and she sensed she was falling.

"Let's sit down, Mrs. McEvoy." The sheriff grabbed her arm and steered her to a chair. "Now we don't know that he's lost or hurt. It's just that his horse came back without him. We'll get a search posse out looking for him. Now don't you worry. We'll do everything we can to find your husband."

Chapter 4

James was sure he'd died and gone to Hell. His skin burned with fire and pain snaked through his body like an angry serpent. If this was hell, where was that bright light coming from? He hesitated before opening his swollen eyes, fearful that Satan himself was waiting for him. The sun's intrusion stung his icy blue eyes. Still, he struggled to assess his surroundings. Damp clothes stuck to his skin like pasted wallpaper. James parted his mouth, trying to lick the wetness from his face when his bottom lip split open like an over-ripe melon. It gave him a jolt, and with that he began to remember what happened.

It was that damned beaded lizard. The locals called them Gila Monsters, nearly two feet long and poisonous enough to kill. Miners said when they clamped onto your limb their iron jaws were fixed. Severing the head from the body was the only way to get free of the pest, but by then it was too late. The black and orange reptile picked his way through the patch of jumping cactus. When Chauncey spied the Gila Monster meandering across his path, his front legs flew into the air, attempting to escape contact. Then the terrified horse reared, loosening James's sweaty palms from the saddle horn. Once again Chauncey's front legs clawed at the air, like Pegasus attempting flight. James reached for the horse's sleek, golden mane, but missed. He was separated from his horse, propelled through the air and cast to the ground like a chewed bone.

How long had he been lying here? The sky reflected a different time of the day than he recalled. He tried to move, but pain was his reward. By lifting his head a few inches, he could see he landed on a large flat boulder. The horse was gone, taking his rifle and water. One leg hung to the side of the rock. He tried to move just the leg, but it would not respond to his head's commands. The most intense pain began in his hip and extended past his knee. Perhaps his leg was broken, or his hip, or both. One arm was still functional.

James reached across his face to the back of his head, locating a pounding discomfort. The hair was sticky with chunks of gooey blood, crusty around the edges. A small, tender indentation verified his suspicions. He must have passed out after the fall. That had been a stroke of luck. The pounding headache, flaming sunburn, and aching hip were all wearing on him. James closed his eyes but told himself he must not go to sleep. He might not wake again. His last thoughts were about the miserable thirst haunting his parched mouth. Surely someone would find him soon. If only he had told Brenna where he was going.

* * * *

"What the hell is this?" a voice questioned. Someone was kicking at James's boot. The jarring sent pain spiraling up his leg. James whimpered, feeble as a sick dog.

"Thees *hombre* has trouble, no?" It was a different voice, thick with a Mexican accent.

"How long you think he's been here?"

"*No se.* He done look so good. He will die soon I think."

"I like these here boots," the first voice continued. "I could use some new boots."

There was a moment of quiet, and then someone was pulling at James's ankles. His legs were being ripped from his body. The voice he heard scream was one he never would have recognized as his own. With what little strength he had left, he lifted his head to locate the strangers tormenting him. He saw two scavengers. One was a Mexican wearing a faded poncho and a frayed straw hat. His dark complexion was the color of adobe. A thick mustache draped over his upper lip. The other was a half-breed white, maybe with Indian blood. Dark brown hair dangled to his shoulders, stringy and matted like a vermin nest. His beard was no better. His cheeks were pitted and pox-marked, and he appeared to have endured a lot during his young life. The half-breed was sitting on the ground, struggling with James's boots.

"Goddamn it! These things is too small." He hurled the boots under a large tree, put his worn boots back on his grimy feet and stood up. He walked toward James, stopping to dig his boots into James's ribcage. "You got any money on you, tenderfoot? Who the hell are you anyway?" He grabbed the flaming hair on James's head bringing his face close to James's nostrils. His breath smelled like something rotten, most likely from lack of hygiene. The only other time James had smelled anything as bad was when he had come upon a dead cow decaying in a ravine. He had lost his balance, rolled down a hill, and come face to hide with the oozing beast. It was an odor that one could never forget and to think of it again was an invitation to vomit.

James felt the other man going through his pockets until he found his wallet.

"Look here, he works for the mines."

"Gimme that." The half-breed grabbed the card, eyeing it closely. You caint read. How'd you know that?"

"I don't need to read. I can tell by the markings on the card." The half-breed looked at the card again.

"Well, I'll be dogged. You suppose he's some official with the mines? Maybe we can get a reward or a ransom.

How much money he got?"

"About twelve *dolares*. That's not much for a rich man." The Mexican leaned down close to James. "What are you doing out here, *Señor*?" James did not answer. The half-breed neared James, like he was preparing to tell him a secret. James heard a gun hammer cock.

"If you don't talk nicely to my friend here, I'm going to share your brains with the buzzards."

"Prospecting," James answered, and then with his last breath, "the mine, over there." He turned his head to the right, toward a hole near the base of a hill that would have gone unnoticed to the travelers. It was his discovery, and they had no right to take it. But he truly believed they would have killed him and needed little excuse to do so. It had been abandoned for some time, but with a little investment, he suspected the mine could become quite productive. Still thinking of his riches, he passed out again.

It was the sound of gunfire that brought him to. The sun had moved closer to the horizon. At some distance, he could see the bandits sitting in the shade of a paloverde tree. They were drinking and playing cards, gambling with his money. Both were very drunk and had just wounded a morning dove that had flown too close. It lay dying in the baking sun, red blood marking the gray breast. It would flutter, rest and flutter again, truly believing it could survive.

James wanted to help it, take it in his hands to comfort the suffering bird. He felt the urge to cry but could no longer produce any tears. Unable to watch any longer, he faced away.

"Water, please," he begged, but they ignored him. Perhaps they hadn't heard. "Please, I need water."

"Did you hear something, *amigo*?" The Mexican was up on his feet, wobbling toward James. "I think he said he wants water." He cradled his bottle of Red Top in his one arm. James's socks had been torn from his feet when the half-breed removed his boots, and now the afternoon sun had colored his flesh an eye-catching red. The Mexican couldn't resist kicking the blistered feet as he passed by.

"We can't spare no water," the other man said. "But we got lotsa dirt. Why don't you give him some of that?"

"Good idea, *amigo*." He bent over, nearly falling on his head. His dirty nails scrapped up a handful of soil; righted himself and sprinkled it over James's face like gold dust. Both men let out a laugh like something possessed. The dirt filled James's nostrils and mouth and sifted into his eyes. Surely death was more welcome than this and the sooner the better.

"Let's play cards," the other man announced. The Mexican obeyed his command and stumbled over to the shade tree. "We're out of *dinero*, so if you win the hand, you get to show off your shootin'."

"What we goin' to shoot at?" asked the Mexican. The half-breed released a large belch and then concluded his instructions.

"Him." Both men decided it was a good plan and the card game commenced.

James ignored the conversation. Though he lay only a few yards away from the men, his mind had drifted to a different time. He was thinking of his childhood and his baby sister and how mean and unfair he had been to her. He was a greedy bastard even then. It was his mother's voice he was hearing.

"Go to the store, James." She handed him a coin. "You may treat yourself and Amanda to some candy and divide it between the two of you." He purchased the candy, hoarding most of it for himself. His sister was too stupid to know the difference or maybe too frightened to protest the inequity. In the past, he had hit her several times when she tried to speak up. Why had he been so cruel to her? Little Amanda accepted her ration of candy, but the disappointment was obvious. She looked into his face without speaking, the sadness in her liquid brown eyes speaking a thousand words.

"Hee, hee, I win this one," exclaimed the Mexican. The half-breed threw down his cards, disgusted with his luck. The Mexican pulled out his revolver, aiming it at James.

Without hesitation he shot off James's big toe. Blood spurted on the desert floor, and what remained of James's toe was scattered a few feet away.

James knew he had been hurt again, but his mind produced an anesthetic, pushing him beyond the pain. For now all he sensed was a dull throbbing.

"You're a good shot for a drunk Mexican," the halfbreed said. "But I bet you caint hit this." He took his time placing the bullet in James's left knee.

The pain was more brilliant now. It was closer, enveloping his entire body. He began to shiver in the torrid heat.

"I can match that," the Mexican assured him. He shattered James's right knee, and more blood spilled on the desert floor.

"Watch this," said the other man. He took a deep breath to steady his inebriated body. His challenge was serious, and with perfect precision, he pointed the revolver at James's damaged body. The explosion of the gun powder echoed repeatedly against the surrounding hills.

For a passage of time, the desert stood perfectly still. The kangaroo rat paused to listen, his long whiskers twitching with curiosity. The peccary lifted his hairy muzzle, momentarily interrupting his rooting to focus on the unfamiliar noise. Even the bobcat perched on the hillside turned his keen eyes to the distraction of the three men below. At this moment, death took precedence over life.

The bullet had succeeded in finding its target, directing its path through James's eye socket. It exited the back of his head to bury its remains in the hardened ground.

Both men began to sober. "We'd better do somethin' with him," said the killer. "It'll be getting dark soon. We don't need no posse lookin' for him nor us."

"How we goin' to hide him?" asked the Mexican. "Even if we bury him, the coyotes will dig him up, and the buzzards will scatter his bones."

"First we get what we can offa him."

They went through his pockets once again, finding little worth keeping. The Mexican tried to remove the gold wedding band, but the heat and sunburn had made James's hand swell. He pulled out his switchblade, cutting the finger off at the knuckle. Gouging what remained of the digit, he freed the ring. Without looking up from his handiwork, he suggested they hide the body in the mine.

"Say, that's a right smart idea, Rico. You're not such a dumb Mexican after all." Rico gave the half-breed a big grin. It was a fairly long distance to the mine, but the two of them managed to drag him to the hole, depositing the shattered body.

"Can you see 'em down there?" the half-breed asked.

"No. It is dark as Hell down there. No one will find him." He threw James's hat down the hole, returning it to its owner. It drifted to the bottom like a weighted cloud.

"Good, now give me the ring."

"I am not going to give you this ring. It is mine."

"Gimme the ring, you moron."

The Mexican pulled his gun, walking toward the unarmed half-breed, convinced all white men were crazy, greedy sons-a-bitches, and he wanted nothing more to do with them. "You know, I am sick of you." He shot the half-breed in the stomach. The man remained standing, clutching at his belly, dripping with blood. He said nothing, but it was clear he knew he was about to die. Shock painted his face. "I am sick of the way you insult me and my people," the Mexican said. "I am sick of your stink. You can finish rotting in that hole with the other *gringo*."

He emptied his gun into the man and dragged him to the edge of the mine. With several sharp kicks he cast the body into the makeshift grave. He stood there, staring down into the black hole, finally deciding he would return home to live out his life in Mexico, despite the turmoil and poverty. Maybe that new revolutionary, Francisco Villa, would liberate Mexico and give dignity back to the people.

By the time the rains came that evening, the Mexican was nearing the border of his homeland. The raindrops were gentle, almost apologetic, on their journey north from the Gulf. Fat clouds drifted across the desert, reaching into the purple mountains. Emptying their water on the land, they cleansed the soil of the blood stains, washing the frightful murders from sight. When the storm had passed all that remained was the blackened night, punctuated by the wails of the howling coyotes, knowing death had come and gone once again.

Chapter 5

Brenna sat at her dressing table confronting the ragged reflection in the oval mirror. Brush in hand, she yanked at her matted black hair, tangled from too many restless nights. Her cotton bed dress emitted a peculiar smell of perspiration, perfume and sour breast milk. It was a disagreeable odor and Brenna wasted no time in removing her gown, dropping it to the plank floor and kicking it to a corner of the bedroom.

Her complexion resembled wax. She raised one hand to her face, poking at the puffy tissue surrounding her eyes. Her mother's face came before her, a young woman, aged beyond her time. The desert would take all it could, undoubtedly an act of revenge. She finished the battle with her hair, content to pin it in a sloppy bun, and walked to the armoire to dress for the day.

Three days had passed, and Brenna knew she would never see James again. If he'd abandoned his family, he would likely never return. If he was injured and alone, he would succumb to bandits or the summer sun. Either way, the situation defined her as one more statistic, a woman left alone. Today she would begin her mourning. Ruffling through her clothes, she found a black dress suitable for the summer. In her mind, this would signify the end of hope.

Crying for James was a forced act. More than anything she was angry. Once she had dealt with the initial shock, there were few tears left. How could she express loss for a stranger? He had lived his life and allowed her to live hers. He hadn't been a bad husband, just a husband who wasn't there. They had never shared dreams, never had hopes, and rarely consoled each other in pain. Now, alone with her pain, Brenna thought it silly to cry for a man she had never loved. It had been a marriage of convenience, one that any man would have envied.

She descended the stairs heading for the kitchen, craving her first cup of coffee. She could hear the clamor of dishes in the kitchen as Marita prepared the children's lunch. What would she do without Marita? Marita had stayed with her day and night for several days, tending to Sara, and always comforting her and the boys. In her grief, Brenna selfishly neglected her family and it was going to have to stop.

In the back of her mind, an ugly truth surfaced. How was she going to support the children? Begging from her father was not an option. She was going to have to get through this without his assistance.

Brenna stopped short of the kitchen. She whirled around to face James's desk, sitting near the entry to the sitting room. Somewhere, among all the papers, records, and his incessant bookkeeping, might be the clue to her financial status. She could determine if they were in debt, if there were accounts and stocks. Certainly she could add and subtract and make sense of her own life. It was abundantly clear that her family's survival came down to dollars and cents and what she might find in that desk.

She was struggling with the desk drawer when Marita entered the room. "What are you doing, *Señora?*"

"This desk, Marita." She tugged at another drawer. "It may tell me what our future holds. God damn this thing; it's locked!" Brenna slammed her open palm on the desk. "Why was everything such a secret with him?"

Marita froze in her tracks like an alley cat about to be chased by a mad dog. "Please *Señora*, calm down. It is not good for you to make yourself upset. I will get coffee for you. Manuel can help. I will call for him now."

When Marita returned with Brenna's coffee, the black liquid's bitter aroma filled her with a sense of comfort while she sipped at it. Cup and saucer in hand, she stood before the picture window with the town spread before her like a glass of spilled milk. Rooftops, scattered in every corner of the hills and valleys, filled the canyon with humanity. What would the tongues be wagging about now? Would they have pity or spite for the new widow? She could imagine the voices trailing through the streets. "Poor Mrs. McEvoy, a new baby and no husband to support her." Mouth would come to ear as each passerby would lean to another, anxious to catch every word, dripping with emotion and false sorrow. Damn hypocrites.

She sensed a presence and turned to see Manuel standing near the kitchen doorway. How long had he been watching her? She must have appeared startled. Self-consciously, Manuel began slapping at the dust on his pants and sleeves. God knew what he'd been up to that morning. She didn't bother greeting him, perturbed that he'd been staring at her.

"It's the desk, I can't get into it. Can you help me?" Continuing his silence, Manuel approached the desk he'd dare not touch before. He ran his scratchy hands over the top of the smooth dark wood. He stopped at a drawer, jerking on the brass handle.

"Is there a key?" he asked.

"Manuel..." Her tone was caustic. "If I had a key, would I have needed you?" Manuel lowered his eyes to the floor, hanging his head like a disobedient dog. Seeing his reaction, Brenna realized what she had said. His hurt had been obvious. She never talked to him that way. She grabbed his hand. "Manuel, wait. I didn't mean to be so short with you. I desperately need you and Marita. You're all I have now."

She collapsed into the desk chair, burying her face in her hands. Her entire body was shaking like a bush caught in the grips of a dust devil. The sobbing grew louder and louder, a swelling river gaining momentum. Manuel glanced around the empty room, looking for a guardian angel to tell him what to do.

"No, no, *Señora*. Don't cry. He dropped to one knee, trying to console her. "I will open your desk. It will be all right. Marita! Marita, I need you!"

Marita burst through the kitchen door still wiping her hands on her apron. "What did you do to her?" she accused her baby brother.

"I didn't do anything," Manuel said in defiance. "I asked her if she had a key." Brenna wiped her eyes with the back of her hand and stopped to catch her breath. With her other hand she wiped the mucus from her nose, drying her hands on her dress.

"That's right," she said. "He asked about a key, and I snapped at him. I'm afraid I've hurt your brother's feelings. I don't want to hurt either of you. Both of you have been so good to me."

Manuel began to fidget, pulling at one ear, rubbing his beard and turning his face away from the women. "She didn't hurt my feelings. I just don't know what you two want. Are we going to open this desk, or not?"

"Yes, of course," Brenna said, composed, almost arrogant. "If you need to break the lock, go ahead. This desk means nothing to me."

In minutes the desk was open. Brenna stared into the file drawers, knowing that the task to come would take weeks to decipher. No matter, it had to be done and would keep her busy until the wounds began to heal.

She pulled up the chair reaching for the first file. A sense of optimism raced through her body, but what if there was something in the desk she did not want to see? There must have been a good reason, maybe many reasons for James to keep it locked. She had no time to dwell on the mistrust and opened the file labeled "Assay". Before her were several mineral reports on samples that James had collected. Each report showed that the ore sample was of poor quality and was best left in the ground. Some reports dated back nearly a decade. How long had he been chasing this dream? Would the contents of the desk reveal the man she never knew? The Assay file was a useless collection of papers to her, and she emptied the file in the trash, moving on to the next folder. If she didn't know James before, she was about to know him now.

* * * *

Autumn blew in on a hot gust of wind, but it was destined to be the last heat of summer. The smell of fall could be detected in the rich, crisp leaves that fell to the ground in a colored mass. Manuel had turned the small family garden preparing for winter's rest. Some crops continued through the fall, but these were a select few. Bisbee was not immune to ice and snow. Although it was a rare occasion, nothing frustrated Manuel more than to lose his prize garden to the frosty will of Mother Nature.

It had been an eventful year for Bisbee. It was still the largest city in the territory. Automobiles had begun to make their unwelcome appearance in the streets. Horse and rider would have to adjust to the racket of the fearless machines, but already there had been an encounter with a pedestrian. With the streets of Main now paved, Bisbee was starting to feel like a real city.

Wages in the mines were up to three-fifty a day, and with the exception of Sam Barn's untimely death, there had been no problems at the mines. Poor Sam. He was a young, handsome man, although no one would have known that when they found his body. The ascent from the mine shaft had been too fast for Sam. While riding in the cage he had fainted. When he fell forward his head was caught between the shaft and the cage. After falling eight hundred feet, all that was left of Sam was his torso, one broken arm, and a belt. His clothing, limbs and head were sacrificed to the mine.

The Citizen's Bank and Trust opened in town, signs of coming prosperity for the young community. Brenna returned from the bank, having made one last withdrawal from her dwindling account. She had opened it with the little cash that was hidden in James's desk and clothing. Within the desk there had been several thousand dollars in stock certificates and land holdings. Many had been gifts from James's family.

They had advised him that his future lay in the west. The McEvoy family had arrived in America well before the potato famine. By the time Brenna's family had left Ireland, the McEvoys had achieved education and position. They had high expectations for their middle son, the most obedient of the trio. James's father had convinced him that being comfortable was not enough; all the riches in the desert hills could be his for the taking. So he left the certainty of his eastern home, looking for his mine that had forever remained an elusive dream.

The banker in town had been kind but honest. "I'm sorry, Mrs. McEvoy. You know it could take years to liquidate these certificates. Making a loan, I'd have to charge you interest. Then you'd need to sign the certificates over to the bank as collateral. That's the only way I can do it."

Her attorney advised her not to follow that plan. "What if the bank goes under?" he questioned. Mr. Donaldson had always been on the conservative side. "Mrs. McEvoy, in your situation, you just can't take a chance like that. You'd have nothing to fall back on." It made no sense to question his authority, so they began the monotonous process of liquidating her assets.

Now the most immediate concern was how she was going to exist for the next couple of years. The house was hers. Perhaps she could have some credit at the stores in town. She could cut corners by sewing the children's clothes and earn grocery money by washing laundry for the miners. She could even do some baking and earn some cash from bread and pies. First thing tomorrow, she would post notice in town. Tomorrow she would also dismiss Marita and Manuel.

She'd thought on it for days. There was no way to pay their wages, and they had a family of their own that needed to be sheltered, fed and clothed. The McEvoys and Higueras were on the same plane of existence now. Life would become a daily struggle. Although her home was much nicer than those on Chihuahua Hill, it wasn't going to put food on the table. Hard work was her only asset, and she needed the nerve to say goodbye to her best friends.

When morning came she summoned Manuel to the kitchen. "I need a piece of board, something about so big." She motioned with her hands measuring two feet by two. "Is there anything in the garden shed?"

"I can look," he offered. "If I don't find anything out back, you want me to check the alleys in town?"

"That's a good idea. I'll meet you back here in two hours." She left to tell Marita she would meet her at the same time.

The agonizing hours had nearly passed when Brenna sat down on the couch parlor awaiting the scheduled meeting.

The weather was mild and cool for a November morning, yet the lace on her high collared dress was sticking to her damp skin. She wrung her hands and then began biting her nails. Unable to sit a second longer, she rose to her feet and began pacing the floor. The methodic ticking of the grandfather clock was the only sound to be heard in the house. For a moment she held her breath, just to acknowledge the quiet. It would be lonely without them.

The back door slammed, and she could hear the two of them conversing in their native tongue. She should have learned Spanish a long time ago. Many whites thought it demeaning to learn the language of the Mexicans. Brenna just thought it would be useful. She would have understood what they were saying and known if they were at all suspicious of her motives.

As they walked into the parlor, she motioned for them to sit on the couch. Manuel sat on the edge of the cushion, appearing very uncomfortable. Maybe he knew what she was up to or maybe he was miserable on the Queen Ann furniture. James always hated the way the wood molding in the couch back dug into his spine. Marita just looked tired and seemed grateful to be resting.

"I found your board, Mrs. McEvoy," Manuel volunteered. "I went behind the company store and found some old crates. I brought back two in case you needed a spare."

"Thank you, Manuel, that was thoughtful." A long silence lingered in the air, hanging like the stench from a spoiled potato. Where would she begin? How would she remove them from her life? She started again. She was the master of the home now. It was her duty to take control and make the decisions. "Marita, Manuel, I know of no other way to say this. I must relieve both of you from your duties." There. She said it. She let out a deep sigh to expel the stress choking her body, but both Mexicans appeared confused, looking at each other, eyebrows furrowed, mumbling quietly in Spanish. Finally, Manuel spoke up.

"Do you mean we're fired?" he asked.

Mother of God, she thought. *I can't even express myself so they understand me. Why am I so weak-kneed?* She would try again.

"No, Manuel. You are not fired. If I were firing you that would mean I was unhappy with your services. I am always so pleased with your work, but you see, I have no money to pay you." She was pacing again, squeezing her hands until the fingertips turned red. "James had a lot of stocks and property, things I can convert to cash.

41

The only problem is that it could be years before I get the money. I don't have money to pay your wages and you won't have money to take care of your family."

"What will you do, *Señora*?" Marita asked. "How will you live?"

Brenna's face brightened. Her plan gave her hope. She explained how she would wash laundry and bake for the miners.

"*Si, si,* that is good. You know…" She lowered her voice like the neighbors were listening. "…they ran the Chinese out of town just last week for trying to do laundry. Can you believe that? If the Chinese did laundry, what would the white widows live on?"

Brenna was reminded again that she was part of the working class and although she was master of her home, she would have to work like a Coolie to keep it. She smiled, acknowledging Marita's compassion, and changed the subject.

"I can give you a couple of weeks to find work elsewhere. I'll be happy to write letters of recommendation. And I'd be terribly hurt if you didn't stop in to visit once in a while." Both promised to keep in touch, but Brenna realized that the chances were very slim that either one would socialize with her. The face of their relationship had a new expression. Brenna longed for a mask to hide under, knowing she would never be the same person she once was.

* * * *

"You cook the apples first and then let them cool." Marita was demonstrating her recipe for fruit cobbler. "Your *niños* love this, so you'd better learn how to make it, *comprende?*"

Manuel broke their train of thought as he passed the kitchen window, taking large strides. His eyes were bright and excited as he ran through the door, scooping his sister up off the floor and swinging her around the room.

"Put me down, you big bull," Marita commanded. She was the only person that could smile while she was scolding.

"What is wrong with you?"

"I'll tell you what is right with me," he said, and planted a big kiss on her cheek. "I got a job today!"

"*Bueno,*" Marita replied. "And where is this job?"

"At the Palace, you know, the livery stable."

"Aieee, Manuel, you always liked animals better than people. Maybe you should have been a cowboy."

"I start first thing Monday. Mrs. McEvoy, if there are things you need done before I go, you let me know." He began to step away, but something caught in his thoughts. "If you need help sometime, if something breaks and you need a man to fix it, I'll be happy to help you. You don't have to pay me nothing. I just want to help."

Brenna took a big breath to keep from crying. Tears were lining the rims of her eyes, preparing to spill. "Thank you, Manuel. I'll remember your kindness." He nodded and left the kitchen. Watching him walk away, Brenna bit at her lower lip. "*Adios amigo*," she said softly, and both women broke down crying like the end of the world had arrived.

Chapter 6

Marita and Manuel had been gone for only a week, and already Brenna's life was in shambles. Two signs in town boasted of her laundry and baking services, but sales had amounted to three loaves of bread and one apple pie. She was behind on her wash and by nightfall, she barely had enough strength to make supper for the boys. Mail continued to pile up on the desk. She avoided looking at the threatening envelopes, sure that there were more bills crying to be paid. How much longer she could exist on credit would be decided by the patience of the shopkeepers.

Looking to her past, she wondered what it was that she did all day. Her time was filled with caring for the children and her husband. Now, there was no husband and the children were neglected. Sara learned to be content on her own. Since Brenna had stopped nursing, Sara seemed aloof, like she had little use for her mother. She would focus on whatever business was at hand as if expecting to complete the task herself.

The boys were quick to fight, with Eric leading them into it. Before they recognized trouble was upon them, Brenna would grab them by the collars and hurl them out the back door.

"Take your fightin' outside!" she screamed. "I'll have no more of your rowdiness in my house." The battle would continue in the fine dirt of the fallow garden, where no one could get seriously hurt. Despite the ruckus, Sara would remain steadfast and serious, both judge and jury of the fighting boys. Brenna tried her best to ignore the disruption.

Darkness enveloped the community early during the winter months, making the long, black nights oppressive. The mountains appeared more threatening than usual, and uneasiness would crawl upon her skin, waiting like a coiled reptile. Sometimes it seemed like the mountains would swallow her whole. While this left her shaken, she imagined what it would be like not to have to worry about tomorrow's troubles; to be able to vanish from sight, being responsible to no one but herself.

The boys had been bathed and for a change, played quietly in their rooms with what few toys they hadn't destroyed. Sara had been asleep for almost an hour, and it seemed like the right opportunity to read the mail.

Brenna lit the kerosene desk lamp trying several positions to get the best light. She preferred electric light but had returned to kerosene to reduce her electric bill. From the top desk drawer she removed James's gold plated letter opener. Her hands were a roadmap of cracks and sores from laundry and dishes. Marita must have skin like a horny toad, for she couldn't recall her ever complaining about her hands. Every night she rubbed carbonized jelly into her skin to ease the searing pain, but nothing healed the sores. She liked to think that in time her skin would become tough enough to withstand her new life.

The first envelope was a bill from the mercantile. It would be smart to make a small payment, at least to show good faith. She put that bill aside, beginning a pile of those that would be paid first. There was a statement of her account at the Citizen's Trust. She glanced at it briefly, noting how little was left. A strange looking envelope contained a letter from one of James's stock companies informing her that they had received her request to sell the stock. Finally! There was hope that she might struggle through this. How she wished she'd held onto James's final check from the mines. They had included a small compensation for his death, but at the time it was used to pay Marita and Manuel, and buy pants for the boys to start school. Now all that seemed frivolous and unnecessary.

The next envelope was postmarked from Tombstone, the county seat. "More legal business that I know nothing about," Brenna mumbled to herself. The return address was from the First National Bank of Tombstone on Fifth Street. As far as she knew, they had no business with the bank in Tombstone, but she wouldn't be surprised if James had been up to something.

12 November, 1906
Dear Mrs. McEvoy,

Please accept our condolences on the death of your husband, James. It has come to our attention that you have not made any arrangements to close his savings account. Is it your intention to continue this account? Enclosed you will find the most recent statement. Please advise.

Respectfully,
Samuel Gates, Bank Clerk

Brenna turned to the next page of the letter. There was a sizeable deposit made the last week before James' death. That deposit would allow her to skirt the poor house for another month. Thank God her prayers were being answered. Her eyes followed the statement down the page to the bottom line revealing a total of $5402.33.

Brenna's bottom jaw dropped open. She stood up, she sat down. Her breathing became rapid and shallow, trying to keep pace with her pounding heart. Over five thousand dollars! If she continued the laundry and baking business she would be able to live quite nicely. The total would continue to dwindle, but not nearly as fast as she first anticipated. In a few years the stocks and properties would be sold. If the boys got summer jobs, she might be able to keep them in school until they could graduate.

Even in death, James had proven to be a mystery. He went through great pains to destroy the statements, leaving no evidence for her to trace the account. None of it mattered anyway. James was gone and now she had a means to exist. First thing next morning, she would surprise Marita and visit Chihuahua Hill to share the good news.

* * * *

By seven o'clock the sun still wasn't up. Gray clouds lined the sky, great brush strokes of dark paint outlining the pale blue horizon. Brenna was fully dressed and sitting at the kitchen table, sipping her steaming coffee. She nibbled on a piece of dry toast, scattering crumbs across the oilcloth. It would be a luxury, she thought, to put some butter on this bread, and then she realized she could afford that now. She removed a piece of butter from the ice box, but by now the toast was cool and the butter sat on the bread in ugly clumps. Next time she'd have Irish oatmeal.

It had been another sleepless night. Several times she had awakened, hardly believing her good fortune. How could one letter change her entire life? The last time she woke it had come to her. She was thinking of Marita and Manuel on Chihuahua Hill and how much nicer her home was and how she'd told herself her big house couldn't feed her family. What a fool she was, of course it could feed her family. The house could feed Marita's family too. It was time to wake the children. She couldn't wait any longer.

It was a long walk to Chihuahua Hill. Chauncey had been sold months ago to pay off the boarding fee. What she needed now was a buggy and a good horse, but that would come in time. Sara was quite comfortable bundled in her carriage and the boys thought of Chihuahua Hill as a great adventure. They were not allowed to play near the dirty community. Brenna was thankful it was fall and the odor of trash and night soil would not be as potent as in summer. The heat guaranteed to intensify the odor of body waste, attracting large green flies that battled over the warm, festering piles. Marita's family always used an outhouse and believed in keeping their adobe home orderly, despite the dozen or so relatives living there. But many of the Mexicans lived in such filth, it was a wonder that any survived to carry on the race.

They passed through Brewery Gulch where the smell of stale beer filtered out from each saloon, mixing with the crisp, cool air. This was one time Brenna longed for a man's company.

She felt out of place among the saloons and working district, and had no business walking through town by herself, much less this side of the street. But the foul water trickling down the road was best to be avoided. It was early Saturday morning and the streets remained quiet. As she passed the Free Coinage Saloon, she dared to slow her walk and peer inside. A sporting girl stood next to the table where two men played cards. It appeared that they had been at it all night.

The painted woman had one foot propped up on the chair seat; her legs spread open with only a hint of her petticoat protecting her femininity from full view. But what did that matter? A good portion of her bosom was pouring out the top of her turquoise costume. She cast Brenna a hateful stare. Brenna turned away, knowing she'd been gawking at the spectacle.

"What's in there, Ma?" Eric asked. He lowered himself to one knee, peeking under the swinging wood door. Brenna grabbed his arm, bringing him to an upright position.

"Nothin' for your eyes, young man." Brenna picked up speed with Michael and Eric scurrying behind her.

The smell of baked goods from the Vienna Bakery was a welcome change. A cheerful woman in a white apron was loading fresh pastries into a wagon, while horse and driver waited patiently. The kindly driver caught sight of Brenna and her family, recognized a lady, and politely tipped his black Fedora.

They were nearly out of the Gulch now, climbing steadily to Marita's home. Her house was located in the middle of town, but exactly where, Brenna was unsure. It had been a decade or more since she'd been to Marita's home, and why she had ventured there in the first place, she couldn't remember. Chihuahua Hill was a mixture of immigrants and those who lived there stayed close to their own kind. She came upon a pretty young Mexican woman, possibly a child, soaping clothes on a washboard. "*Dondè esta la casa di Higuera?*" she asked awkwardly. The girl stopped scrubbing and looked at her with a quizzical expression.

"Which Higuera family do you look for?" the girl replied. "There are many." Brenna felt her face flush, assuming the poor girl would not have been educated.

"Marita and Alberto."

"They are down the road and to the, the —" She directed with her hands.

"The left," Eric shouted.

"*Si*, left. It is the house with the shrine to the Virgin in the yard."

"Thank you." Brenna bowed slightly and continued her walk through the neighborhood. At the next house two old men sat in two crippled chairs, partially hidden by the side of the house. They shared a bottle of tequila, laughing at each other as they'd been friends for a lifetime. A short, fat woman with braided gray hair came out of the house, looking like a cat in search of a mouse. She found the *compadres,* spied the tequila and her shouting could be heard for several blocks. She scolded with her body as well as her voice, flailing her arms and circling the men like an angry bumblebee. It now became clear why the two men obtained so much pleasure from their bottle.

"I don't like this place," Eric whined. "It smells and so do these Mexicans."

"Eric, stop that kind of talk," Brenna reprimanded. "Wouldn't you be ashamed if one of them heard you?"

"Why should I care?" asked Eric, kicking his brown lace boots in the dust. "They're just stupid Mexicans."

"Quiet down. We're coming to their house."

Marita's house was easy to recognize. Though the adobe was in need of repair, the tin roof appeared sound. Used flour sacks in pastel pink hung in the window, serving as curtains. Several chairs, placed in a semi-circle, were arranged in the patches of grass and caliche that made up the front yard. Across the dirt path leading to the front door, was the Virgin Mary. She stood atop a pedestal of river rock and cement. An archway of bricks protected her aqua and red paint from the ravages of the weather while a gold arch painted inside the dome symbolized a heavenly glow. Brenna was amused that the Higuera home was made of mud but the Virgin's home was made of bricks and mortar. All things considered, both homes were slightly worn but extremely neat and orderly.

A small child had seen her coming and opened the door to meet her. He appeared to be about four. His straight black hair sat like a bowl on his head, and he was already dressed for the day in a pair of worn overalls and an oversized flannel shirt. Warm brown eyes turned up to greet her. He said nothing but offered her a big smile.

"Who ees it, Miguel?" called Marita's voice. Her accent sounded heavier in her own neighborhood. Her back was to the door where she stood at the kitchen table. She glanced over her shoulder, paying little attention to the strangers. Then, recognizing the McEvoy family, her strong hands fell limp, and the tortilla dough she'd been molding, dropped to the dirt floor. A mongrel dog quickly captured the ball of dough and exited a back door, but not before Marita had thoroughly shamed him.

"Señora! It is so good to see you!" Marita darted across the room to give Brenna a hug. For a moment Miguel stood in wonder, amazed at the reunion, but then became bored. The little boy wandered to the table, and imitating the dog, stole a fresh warm tortilla. Eric and Michael stood by, waiting their turns for the hugs that were destined to come their way.

Marita dropped to her knees, grabbing both boys at one time. "Have you both been behaving?" Both boys nodded in agreement. At Eric, she raised her eyebrows as he shrugged.

"Well, I'm sure you are trying," she replied.

She turned to Brenna. "Did you walk here by yourselves? If you had let us know, I would have sent someone to get you."

"We wanted to surprise you," Brenna said. "I have some very exciting news."

"Come then. Have some coffee. We can talk. Alejandra, take the little ones outside to play." Children, scattered like jacks upon the floor, obediently stood to go outside. "Boys, do you want to go along?" Michael got up to follow, but Eric remained fixed to the wooden chair, making it clear he did not want to play with the cocoa-colored children.

Marita placed two china cups and saucers on the kitchen table. They appeared to be the only matching dishes in the house. An open can of Arbuckle's Arioso sat on the dry sink. Marita measured the ground coffee into the pot and moved it to the wood stove, placing it next to a bubbling kettle. The room was filled with the familiar smell of cooking pinto beans and the fragrance of fresh dirt, and Brenna was reminded of her childhood in the old adobe house. Marita poured the coffee and sat at the table to join her friend.

"I wish Manuel was here to join us," she said. "He is working at the stable this morning."

"How does he like his new job? Is he happy there?"

"The man that supervises his job, he is stern. But you know my brother. He loves working with the horses and he is learning a lot. And you? How have you been getting along?"

"Until yesterday, we weren't getting along at all," she said, shaking her head. "No one had brought laundry and the baking was no better. Honestly, Marita, I didn't know how I was going to make it. Then this letter came." She pulled an envelope out of her purse and removed the letter from inside. She read it to Marita, revealing the five thousand dollar account in Tombstone.

"That is money you can have now?" Marita asked.

"Better than that, Marita. This is money that can work for us now."

"I do not understand," Marita said. "Here, have a sweet." She handed Brenna a small round cake. Brenna took a dainty bite of the sweet bread, surprised at its pleasing taste.

"Like this," Brenna said, holding the cake in her hand, while trying to talk with food in her mouth. "I want you to bake these for our boarders."

"*Señora*, you are making no sense."

"Marita, you have been with me all of my life. You are as much a part of me as any other in my family. This money, the five thousand dollars, is enough to start our own boarding house. I want you to be a partner with me. As long as you live, you will always have an income for your family." The poor Mexican woman looked suspicious.

"I have no money to buy this house with you, *Señora*."

"Let me explain. I will use some of the money to add rooms to my house. You will stay on as my cook and housekeeper and over time, earn a percentage, a part of the house collections. When my boarders pay me, I pay you. You will continue to get your wages, but I'm going to need your help to make this work. I will also need Manuel back to help build my rooms."

Marita sat quietly as she absorbed all the news. Finally she spoke.

"I must talk to my husband, Alberto, and Manuel too. I don't know if Manuel will leave his job now. Monday I was to start at *Señora* Moore's house."

Brenna could see she wasn't getting through and decided to appeal to Marita's sympathetic nature. She reached out for Marita's hand.

"I know this is all very confusing for you. First I send you away. Then I beg you to come back. But this letter has changed our lives. Don't you see? The three of us can make this work." Brenna stood up to leave. Sara stirred in the carriage and on instinct Marita picked her up.

"I miss her," she said, and stroked the infant's cheek. "I miss all of you. Tomorrow, after church, I will bring Alberto and Manuel to visit. We will see what we can do."

Brenna gathered her children and made her way out of the community, returning to her quiet home in Bisbee. There was so much to do now: building plans to draw, menus to write, linens and furniture to collect.

As she was approaching her front walkway, a spot of red caught her eye. On the last rosebush sat a single bloodred rose, fully extended, petals reaching out to soak up the warmth of the fall day. It seemed delighted to have survived the cool weather and to have reached full bloom so late in the season. It was just like the Bible verse she'd known as a child. "The desert shall rejoice and blossom as the rose." Brenna took this as a good omen. Tomorrow she would show Manuel.

Chapter 7

"Why would a white woman want you to be her partner?" Manuel questioned Marita.

"Maybe because she tells the truth, Manuel."

Alberto broke into the conversation. "How could she feed all those boarders by herself? Marita, did you see this letter she talked about?"

"*Si*, I saw it."

"And what good would that do?" asked Francisco, the oldest Higuera son. "You cannot read English."

"No, but I saw her read it. Manuel can read English. He would know if it was all true. Besides, what is there not to trust? I am getting my old job back. She said I could buy part of the house when I was ready. I give her no money."

"She is a desperate woman." Alberto said. "Maybe she would cheat us."

"I've heard enough," said Marita. She rose from her chair at the kitchen table where the family gathered. "While you men sit here and talk about your worries, I am going to visit. Are you coming with me?"

"Yes, we are coming," Manuel replied. "Marita?" He faced his sister. He was a full head taller than her, rather big for his race. He looked down at her and took hold of her pudgy hands. "I don't want you to get hurt. Your children could go hungry. I do not trust these white devils."

"I understand," said Marita. "But the *Señora* is no white devil. Francisco, go get the burro. We will take all the little ones he can hold."

* * * *

Brenna was delighted to have so many people fill her house. Neighbors stared at the procession of Mexicans entering the McEvoy home. Three children were stacked upon the burro, with four adults leading the reluctant beast. Manuel was angered by the neighbors' stares. It was a Sunday afternoon, and by white standards, they had no business in this neighborhood. He started thinking Marita was right. Wouldn't it be sweet revenge if a Mexican owned part of this lovely home and neighborhood?

"Manuel, Alberto, it is so good to see you. Please come sit at the table. I have plans to show you."

"I brought Francisco, my nephew." Manuel said. "He is a hard worker and if we build these rooms he will be a big help."

"Welcome, Francisco. All of you please sit down."
Michael whisked the young children up the stairs to his bedroom. They would be entertained for hours with so many toys, some that they had never seen in their lives.

Brenna eagerly brought out her plans. They had been sketched on a large piece of brown wrapping paper and were difficult to read. Still, they were straightforward and her designs could be identified. The addition would be built on the west wall. The boarders would be separated from the family quarters and have their own bathing room and water closet at the end of the hall. By placing the bathroom near the kitchen, it would be easy to extend the plumbing. Six small rooms could be built if a section of the front porch area was enclosed. Each room would hold one dresser and one bed, and one bedroom might be big enough for two cots. It would still be attractive from the walkway, and the addition would be unnoticeable.

Manuel was impressed. Whether it was divine guidance, enthusiasm, or intelligence she seemed to know what she was doing. The adult assembly walked outside to take measurements and estimate how long the project would take.

"How long before you get the money, *Señora* McEvoy?" It was the first question Alberto had asked her.

"I'm sending the bank a letter tomorrow."

"This letter," Manuel asked, "it is from the bank and says you have five thousand dollars?"

"I have it here, in my pocket." She pulled out the familiar envelope and handed it to Manuel. He unfolded the papers and slowly began reading aloud, stumbling over every other word. He knew his English was child-like, but it was important to him and his family that he read the letter word for word to quell any mistrust.

"That letter you are writing tomorrow," Manuel began. "I have a better idea." Alberto turned to him, shocked at his boldness. "Forget the letter. Why don't you and Marita take tomorrow's train into Tombstone?"

"Manuel," Marita spoke up, "it's up to the *Señora* to decide how she would like to do this.

"No, no, Marita, it's a grand idea. I haven't been to Tombstone in years and I wouldn't want to go by myself. Can Alejandra watch the children for the day?"

"Of course, she is a very good mother when I am not around."
"Then it is settled. We can take the early morning train and go directly to the bank. Manuel is right. We can get the money quicker and start building immediately."

Marita gathered her family to begin the journey home. Exiting from the side of the house, Brenna called Manuel to admire her rose. "It's beautiful, isn't it? And you didn't think I could grow anything." She bent over and picked it from the bush, handing it to Manuel. "Here, give it to your Virgin. The Lady of Guadalupe brought roses to winter; maybe the Virgin of Bisbee can bring us luck."

* * * *

Brenna arranged to meet Marita at the station ticket window the next morning. The November day was cool, bright and clear, and Brenna was anticipating a wonderful day. She handed the man three dollars for two round trip tickets and they boarded the train.

Marita was jittery as a butterfly. She slipped the black crocheted shawl off her head and down to her shoulders, and then fidgeted with her bun. Next she smoothed the wrinkles from her gray skirt and brushed at the dust on her black button shoes. Most everyone was wearing shoes with laces now, but Marita was not likely to purchase new shoes unless the soles were worn through.

Brenna was doing her best to hide her uneasiness. She had become accustomed to expecting surprises when it came to James's past. Above all, she hoped her plans would come to fruition and that soon she would be able to provide for her family. She was still dressed for mourning, wearing a black wool suit and a proper, but attractive mourning hat. A woman walked down the aisle in a stylish royal blue suit, trimmed with a black velvet collar and black satin ribbons circling the sleeve cuffs and hem of the skirt. Her outfit was completed with a black box turban draped with silk taffeta that accentuated her auburn hair. It was a stunning look and as Brenna watched the heads turn, she longed to be rid of her black wardrobe. She hated being an object of pity and in disgust turned her attention to Marita.

"Is this your first time in Tombstone, Marita?"

"No, but it has been many, many years. The last time I went I was a young woman and I took the stage coach with Alberto. I never let go of my Rosary beads."

"I heard that was a frightful experience. They said the wheels of the coach nearly hung off the road with a straight drop down the canyon."

"*Si,* and then there were the Indians. Geronimo was an animal. He would slice your throat, steal your money and think no more about it. And then there is the dust. You would blow dirt out of your nose for days. The bouncing made my stomach turn like a windmill." She motioned in the air with one hand while holding her abdomen with the other.

"I don't think we can expect any of those adventures today. I'm just anxious to get to town, collect my money and return home."

Marita furrowed her brows and discretely shook her head. Brenna got her signal, hardly believing her own stupidity. How could she boast on a crowded train about a large sum of money? Dressed in black, she'd be a likely target. She stole several quick glances around the car but most everyone seemed engrossed in something. The two women behind her were deep in conversation, and the man across from them was reading a copy of the *Daily Review*. She'd have to be more cautious and gave Marita an appreciative look.

The ride to Tombstone took over two hours, but the time passed quickly. Brenna was so happy to have Marita to talk to again. They lunched on finger sandwiches that Brenna had prepared and caught up on all the gossip from the week they'd been separated.

After the train arrived in Tombstone they disembarked, seeking directions to the First National Bank. Compared to Bisbee, Tombstone was as flat as the bottom of an iron skillet. It was laid out in a grid pattern and easy to follow the directions from the station master. The passengers emptied off the train, drifting like tumbleweeds, each choosing their own path. The two women turned down Toughnut Street and headed up Fifth, making their way toward Allen Street.

"I want to stop by Wells Fargo before we go on to the bank," Brenna said. "Let's find out how much it will cost to transfer the money to Bisbee. There." Brenna pointed toward a small plastered structure, and made her way across the street.

Marita was the first to speak up. "*Señora*, this is not Wells Fargo. We are in the wrong part of town. See next door? I think that is the whore house they call the Bird Cage."

"Oh no, we must be turned around." They stood there in the warmth of the sun, not knowing which way to turn, but thoroughly entertained by the characters on the street.

"Look at that hombre," Marita said. "His legs are so bowlegged, they look like a lariat." They giggled together like school girls, their eyes finally resting on the prostitutes lining the balcony of a saloon on Sixth. The prostitutes, two in particular, had already spied them. "What are those whores staring at?" Marita asked angrily. "Do you see how they watch us?" It was true. They were staring in their direction. Brenna looked around and saw a group of cowboys standing in front of them.

"Oh, Marita, you're so suspicious. They're probably eyeing those men and planning how they'll spend their money."

"No." Marita was insistent. "I can feel their evil eyes, they go right through us."

"Nonsense, you've got to feel sorry for them. Lord only knows how they got to be working girls. We need some directions, but we have to get off this street."

They started to leave when a small boy approached them. He gave them an impish smile, revealing a large chip in his front tooth. Part of his shirt tail hung out of his pants which were too short for his sprouting legs. His hair was a dull brown, lightly dusted with powdered dirt. Large freckles camouflaged most of the grime on his face.

"Do you have any spare change, ma'am?" he asked.

"Do your parents know you're begging, young man?" Brenna asked in return.

"Ain't got none," replied the boy. My brother and I live with my uncle. Lotsa times he's not around." Brenna reached into her bag for her coin purse. "You sure are purty, ma'am," he continued. "What's your name?"

"You sure are nosy," Marita snapped. She allowed Brenna to give him the coin. "Where is Wells Fargo?" she asked curtly.

"It's up on Fifth, toward Fremont, thata way. They moved from this street a long time ago."

The two ladies turned around heading in the same direction they had come from. The youngster waited for a moment and then followed toward the express station.

"There's First National," said Brenna. "We might as well stop there first."

The bank was soothing and comfortable, taking them out of the bright sunshine and bustle and into the warmth and quiet of the money world. It was here that men's futures were decided and fortunes lost or gained. The bankers reigned with power and control, not unlike the mining companies.

"May I help you, ma'am?" the polite teller asked.

"I wish to speak to a Mr. Samuel Gates," Brenna replied.

"Mr. Gates," he called from his barred window, "this lady would like to speak to you." A small man with spectacles, wearing a brown herringbone suit, looked up from his paperwork. He immediately came around the counter wearing an eager expression, almost as if he'd expected this widow. Brenna held out her gloved hand.

"Mr. Gates, I'm Mrs. McEvoy." While the two engaged in conversation, the small boy that had been hiding in the corner casually left the bank building, darted in front of a motor car, and ran to the alley to wait for Miss Rose.

* * * *

"Her name is Mrs. Mac."

"McEvoy," Rose finished. "Here you go." She tossed a coin to the child. "Don't' lose it playin' marbles." He gave her that same chipped-tooth grin and ran off to find his friends.

"You knew it was her, didn't you, Rose?" A willowy woman with light brown hair and porcelain skin put her arm around Rose's waist and gave her a hug.

"I seen a picture of her once," Rose replied. "It'd make sense, her coming to town to collect his money. He said that money was for us. Money for having a good time." Her voice was bitter.

"Nothin' you can do, honey. Don't eat your heart out over this."

Rose walked away from the conversation, returning to the saloon. She called to the barkeeper.

"Harold, have you seen Simon? I have a job for him."

* * * *

"That was easy, wasn't it, Marita? I think we have time for some shopping before we catch the evening train."

"I'm glad you decided to let the bank worry about moving the money," Marita said. "It would have been dangerous for you to carry that much money."

"Yes, you're right. Two hundred dollars is more than enough to get us started and Wells Fargo will transfer the rest of the money next week."

There were so many sights to see in Tombstone. The town had spread like the silver-fever that gave it life. They started back down Fifth, passing the Occidental and Grand hotels, crossing Fourth to Wolcott's General Store. "That's Rotten Row," said Brenna, pointing down Fourth Street. "I understand all the lawyers work in this part of town."

Wolcott's store was filled with all kinds of goods from staples to specialties. "Would Manuel like one of these?" Brenna was admiring a tray of switchblades.

"Oh I'm sure he would. But, *Señora*, you do not have to be so generous."

"I want to, Marita. If it hadn't been for Manuel, we'd still be waiting for the money." She handed the shopkeeper the ebony handled knife and a dozen candy sticks for the children. I'll take these and the rouge," she said.

"Rouge, *Señora*? You are still in mourning, no?" Brenna leaned to Marita's ear.

"I never was in mourning, Marita. And you know it." Marita made a few clucking sounds like a disgruntled hen.

"Look at the time. We have to get to the station." Brenna paid for her purchases, slipped the rouge and knife into her purse, and carried the candy in a brown wrapper bundled with string. By the time they got to the station, Marita was convinced there was someone following them. "Not again, Marita. You are taking all the fun out of our trip."

"He was in the store and now he follows us to the station. I do not want him sitting next to us." The ladies chose seats where a family of four was sitting, leaving only two vacancies. The stranger that Marita observed sat at the end of the car.

"Now, are you happy?" Brenna whispered to Marita. Marita seemed to relax and prepared for the long ride home. In no time the gentle swaying of the train had nodded her off to sleep. Brenna continued to read her copy of *The Epitaph*. When she looked up she caught the stranger staring at her. He wasn't an evil looking man, he was quite handsome. But he averted his eyes like a guilty child, rather than an admirer. Brenna wrapped the drawstring on her purse around her wrist several more times and placed the paper over it. She turned away from him but was determined to stay awake.

It was dark when they arrived in Bisbee and neither looked forward to the walk home. "Let's go get a buggy," Brenna suggested. "I'm too tired to walk." They staggered from the train, stiff and blurry-eyed, looking for a driver. "Do you see a carriage?" Brenna asked. But Marita's attention was focused on the mysterious man making his way toward the women. As he was quickening his pace, Marita watched him reach into his jacket pocket.

"Marita, Mrs. McEvoy!" Brenna twirled around in the direction of the familiar voice. It was Manuel and Francisco. Exactly then there was a hard push from behind and both women were jarred, nearly falling as the rude man rushed by. Manuel was instantly at Brenna's side, catching her by the arm to stop her fall.

"It was him again," Marita said. "See I told you I didn't like him. Why he didn't even apologize." Brenna reached for her purse. It still dangled from her wrist yet one of the cords had been broken. She fingered the cloth bag to identify its contents, relieved that the money and gifts were still enclosed. She opened her purse and pulled out the knife.

The stranger had vanished.

"I borrowed a carriage," said Manuel. "We didn't want you walking in the dark."

"How nice," Brenna replied with a smile. She continued to search the crowded station for the man's face. "Look what I got you." She handed Manuel the knife and ripped open the bag of candy for Francisco. Manuel opened the knife, admiring it, but seemed embarrassed to receive such a nice gift. Brenna looked up once again. Her eyes locked on the stranger watching Manuel handle the knife, turning it deftly in his hand. He remained fixed, rolling a cigarette as Manuel helped the two women into the carriage. Marita arranged a blanket over their laps. A quick tug on the reins brought the chestnut horses to life. The black carriage was off with a jerk, escaping with James's hard-earned money.

Chapter 8

The last fork dropped from Alberto's hand to the plate, clattering as it fell. All that remained on the dining room table was the turkey carcass and the empty serving bowls.

"Manuel, that was a wonderful Thanksgiving turkey," Brenna said. She dabbed her mouth with the linen napkin.

"Where did you say you shot him?"

"In the canyon," Manuel replied. "But you know, it's getting harder and harder to hunt. The more people that come, the less game there is."

"Well, I'm afraid we've left nothing but the bones,"

Brenna replied. "There certainly won't be any leftovers."

"No, no," Marita defended the pathetic looking cage of bones and skin. "I will take him home and cook soup. It will make a good broth for the *menudo*."

"Ugh," whined Enrique, Marita's ten-year-old son. "I hate cow stomach! It's too chewy." The other children giggled.

"Good." said Alberto. "Then there is more for me. I still have a lot of room in this beeg belly." He patted his stomach like he was greeting an old friend. Alberto was proud of his protruding abdomen and well-fed family. The color of his skin had placed him in the smelter where the pay was considerably less than the white men and the Cousin Jacks. The work was dangerous and the heat often unbearable for most men. But Alberto considered himself a success, having immigrated from Mexico so he and his mate could birth American children, sure to have more opportunities than his generation.

"Well, don't be too boastful of that big stomach," Marita chided. "Mine will be just as big very soon." The room was silent.

Alberto's round face lit up like the morning sun. "Another one, Marita?" He held up his fingers to count. "This one will make number eight!" He stood up from the table and went to his wife, planting a big kiss on her cheek. The younger children covered their eyes while the older ones cheered. More laughter broke out as Marita blushed a warm pink. "And when will this blessing arrive?"

"Early this summer. So you'd better plan on working harder to feed this extra mouth."

"Why should I," Alberto questioned. He stopped to pick a piece of food out of his teeth with his fingernail. "My woman is part owner of a boarding house."

"Don't count your money so fast, *Señor*," Manuel said. "I may never finish building."

"Oh, we're not that far from opening, Manuel," Brenna replied. "Why we'll be able to board out the first room by next week."

"But the last two rooms won't be finished for months," he said half-heartedly.

"That's right," Francisco added. "The lumber we ordered last week, they sold it to the mines."

"Well, I never...." Brenna started. "What gives them the right?"

"They don't need the right," Manuel said. "They are the mines and they do what they please. I've had to reorder and it could be two more weeks before our lumber comes in."

"Well, we're going to have our grand opening anyway. Alberto, can you get word around at the Copper Queen?"

"Si," Alberto replied. He reached up to smooth his graying mustache. "My mouth is as beeg as my belly. I will tell all the miners about Mrs. McEvoy's boarding house."

* * * *

Alberto was true to his promise. A town full of lonely miners longing for home cooking, would fill a boarding house faster than a starving man could empty a bowl of beans. Manuel worked into the late hours of the night, ashamed that his work had not yet been completed. There was still his part time job at the stables, but his evenings were spent building. Often he was so tired, he wanted to lie down in one of the small rooms, curl up on the wood floor and drift off to sleep. But what would Mrs. McEvoy say if she found him there in the morning? What would the white neighbors say about her?

It was nearly ten p.m. and he had already sent Francisco home to finish his school work. That boy was going to graduate high school whether he liked it or not. He was already older than most of the other students and that was often cause for his embarrassment. But he was made to understand that he needed to put his embarrassment aside. In this new century, the only way out of poverty was through education.

Driving one last nail into the window frame, Manuel heard gentle footsteps and the rustle of a skirt, trailing down the corridor to the last two rooms. The hall filled with an amber glow from a kerosene lantern, as Brenna made her way into the room.

"I need one of those miner's hats with the lamp", she said and laughed. "How can you see in here?"

Manuel laid down his hammer. "The wiring will be finished this week. When the electricity is in, we won't need lamps."

"I brought you some fresh coffee." Brenna placed a tray on a half empty keg of nails and pulled up an old wooden case. She filled the two coffee cups, handing one to Manuel, before seating herself on the wooden box.

In the soft light of the flames her dark coloring called to him. Her long black hair was pulled back off her face and tied with a yellow ribbon. He had seldom seen her face painted except for a little cheek color which she sometimes used on her lips. The dusty room had filled with the fragrance of fresh flowers and he breathed deeply, inhaling her scent. What a shame she didn't have a husband or even an admirer to appreciate her beauty.

"I just finished putting up the curtains in room one," she announced. "Lydia Maxwell has a bed and dresser to sell since her youngest son moved out. They're going to bring it by tomorrow so our first room will be finished."

She had a way of making it sound like it was his house too; a way of making him belong here. Marita had been right all along. She wasn't like the other white devils. Something about her was different. For some reason she thought of the Higuera family as her own and failed to pass judgment on any of them.

"Manuel? Are you all right? You look exhausted."

Manuel realized he'd been dreaming and not paying attention to the conversation. If she only knew he had been dreaming about her. How would she judge him then?

"I think it's time for you to quit working and get some rest."

"You're right. The coffee was good but I am very tired." He rubbed both hands over his eyes. "I'll be back tomorrow night."

"I'll be sure to save you some dinner." She helped him gather his tools and walked him to the front door. Brenna handed him his heavy coat and hat to shield him from the cold. He walked down the porch steps. Compelled to turn around, he looked at her one more time.

She was standing in the doorway, the light shining from behind her, making her image glow like an angel. She gave him a broad smile, tilting her head just to the left, a curious expression of expectation on her face. He was filled with an overwhelming urge to kiss her goodnight, like a man parting with his lover. Instead he smiled back and waved goodbye. What the hell was wrong with him? My God, he must be loco. That was it, the fatigue, the long hours drifting into the night. It could make a man crazy.

* * * *

When Manuel entered the back door to the kitchen, he found Marita peeking out the dining room door like a thief preparing to steal a pie. She failed to notice his entrance, focusing on whatever business was being conducted in the parlor. Her enlarged belly, expanding with the impending pregnancy, was pressed close to the swinging door. Only the top of her head, her nose and two eyes extended over the slab of wood. She remained out of sight, but well within earshot of the conversation. Feeling mischievous, Manuel snuck up behind her, grabbing her by the shoulders.

"What is so interesting, woman?" Marita shuddered. Turning to see it was her brother, a scowl crossed her face and she raised her arm to slam him in the chest.

65

"You are a fool," she hissed in a low voice. Manuel took her abuse in stride and chuckled. "Shhh, there is a gringo at the door, a Cousin Jack I think. Maybe he will be our first boarder." Hearing this, Manuel suddenly became interested. He stretched his neck to peer over Marita's head, the two of them spying while Brenna and the man spoke.

The man's face was not a familiar one, but it was one that had been seen around town. Undoubtedly he was a new miner, perhaps fresh from Cornwall or maybe an Eastern transplant. He sat on the tapestry couch, hat in hand, with his best manners on display. He looked moderately strong for his size. His skin was pale as clay and colorless as he was, either he was nervous or had never endured a desert summer. Marita and Manuel strained to hear the conversation, occasionally holding their breath to maintain the silence.

"Yes, ma'am, I heard through one of the other miners ya might be openin' up a boardin' house." His language was thick with a cockney accent. "It would be nice to have a home cooked meal. I get good and sick of the food on Brewery Gulch, if you can call it food."

"And would you mind Mexican food once in a while?" Brenna asked. "I have a Mexican cook."

"No ma'am, I've taken to it nicely. I was thinkin' the hot peppers would be far too potent, but I find it a pleasant change."

"Where would home be?" Brenna asked.

"England, ma'am, grew up outside a London, but me Mum moved us to Cornwall when I was a young lad. I surely do miss the green and the rain. But this was m'only chance to make it to America."

There was no remorse in his voice. It was almost as if he knew he'd never see his homeland again and that special part of his life had been lost forever. How sad, Manuel thought. My people are only a few miles away and I can always return home. This man was not likely to ever see England again.

"Well Mr. Hol—did you say your name was Hollan?

"Hollands, ma'am. Michael Hollands."

"Mr. Hollands, we would like to make our home, your home. We have our first room ready, closest one to the water closet so it will be very convenient. Would you like to see it?"

He followed her to the boarding rooms, passing the large, mahogany dining table, decorated with a lace runner and a large, bushy green fern. Walking through the room, his head turned side to side, eyeing the comforts of his new home. When he was well out of view, Marita and Manuel crept out of the kitchen and into the dining room.

"Here you are, Mr. Hollands." She opened the door to the small room, removing the skeleton key from the lock. The door opened to a cheerful space, bright with the morning sun.

The quiet gentleman sat on the bed, testing the softness of the mattress. Worn springs squeaked in response. He pressed down on the pad with both hands. Manuel saw Brenna flinch as she let out a gasp, concealing her reaction with a dainty, feminine cough. Manuel strained to see what had startled her. Hollands scanned the room, pausing to admire the blue and yellow wallpaper. He stood and walked to the dresser. While he fiddled with the dresser drawers, Manuel noticed several of his fingers were missing on one hand, cut clean down to the palm.

For a moment Manuel wondered what it was that they found so shocking about a man without all his fingers. Was it the oddity of an incomplete human being? Or knowing he endured terrific pain to sacrifice a part of himself? Hollands walked to the window. "Not much of a view," Brenna contributed. "But it will help cool the room on a warm night."

"Mrs. McEvoy, I couldn't ask for better lodging. This will be a fine room."

"When would you like to move in, Mr. Hollands?" Brenna fingered the key that was still in her possession. She seemed anxious to make it Mr. Hollands' property. "If you want we can complete the contract today."

Hollands lowered his gaze avoiding eye contact with Brenna. "I got me goods with me, ma'am. Hid 'em out in the bushes while we talked. I been so lonely in the Gulch, so unhappy." He shook his head while he spoke about his misery. "I was hoping more than anything this would work between us."

Manuel liked Hollands more and more. He was such a humble man; not at all arrogant like some of the Cousin Jacks.

"Please step over to my desk," Brenna suggested, "and we'll go over the contract. Why don't you retrieve your belongings while I get the papers ready?" Marita and Manuel scampered back to the kitchen. Mr. Hollands nodded politely and, capping his head, dashed out the door, returning before Brenna could find her ink bottle. She began to explain the terms. "As you can see, this paragraph states that room and board is a dollar fifty per week and includes your three daily meals. Laundry is extra but you are always welcome to use our facility to do your own wash. Marita can pack you a lunch for your shift should you be missing a meal during your work day." Brenna continued for several more paragraphs before she noticed the blank look on the man's face. She hadn't questioned his literacy. "Mr. Hollands, can you read this contract?"

"Not very well, Mrs. McEvoy. But you're doin' a fine job of tellin' me."

Brenna continued slowing her pace to be sure he understood all the terms. "Now these are the house rules. They're quite plain and straightforward. If you break the rules you get a warning. After that your contact is revoked, cancelled. Do you understand, Mr. Hollands?"

Brenna didn't wait for an answer. "Rule number one. No drunk and disorderly behavior. If I find you're annoying the other boarders, I'll confine you to your room to sleep it off. You'll also be expected to pay for any damages made during a drunken spree. Rule number two. No women in the rooms after midnight. No exceptions."

"Yes, ma'am," he complied.

"Number three is no spitting on my floors. That's disgustin'. And we don't use spittoons either." At this announcement the man took a hard swallow. "Number four. Always clean up after yourself in the water closet. Rinse the tub and keep it tidy."

"We have a tub?"

"Yes, a lovely tin tub. And there's a small stove to warm the water should you be wanting a hot bath. Very soon we hope to add a hot water heater to the house, but for now the stove will warm the water and the room." Mr. Hollands let out a contented sigh. "Now, are you having any questions about the rules?"

"No, ma'am. I'd like to mark my X and settle into my new home." She handed him the pen which he grasped awkwardly. The pen dropped from his hands and he retrieved it. Feeling a need to explain his difficulties, he began to tell his story. "Was a mining accident, ma'am." He held up his disfigured hand like he was looking at it for the first time. "Got my hand caught between two a them cars. There was no way to save my smaller fingers, they were bloody goners already. The Doc, he just finished cuttin' them and threw them away, like they was nothin' but trash. Guess they were by then. But I still have my big one and my thumb." He gave the claw-like hand a wiggle. "I do all right by them."

Hollands marked his X and Brenna finished the contract with her signature. She filed the paper in her desk and bid good morning to Mr. Hollands, promising to try her hand at English cooking sometime. Then, she headed for the kitchen.

"Marita!" she called from the parlor. There was no answer. Marita and Manuel scrambled from the kitchen door to the table, trying to contain their excitement. She pushed through the door and there they sat, with the innocence of two children that had set fire to the barn.

"Marita, we'll be having one more for dinner," she announced flatly. "A Mr. Michael Hollands." She walked toward the table, bending low to get close. "We have our first boarder," she announced quietly.

"*Si, si*, we were watching! It is so exciting." Marita had jumped up from her chair, holding tight to Brenna. She was buoyant with enthusiasm and bounding like a desert toad.

Manuel stood, preparing to leave for his stable job. "I will be back this afternoon, Mrs. McEvoy. Soon you can fill all your rooms." He stepped out the back door, anxious to work with his horses.

"Manuel." Brenna stopped him. "You know this would not have been possible without you."

"Yes, I know, but it works both ways. We would not have jobs without you." He paused. "We are here to help each other."

He stepped out into the quiet December day. The air was cold and clean, hanging like a fresh washed sheet. Everybody and everything seemed chilled and unwilling to move fast. Soon the day would warm and the crispness of the morning would be forgotten.

In the city activity began to stir. The puffing of the train could be heard in the distance, resting before its departure for Tucson. Along Main Street, door bells were jingling. Customers wandered in from the cold, hoping to locate the perfect Christmas gift while warming themselves in the cozy stores. People mingled everywhere, concerned with their business of the day. Did they know how happy he was?

For the first time in his life, he had been allowed to take control of another person's destiny. God had given him a reason for being here. Who would Mrs. McEvoy have turned to if he had failed her? He had never seen her so confident; proud and determined that she would make it this time. He had been a part of what made her whole. A vision came before him. He saw a swallowtail butterfly, black and yellow and bold, with fresh, tender wings, emerging from a brittle cocoon. Clinging to a budding tree branch, it waved its new wings in the spring sun, stretching to capture each warm ray of light. He had seen them often in Mule Canyon, struggling with their new lives, trying to make a place for themselves. Yes, she reminded him of a swallowtail. And there was a whole new world out there waiting for her.

Chapter 9

Marita had a dream. It was a fitful nightmare that startled her from sleep and threw her into a wakeful panic. She sat up in bed, glancing around the room to make sure the demon woman had not followed her to reality. Gently she lay back down so as not to disturb Alberto. She reached out for his hand to calm her pounding heart. Soon it would be time to rise and prepare breakfast. For now she would remain in her warm bed and wait for the minutes to pass.

What had the dream meant? She knew that the devil woman in her nightmare was La Llorona. Why had this spirit come to her now? The dream played in her mind like one of those new moving pictures at the theater. The river she stood near was a channel of churning muddy water, frothing with dirty, white foam. La Llorona, draped in black, knelt beside the river bank, screaming for the children she had thrown to the hungry waters. Her silhouette revealed claw-like nails reaching into the black sky, grasping at nothing. She wailed with the howl of the coyotes, and all that answered was the roar of the angry waters.

Marita began walking toward her, taking small cautious steps. She was terrified but drawn to the ghost and her plea. Closer and closer she advanced, and now there was only a few feet between them. The terror was making her skin crawl like a nest of spiders.

Marita reached out to La Llorona, touching her on the shoulder. At any moment now the woman would turn to face her. No one had ever seen her wicked face before. At least no one who had lived to tell about it. In a blur of black and grey La Llorona turned to confront her. Marita was awake, gasping for air and shaking from terror.

She said a silent prayer to the Virgin, thanking her for waking her from her torment. It would be some time before she would be able to put her fear aside. For now she would tell no one about the dream.

Marita pulled back the patched quilt and the striped wool serape covering her bed. Her toes curled as they touched the damp dirt floor. In the darkness she reached for her brown leather sandals hiding underneath the sagging mattress. She longed for warm bedroom slippers that would comfort her stiff arthritic joints. Perhaps she could buy some slippers for Christmas when she got her bonus from the *Señora*. Most likely she would buy some special treats for the children.

She grabbed her wool wrapper to help fight off the morning chill. Dawn was still two to three hours away but a full moon illuminated the bedroom, sending streams of light through the thin, cotton curtains. She pulled back the heavy drape that separated her sleeping quarters from the rest of the house. Graceful as a deer, she made her way among the sleeping bodies scattered around the rest of the house. Little Bianca was having a fitful dream herself, talking out-loud, first in English, then in Spanish. Several other children were snoring in varying degrees of loudness and depth. They slept peacefully in their own little worlds, following whatever dream their hearts would lead them to.

The baby stirred inside her. It was a gentle flutter, not unlike a gas pain, and it was several seconds before Marita understood what had happened. Her hand responded without hesitation, caressing her belly to comfort the unborn child. Was it a bad omen, the baby kicking for the first time after she dreamed of the Weeping Woman? Manuel and some of the older children would think she was crazy for sure. She would have to pray very hard over this one. Maybe she would talk to her priest.

She poured herself a strong cup of boiling coffee, standing close to the iron stove to warm her body. This baby would have to be the last. She was getting too old to bear the physical burden of childbirth. But how would she make Alberto understand? Many a marriage had soured when wives had refused to bed with their husbands. She loved him with all her heart and after all these years he still lit a fire inside her. If she refused him, he would find solace somewhere else. If she didn't and birthed another child, it could kill her.

She parted the drapes underneath the dry sink and pulled out the flour tin. The lard was kept outside in the desert cooler, but she had brought it in the night before to avoid the crisp morning air. Her experienced hands blended the meager ingredients that would fill the empty stomachs of her family. As she kneaded the dough and patted the dough into shape, she thought of Magdalena. That whoring widow had been eyeing her Alberto for years. Magdalena would love to have a hard-working man to keep her and feed her children. There must be another way to stop having babies besides refusing her husband.

She had heard of a pessary, something you put inside you to keep their seed from entering. It was against her God not to want children, but who was to know? She would only have to shame herself, and maybe God would even forgive her. Perhaps she could talk to the yerberia. Maybe there was an herb to kill the seed. Several women had drunk pennyroyal tea to end their baby's lives. The blood would peel out their wombs like the inside of a ripe tomato, taking the life from the child. Again her protective hand went to her abdomen to shield her baby. She could never kill her own child, and wondered what sort of pain a woman would have to suffer to commit such an act.

When she was a younger woman, there had been an Italian girl who got pregnant before her time. The selfish pig who did this to her refused to marry her. As the baby grew, so did her anger. In her seventh month she threw herself down a flight of stone stairs, trying to kill the baby. Instead he clung to life. When he was born he was a beautiful child with the face of a cherub. But he was never quite right in the head. He was dull in school and taunted by the other children. Johnny absorbed his mother's anger and was often violent. He left home when he was a young boy and was never heard from again. And as penance for her hatred, his mother was cursed and made barren for the rest of her days.

The tortillas were done and laying in a large heap on the stove, patiently waiting for the morning feast. Yesterday she collected enough eggs from the hens to give everyone a full breakfast with today's tortillas. Alberto staggered into the kitchen, pulling his suspenders over his plaid flannel shirt.

"Alberto, you are up? I didn't get a chance to warm the water for you to wash."

"That is okay, Mama," he replied, placing a tender kiss on her cheek. "The ice cold water woke me up." He patted her behind and seated himself at the table waiting for his coffee. Dear Lord, how could she ever refuse this man?

* * * *

The Mexicans would have called it *huevos*…balls. No fear. Marita needed to get up enough nerve to talk to another woman about her problem. It just wasn't a topic that women discussed lightly, and she didn't know how the Señora would react.

She waited several days before deciding to ask about the pessary. Manuel had left for the stable, so the two women were left alone to discuss life.

"Marita, you're confusing me. What is it exactly you're trying to say?" Brenna was sitting at her desk in the foyer. She wheeled around the brown leather chair to Marita's direction, as if facing the poor woman would clarify her hearing.

"*Señora*, I don't want any more babies. Do you know how to stop this?"

"I'm not sure," Brenna responded. "James and I were never together enough for me to worry about such things."

"To tell Alberto I do not want him," she shook her head, "he will leave me, *Señora*."

"But that's not so, Marita. You still want your husband, don't you?"

"*Si, si*, it is the babies I don't want. I love my family. I just don't want any more of them. It is hard to feed and clothe a large family. Besides, there is no more room in the house. What do you know? What is a pess, pess…aieee!" She threw her hands up in the air and began to walk away.

"Wait, a pessary? Is that what you want?"

"I don't know," Marita replied. "What is it?"

"I'm not sure myself. I know there's something that will go over the man's…" She motioned with her hands like she was covering her finger.

Hollands burst through the front door. Brenna, caught completely off guard, gave a jump and reached to the back of her hair with both hands, adjusting a comb.

"Good day, ladies," he said, tipping his hat. "Forgot my lucky coin. Don't go in the mine without it." He made his way to his room in large easy steps. He returned quickly, capturing lost time, while the women pretended to busy themselves with the day's work. Politely, he tipped his hat again and closed the door. Marita waited until she heard his steps fading down the rose path. She remembered exactly where they had left off.

"Alberto would never do that," Marita scoffed. "He would say we were sinning against God."

"Sinning against God," Brenna repeated with contempt. "No doubt a man came up with that sin. Tell a man to split his legs like a wishbone, push out a watermelon, and then ask him about sin." Both women snickered.

"What if I wash afterwards?" Marita continued.

"You mean douche?"

"I do not know what it is called. Whatever it is that washes out the seed."

"I've heard that doesn't work," Brenna said. "You can still get pregnant." Marita tried again.

"What about jelly? They say a greased egg won't hatch."

"Marita, this is all wrong. We don't know what we're doing. You need to talk to a doctor. They'll know what to do. They won't tell anyone and I'll go with you if you want."

"It will be embarrassing."

"Why should it be? Isn't your marriage and your health worth it?"

"We will see," Marita concluded, picking up her dust cloth. "I have a long way to go before I worry about such things." But Marita was lying to herself. She was very worried. Mostly about Magdalena and her wandering, evil eyes.

* * * *

The success of the boarding house gave everyone reason to feel good about the Christmas season. Dark green pyracantha branches laden with red berries decorated the fireplace mantle, while the fragrance of baking gingerbread and holiday treats lingered in the cozy home. Brenna had draped the dining room table with a magenta cloth. At each end of the table, a plate of tempting sweets beckoned the hungry miners returning home after an exhausting day in darkness.

Two new boarders had joined the house. An Italian man named Vincenzo Toro, who went by the American name of Vince. He left his bride of twenty-two days in Sicily and promised to send for her when he could afford her passage. He barely had time to consummate the marriage and for all he knew, he might need passage for two by the time he saved enough money for the boat trip. He still spoke more Italian than English, but often the Englishman would spend time with him trying to share his language. The conversations were comical and Marita enjoyed eavesdropping.

"I no understand," Vincent would start. Chi gaga, thatsa not a nice word."

"I'm trying to explain," Hollands said. "Maybe in Italian, chigaga isn't nice. But in English, Chi-ca-go is a big city in Illinois."

"Oh?" Vincent was pleasantly surprised. "What's Ill-enoy?" Hollands would get out his map and with his two good fingers patiently point out the different states. Vincent absorbed the information without hesitation, and it was easy to see he would not remain in Bisbee for long. There was too much to discover in this new land for those that were willing to work hard.

Each evening the dining room table was filled to capacity. Several nations sat around the table: the English, Italian, Mexican, Irish and French, all speaking the only common language they knew, American. Here and there American slang began to emerge and even the Englishman's words were softening, no longer speaking the Queen's language.

It was Brenna's custom to dine with the boarders each evening. If seats were available, others would drop in for a meal. Brusque as they were in the mines, the men would maintain their best manners with Mrs. McEvoy. In time Brenna became known as Mrs. Mac, largely due to one particular boarder.

When the boarding house had been open for only a few weeks, a man came to the door looking for a room. He stood tall and lanky, unsure of himself. When he opened his mouth it was clear to see why. He had the most hideous stutter Marita had ever heard. He was at his worst in unfamiliar circumstances, and as he stood at the door requesting a room, Marita remembered thinking what a pathetic sight he was.

"Mmmm, m-m name's Lll, Leroy," he stammered. "Do, do, do, do ya, you have a room, ma'am?"

"My name is Mrs. McEvoy, Leroy. And yes, we have a room available. Won't you come in?"

He stumbled in and Marita rolled her eyes at Manuel. She had no patience for such misfits. Manuel shrugged his shoulders, knowing there was nothing they could do. Both knew the *Señora* would take him in like a stray cat from the alley.

Once he was comfortable, the stuttering improved. But through the course of the evening and the conversations, he was never able to pronounce Mrs. McEvoy. He would get as far as Mmmm missus, mm, mm, Mac and then he would start all over again with the missus. Surely it was something about the repeating letter, M, but finally Brenna reached out to him, placing her delicate hand on his leathery forearm. "Leroy," she said, looking him directly in the eyes, "call me Mrs. Mac." He gave her a smile that said a thousand thanks and before the next dinner everyone at the table addressed Brenna as Mrs. Mac. She seemed to enjoy her new identity as the fragile Mrs. McEvoy had been replaced by the stronger Mrs. Mac.

Yet another stray came to frequent the boarding house. A wrinkled old man, aged well beyond his actual years. He lived as a hermit, believing he was unfit to share a home with anyone else. Years ago, his only companion had been his younger brother, Jacob. Working a claim, alone in the hills, his brother had been taken with fever and died within days. He blamed himself for the boy's death and had lived alone ever since. Roosting in a tiny shack, tucked up in the sparse hills, he worked odd jobs to keep his belly filled with food.

When Brenna met him for the first time, he came to the back door, cash in hand, asking to buy a meal. Not knowing any better, Brenna welcomed him to her table. He was seated at the table and immediately recognized by the men.

"Ahhh, eet ees Pinto," said the Frenchman in a loud voice. Meesus Mac, I am grateful he seets at the far end of your table." All the men laughed at his comment but Brenna failed to understand.

"Your name is Pinto?" Brenna asked. Marita began serving the soup. "How did you come by that unusual name?" Hollands began choking, gagging on his broth and nearly spitting it back in his bowl. The other men were laughing again while Brenna tried desperately to keep up polite conversation. She had never seen them behave this way.

Marita reached across the table to serve Pinto when a penetrating odor crawled into her nose and mouth. It left her with a burning sensation in her throat. She twitched her nose and widened her eyes. Then she pinched them shut as they began to water. Perhaps she had stepped in something foul. She checked her shoes and then caught Manuel laughing at her. All the other men were watching her too. Marita remained behind Pinto, somewhat stunned by the odor. Then it occurred to her. The man had broken wind.

Again her eyes widened and she took a quick step back, crashing into the couch, nearly spilling the kettle of soup. By now it had reached Brenna. She gulped her soup in a most unladylike manner and raced from the table, excusing herself to help Marita with the serving. Once in the kitchen, they could breathe again.

It was the fastest supper on record. Most of the men ate in twenty minutes, made a fast exit and promised they would return for coffee and tea later that evening. Pinto thoroughly enjoyed the dinner, remaining for Marita's famous spiced cobbler. As he left, he expressed his gratitude, remarking he would like to return after his next payday.

Once he left the kitchen, Brenna collapsed on the couch. She reached for her black lace fan, resting on the coffee table, waving it as fast as a hummingbird wing. "Now what would be his problem? He's stunk up my whole room. Even with all the diapers I change, even when Sara's filled her pants, she doesn't smell that bad."

Manuel fell to the floor laughing while tears streamed down his face. Never before had they heard the *Señora* talk so frankly about body functions.

"What is wrong with him?" Marita fired her questions at Manuel.

"They don't call him Pinto for nothing," he said while wiping his eyes. "He has this problem digesting beans. He says that it gives him terrible gas. The problem is, that's all he has to eat."

"Well now," Brenna said. "I guess we all know what Mr. Pinto had for lunch today."

"Mrs. Mac, you mustn't let him back in the dining room," Manuel cautioned. "He will start driving the men away."

"Manuel is right, you know," Marita chimed in. "He can't come back." Brenna released a big sigh, grateful for the fresh air.

"I'll feed him in the kitchen," she said. "I don't have to charge him and he can't do any harm in there."

"No harm," Manuel said. "Who knows, he may even do us a favor and choke the poor flies foolish enough to wander into the kitchen."

Marita shook her head and left to finish tomorrow's shopping list. When was that woman ever going to learn? Her heart would always be bigger than her head.

Chapter 10

Winter's frost melted with an early spring. Manuel strolled around the backyard, analyzing the garden plot as seriously as a man building a castle. Instead he made plans to build a home for his summer vegetables. The swollen brown buds on the trees, nearly ready to burst with tender new leaves, told him it was time to turn the soil and begin.

There would be plenty of fresh horse manure from the stable. He would have to enlarge the garden to satisfy the appetites of the new boarders. No doubt they would appreciate the fresh vegetables, so hard to come by in the mountain community.

He reached for the soil, grabbing a fistful of rich dirt. The soil compressed into a firm ball and then broke easily with his fingers. The ground was easy to work, and the smell of the damp earth made him eager to grab a shovel and begin turning the beds for the new seeds.

When the screen door slammed he looked up to see the two boys tumbling out of the kitchen. They went running toward him to see what he was doing.

"Are you gonna start the garden, Manuel?" Michael asked. "Can I help dig and plant?"

Manuel rubbed his chin thoughtfully. "I don't know, *hombre*," he replied. "Are you man enough?"

"I got muscles," Michael responded. "Come feel," he said, defending his manhood. Manuel walked over to the child, grabbing his arm to appease the request. His big hand nearly wrapped around Michael's arm. The flesh was as tender as chicken meat but his eyes enlarged as he released his grip and let out a big whistle.

"*Hijola*! That is some muscle. Okay, you get the shovel and start digging over there." He pointed to a far corner of the yard where the child could do no harm.

Eric, in the meantime, was chucking dirt clods at the hens that had wandered in the garden plot. His aim was sure as he hit a small white bird square in the behind, sending her squawking and flying through the air. With one sweeping motion Manuel took his hand and caught the top of Eric's head, reminding him to leave his hens alone.

"Wha'dya do that for?" Eric complained.

"Why do you throw clods at the chickens? She won't lay eggs for days now. Besides, you shouldn't be mean to animals."

"It's just a dumb chicken," Eric taunted. Manuel was disgusted. The child was mean spirited and seemed to have a desire to cause pain. How much of it was from his father? He should not be thinking such things of the dead but it was easy to see the continuance from father to child.

Over at the clothes line, Marita was hanging laundry. It was Monday, wash day for the women. The boarding house supplied plenty of soiled bedding and then there was the men's laundry which provided extra income. Marita was big now, ripe as the buds on the tree. He saw her stop and reach around to rub her back after bending to pick up the clothes. She seemed exhausted this time. Maybe this baby was to be the last. The garden could wait. He walked to the clothes line and picked up the basket of clothes. He didn't know anything about hanging the wash, but he could keep her from bending and ease some of her pains.

Marita looked at him with a quizzical expression and then reached out to place a hand to his cheek.

"You will make some woman a fine husband someday," she said, grateful for the help. "Do you look for a mate?"

"There is not much to pick from in this town," Manuel replied, wanting to change the subject.

"You should have had three babies by now."

"How do you know I don't?" he asked. Marita was not sure whether he was telling the truth or making up lies. She looked into his eyes and he began to smile."

"You are full of yourself," she said. "I still say you need to find a woman."

"When I find the right woman, you will be the first to know."

* * * *

It was not long after Michael and Manuel had planted the garden that Marita gave birth. Alberto could not stand to be present and had gone to Brewery Gulch with Manuel to await the arrival. After so many babies and so much suffering, Alberto expected he could have endured just one more birth. But he could not stand to see Marita in pain, and Manuel, knowing this, took him to St. Elmo's saloon to dull his senses.

Within the thick walls of her adobe home, with her oldest daughters and a *comadrona* to help, she brought forth another daughter. A thick mat of black hair crowned the baby girl, whose bright pink complexion told the mother that this would be a healthy one.

Angelina washed the blood from the baby and swaddled her in a blanket. She walked to the front entry and yelled for Enrique, busily engaged in a rock fight with the neighborhood boys.

"Go get your *Papà*," she bellowed. "Tell him to come see his beautiful wife and new daughter." She smiled at her baby sister and walked inside to place the infant at her mother's breast.

Struggling for air, chubby Alberto half ran, half staggered into the bedroom, where the child had been conceived. Manuel followed, where his sister lay in bed, cradling the infant. Nearly asleep from hours of labor, she had worked as hard as any man in the mines.

"This has not been easy for her, *hombre*," Manuel reminded Alberto. But it seemed that Alberto knew this already. His tongue ran more freely than usual, pickled from several hours of tequila shots.

"Marita," he exclaimed, "you have given me another beautiful daughter. What have you named her?"

Marita stirred from her daze. "Theese is Ana," she slurred. "Alberto, this one will go to Normal school and make something of herself."

"*Si, si,*" he agreed willfully. "She is so plump and fat and healthy. You have done a good job, wife. But Marita," he sat on the bed and took his wife's hand in his scratchy palm, "this should be our last, no? You have worked very hard to give me so many beautiful children, but I cannot bear to see you do this again. We can do something about this, no?"

To this Marita awakened. Her eyes puddled with tears and as Manuel stood by, consumed by the miraculous event, he witnessed a love he was sure was matched by divine guidance. Not many Mexican men would be able to express their feelings like Alberto could show his Marita. If he could find a wife like this, life would be complete.

* * * *

Summer's intense heat caused the gardens to thrive, but Manuel feared if it did not rain soon, the living things would die from the parching heat. Almost every evening, he could be found watering the roses, vegetables, or the tiny patch of green lawn in the front yard. The women were counting on his efforts to bring food to the dining room table, and so were the hungry boarders.

Pinto was a regular now. He would stop by every Saturday evening, clean shaven and just a little drunk. Manuel was always surprised at how tidy he was. It was just that problem he had with gas that made him so offensive. He had an agreement with Mrs. Mac that he would get his leftovers in the kitchen for no charge, and he was welcomed to stay until he'd had his fill.

Often he would bring some token gift, like a child bringing flowers to his mother. One week it was a special rock he had found near the mine. Another day it would be a shiny bird feather or an unusual bottle. Pinto could find beauty in objects that other people would discard, and perhaps it was the simplicity in his life that helped him see beauty in almost everything.

Brenna never discarded his gifts. They lined the window ledges and corners of her home like special treasures waiting to be rediscovered. Marita complained that it was "trash that needed to be thrown away," but Brenna insisted that the goods be retained. Whether she took a liking to his tokens, Manuel didn't know. But the collection continued to grow with each dinner Pinto enjoyed.

The sun was burning on the horizon like the devil's torch when Marita sat beside Manuel to watch the day end. "No water tonight, Manuel?" she asked.

"It will rain before tomorrow," he replied. "I can smell it in the air." Puffy clouds curled in the sky, shaped like giant smoke plumes rising after an explosion. "Look at that one," he said, pointing to a pink and purple cloud. "It looks just like a big bear." A flash of lightening in the distance, somewhere over Mexico, seemed to confirm his prediction. Marita appeared distracted, like she was not herself. She was smoking heavily since Ana's birth. How she kept it from Alberto, he would never know. She finished her cigarette, crushing the burning tobacco in the powdery dirt.

"What is bothering you, woman? For days now it is as if you have something else on your mind. Your body is here, but your thoughts are somewhere else."

"If I tell you, you will say I am a crazy old woman."

"If you don't, I will know you are."

"Manuel, I had a dream. No, eet was a nightmare, so frightening," she said, shaking her head. "I don't know what to think."

"It probably means nothing. Maybe you were worried about something. What was your dream?"

She hesitated. "There was water, a river full of churning water. La Llorona, The Weeping Spirit, knelt by the water screaming for her children. Did you hear Jesus and Armando Montoya saw La Llorona just last week by the San Pedro River?"

"Marita, they had been drinking for days."

"Well anyway, I was afraid of her, but I felt sorry for her too. I walked toward her and reached out to touch her and then by God's grace, I woke up. *Es la verdad*, Manuel, eet was real. I was so scared I couldn't go back to sleep. Then that morning Ana moved for the first time. I keep thinking something is going to happen to her."

"So it's Ana you are worried about?"

"I don't know. I don't understand. Should I go see *Señora* Robles?

"That old witch? No, Marita. Don't get involved with that woman. She is linked to evil."

"She can see the future."

"If *El Señor* had wanted us to see our future, he would have given us all that gift. Stay away from her. Alberto will be furious if he finds out."

A baby let out a wail, signaling Marita to return to the house. "Someone calls to me," Marita responded. She stood in haste to go to the crying child. "With Ana and Sara side by side, if one started crying, you can be sure the second one will follow."

"Marita." Manuel stood to follow her into the house. "It will be all right. You mustn't worry about such things as dreams. Maybe tomorrow you can go to the church and say your Rosary and you'll feel better, no? Light a candle too. You are not a crazy old woman, just a confused one."

Manuel glanced up at the sky before entering the house. The clouds were collecting faster than flies on horse shit. Maybe this would be a good rain.

* * * *

For two days the clouds continued to build but the rain they delivered was a sorry output. The weak drizzles were hardly enough to settle the dust and Manuel could not understand why the sky would not open up. But on the third day, it began.

The sky was red and gold that morning when the sun caressed the clouds. They melted into shades of gray and black and by early afternoon it had begun to rain large round drops that marked the desert floor. The crusty ground made it difficult for the earth to absorb the water. It filled every channel of the hills, pursuing the closest ravine. The mountains had been plucked clean as a chicken's hide from when the Mexican cutters had supplied the insatiable mines with wood for their furnaces. Now there was nothing to hold the soil, and it ran with the water that eroded the hillsides.

The town began to agitate as if someone had kicked an ant hill. Floods had tainted many lives, and like animals anticipating an earthquake, many suspected the worst. When the men came home from the afternoon shift, there was word that water was coming down the canyon and headed for town.

"Ssss someone says there's water coming," Leroy blurted out when he walked in the door. He was dripping wet and what wasn't touched with water was covered with mud.

"We're safe here, mmm, Mrs. Mac, aren't we?"

Brenna was drying her hands on her apron. "My father built this home here for that very reason."

"Let's go down and see the water!" Eric pleaded.

"Can we, Mama? Can we see the water?" Michael asked. Brenna looked to Manuel.

"Is it safe?" she asked.

"If the rain lets up, I can't see any harm. There's a spot up the canyon where you can get close to the wash and see what's floating down." Manuel could see that Brenna was as curious as the boys. "We can leave Marita with the babies. Let's go take a look."

They could only go so far in the wagon. For a short distance they all got out to walk. Leroy was quite the spectator, venturing down toward to the water's edge.

"Looka there," he exclaimed. "There goes a table." Sure enough, someone's kitchen table floated down the wash with a red checkered cloth snagged on one corner. Up ahead more spectators had gathered to observe the unusual event.

But no one noticed Michael's absence from the group. Always a trusting child, he had no fear of harm. When the roar echoed up the canyon, it was a voice heard too late.

A large rush of water burst around the corner of the wash. It had gained momentum that had been collected from a fresh downpour. It chewed at the embankment and in one easy gulp, took the chunk of ground that Michael stood on. His hands flew up in the air and the ground disappeared beneath him. There were no cries from his throat. He simply vanished.

Brenna saw, far too late, the one thing she loved most in the world, taken from her in an instant. She went running down the bank, parallel to the wash, calling out his name, begging for a response. She ran as far as the land would let her, with Manuel and Leroy running behind her. When she could run no more, she fell to her knees, fingers digging into the mud in front of her. Still, she screamed out his name.

"Michael, Michael," she wailed. "Oh God, Michael, where are you?" She shook with her sobbing as Leroy and Manuel lifted her from the mud. "It took him from me," she continued. "The river took my baby."

Manuel's skin crawled like a black serpent had slithered across his heart. "Marita's dream," he whispered to himself. "My God, it's Marita's dream."

Chapter 11

Manuel sat on the steps to remove his boots. He knew Marita would crucify him if he tracked soot into Mrs. Mac's house. He struggled with each shoe, weak and exhausted from fighting the fires that had destroyed so many homes and dreams. As he stood, Marita came to the door.

"What did you see, Manuel?" Marita asked. "Is there anything left?"

"Most of it is in ashes," Manuel replied, dusting off his pants. "Tonight there will be many families on Chihuahua Hill without homes."

"And my home?" Marita asked without looking up. "Do I have a home?"

"You have a home and your family is safe." Marita crossed herself.

"I knew we would be spared," she said. "You say Alberto and the boys are all right?"

"*Si*, Francisco got some smoke while he was helping the Cruz family empty their home, but he will be fine."

"Did they lose it all?"

"They got out with their children and what goods they could carry away. But you know, their home was made of wood. It burned like kindling. The church is putting up some of the families until they can start building again. It will not be easy with the rains but the rains are what saved the rest of the Hill."

Manuel finished scrubbing the soot off his face and arms, drying himself on a cloth that Marita handed him.

"How is she today?"

"About the same. Doctor Benson says there is nothing more he can do for a broken heart. He can't help her unless she wants to help herself. You know, she did so well after *Señor* James disappeared. But to lose a child…a child should never die before their mother or father."

"If she doesn't get better soon, she is going to lose everything that is important to her. We need to get her out of the house."

"Maybe we should invite her to Lewis Springs," Marita offered. "It would be a good day for a picnic and would give her some time to stop thinking about her loss."

"She would not go with a Mexican family."

"It never hurts to ask. At least she knows we think of her."

* * * *

Brenna looked so sad sitting alone in the parlor, clothed head to toe in black and sipping the same cup of tea she'd been drinking the hour before. Her face was drawn and blanched, paler than he'd ever seen. Now and then Manuel would peer over the banister he was repairing. It seemed a large part of her had been lost with Michael. There was a dull ache in his chest as he recalled the garden he and Michael had planted together. It was only a few months ago. The plants continued to thrive, but Michael's life was gone forever.

He hoped the drowning had been quick. He imagined Michael's delicate pink lungs filling with the foul water and shut his eyes to rid his mind of the image. If he felt this way, what did she feel? He put his hammer down and walked to her.

"How are you today?" he asked. She failed to utter a word, only looking at him with drooping, puffy eyes and a faint smile.

"It's hard," she finally responded. "I miss his hugs, his gentleness. Sometimes I expect him to burst into the room and… " Her voice began to crack. "But I'll never see him again." She exploded into tears. Manuel expected she spent most of her wakeful time crying.

"Come to the Springs with us, Brenna." He had never dared call her by her first name before. He was sitting beside her on the couch, trying to console her. He wanted to hold her, tell her someday her pain would ease. Even now, he choked back the tears.

"Two of my family members dead and not even a grave to mourn," she continued. "Is it the hand of God or the hand of Satan that's dealt me this fate?"

What was he supposed to say to that? He allowed the silence to fill the void between them before speaking again.

"You know, in October we will celebrate *La Dia De La Muerta*, The Day Of The Dead. You call it Halloween. Mexicans have a different way of dealing with death. We live with it all the time; it is always there to face us. But we tease death, dare it to destroy us. And in the end, we know we will not escape. In the meantime, we live our lives. Above all, we go on."

Brenna's tears stopped. She wiped her eyes and nose with a black handkerchief, trying to stifle the spasms in her chest.

"This Lewis Springs, what is it? My father never took me there and James couldn't be bothered. Marita mentioned going there, but I refused her invitation."

"You can change your mind. You would like it," he encouraged her. "We ride in the flat cars out to the Springs and find a shady spot to settle the *niños*. We bring food and music. Later we swim and the children take a *siesta*. When the sun starts to set, we go home." He put his hand on top of hers. Startled, she tried to read his face. "Come with us," he said. "All you have to bring is yourself."

Brenna gave him a weak smile and a nod of her head. "All right. I accept your invitation."

They met at the station. The dozen or so brown, Higuera family members were a contrast to the white Irish woman. Manuel was relieved to see she was not wearing black. A straw hat trimmed with a pink ribbon shaded her from the sun. She was holding Sara and was wearing a calico dress, one that Manuel had never seen before. He was sure she'd bought the new outfit just for the picnic. For the first time since Michael's death, she appeared less vulnerable, more relaxed, and at peace with her demons.

Marita waved to her and she returned the expected feeble smile. Like a good mother hen, Marita directed her brood and Brenna onto the flat car with Eric trailing by her side. Almost on instinct Brenna opened the white lace parasol, shielding her face from the dangerous sun. The Higuera family paid no attention to the sun, yet Manuel watched Marita making a futile effort to keep their faces shaded. Some of the children were very light, and Marita was certain that they would be treated better with whiter skin. Manuel knew it would never make a difference. They would have to abandon their names and culture to become white. And who was to know? Maybe in time the girls would breed out their Mexican blood and marry *gringos*. This was often the way in America.

Someone started singing "In The Good Old Summertime" and before long most of the train was singing along. The music filled the desert void causing hawks, roadrunners and jackrabbits to scurry from the track and the unfamiliar sounds of human voices.

It took three picnic baskets and several blankets to complete the Higuera outing. Once scattered into small groups, the families became more manageable. The youngest children piled onto one blanket and the older youngsters sat off to the side. The adults and infants took the last cover, finding a cozy knoll overlooking the watering hole. People that had once crowded the train scattered to the shores, many fussing and arguing about the perfect spot to spend the warm summer afternoon.

Marita opened the baskets and began the parade of food: Chicken, sausages, salsa and tortillas, sweets melons and jugs of chilled tea. The children were upon them, scrambling for any food they could hold in their hands. They engulfed it and then were gone to romp in the cool spring. "Is there anything left?" Alberto asked.

"*Pobre niño*," Marita teased, while attaching Ana to her breast. "There is plenty for everyone."

Brenna responded to Alberto's plea, making plates for the rest of adults. When the food had been passed around, she let out a sigh as if she'd reassured herself she was useful again.

"That's all you eat?" Alberto asked, waving a chicken leg through the air like the United States flag. One cheek was still packed with food. "You will never get my nice, shapely figure if you eat that way."

Brenna actually managed to laugh a little. Alberto always amused her with his child-like ways. In that moment, she put her pain aside for the child that was missing from her life. Was it possible that she had almost forgotten how good it felt to be happy?

Dinner was a long, relaxing event, culminated by the splitting of red and orange melons that filled the air with their sweet fragrance. Instinctively the children flocked back to the blankets. Watermelon seeds flew everywhere. Brenna found herself laughing again as she watched the children running through the brush, spitting seeds under bushes and trees. "What are they doing?" she asked.

"Oh, it is silly," Manuel said, "but I've taught them to reseed the watermelons by spitting the seeds in the bushes. It gives them something to do."

"Has it ever worked?"

"Only for those seeds strong enough to survive."

Brenna stilled again and turned to face the gathering at the water, where children's voices rang through the air. Manuel wondered if the water awakened unpleasant memories for her.

"Come on," he said and offered her his hand. "I want to show you something."

Brenna wiped her hands on the green grass beside her and obediently accepted Manuel's help to stand. "Where are we going?" she asked.

"Are you afraid to be alone with me?" he asked, his brow creasing in concern.

"Of course not. I was just curious."

"It is a secret," he answered. After that she said nothing more, but clung to the arm he'd offered. As they left the picnic grounds Manuel caught site of Marita raising an eyebrow to Alberto.

They followed a grassy path through a clearing and turned a corner to climb a small hill. In a moment they came upon a large collection of sandy boulders which he led her behind. Her grip tightened as they disappeared from sight. She turned to look behind her one last time like a captain would view his sinking ship.

Manuel stopped in his tracks. "You are frightened," he said again.

"No, I'm not," she emphasized. "It's just that it's not proper for a woman, by herself, to be un-chaperoned."

"I am chaperoning."

She tightened her lips. "That's not at all what I mean, Manuel, and you know it."

"Shhh," he said, putting a finger to her lips. "Listen." Again he could see she was shocked by his boldness, but quieted herself. Then something caught her attention.

"What is that?" she asked. "It sounds like the river, but quieter, gentler."

He directed her to an opening where young trees and tall willowy grasses stood, enclosed by the large rock formation. In the center was a small bubbling spring, no larger than a wagon wheel, filled with crystal clear water. It took Brenna's breath away, and for a moment she stared at the water hole like someone had handed her a sparkling jewel. "Who knows about this?" she asked.

"Just me, and now you. And maybe the family that lived here before."

"Someone lived here?"

"I've found some old bottles and iron scraps. It's hard to tell."

"I would never leave a place like this."

"Sometimes I come here when I need to think, or to be alone. It is hard to do that at my sister's house," he added with a chuckle. "A couple of times I've come across deer or javalina drinking and resting in the grasses. It is a good place to be."

They were quiet, but comfortable with the stillness. Then Brenna spoke.

"This Day Of The Dead that you celebrate, how can you mock death?"

Manuel was picking at the grass, searching for small pebbles to toss into the spring. Each tiny stone sent a circle of rings that quickly reached the other side and bounced back to him; each separate circle penetrating the space of the one before it.

"We are not being disrespectful to those that die, but we must continue with our own lives. Those families burned out on Chihuahua Hill, they had nothing but they lost everything. They will go on because it is all they know how to do. You are a strong woman, Brenna. Life must go on, but only you can make that decision."

He thought he'd better close his mouth. He'd said enough without sounding like an old woman. On one knee, he bent down to the water, filling his palms with the sweet liquid. "I'd better return you to Marita. I will catch hell for dragging you away for such a long time."

"Luckily for Manuel, Marita and Alberto were resting when they returned. Both were sleeping on their backs, mouths wide open. "Look at them," Manuel whispered, "they even sleep alike. Watch this." He rearranged the blankets and motioned for Brenna to sit. He sat beside her and began speaking in a booming voice.

"*Si*, they say that Tombstone will be a ghost town soon." He directed her to pick up the conversation.

"Is that right?" she yelled back, not really knowing what was to come next.

"They can't seem to get rid of the water. What they need are some good miners, like Alberto."

Alberto, on hearing his name, rolled over like a floating log, stuttering, yawning and arousing Marita. She came up on one elbow.

"Oh, so you are back," she announced, rubbing her eyes with her fingertips.

"We've been back for quite some time," Brenna lied.

"How long would you say, Manuel?"

"Oh a good while," he replied. "Did you have a good *siesta*?"

"*Si*," Alberto said, but I hardly feel rested."

"I'm sure it's the sun," Brenna reassured him. "It takes so much out of you." Brenna had to bite her lower lip to keep from laughing. She didn't dare look at Manuel who had instigated their disrupted sleep.

Marita gave a long, lazy yawn. "We need to gather the *niños*. Soon it will be time for the last train." Manuel scanned the collection of children. "I see all of them but Eric."

"My God!" Brenna bolted to her feet, eyeing the water.

"No, Brenna." Manuel stopped her. "Eric is a strong swimmer and this spring runs still. Maybe he is somewhere in the brush making water. I will find him." He left in a rush, headed for the closest thicket. He was not superstitious, but in the back of his head he heard Marita's voice reminding him that tragedies come in threes.

He ran several hundred yards before a young Mexican girl came running out of the bushes. Her dress was marked with dirt and grass stains. She plowed into Manuel and with a startled tearstained face, looked to him as if she would say something, chose not to, and continued running. He heard voices and followed them into the brush. Eric and a strange young face emerged, a white boy he'd never seen before. They were laughing and talking in low voices.

"Your mother looks for you," he barked. "What were you doing back there? Did you hurt that girl?"

"We was just havin' a smoke," the stranger said. He was an older boy, scruffy and ragged looking. Manuel could smell smoke on their clothes but suspected more had been going on.

"Let's go," he said. "You are holding everyone up."

"Quit bossing me," Eric snapped. "You're not my father. You're just the hired help."

"And for that, I am grateful," Manuel replied and shoved him down the trail toward the train stop.

* * * *

"I believe that's the last of it, Manuel." Brenna finished by wiping her dusty hands on her apron. She stood authoritatively with her hands resting on her hips. "Bring the carriage around to the back. You can lay a blanket down and haul these clothes over to your church. I hope someone can make use of Michael's belongings."

"It is a good thing you are doing, Brenna."

"Well, Eric certainly can't use his clothes. This will help me put the past aside. Oh, and before you go, check the garden for any surplus vegetables. You can pass those on too."

She's back, Manuel thought. Like a soul that had been sleeping and finally acknowledged its purpose, she was busy giving orders, making plans and he couldn't have been happier. The house was alive again because of her renewed presence.

Sometimes at night, when sleep would not come, he would think of her. He pictured her sitting in front of the dressing table with the large, oval mirror, combing out the twist she wore on top of her head.

This time of the year when red and gold leaves fell from the trees, she would be wearing a long sleeve sleeping gown, most likely white but maybe with a pattern of small flowers and lace trim. He dared to think what it would feel like to unbutton the front of that gown and run his calloused hands over her cream-colored skin. And how would he feel waking up next to her every morning? Would it be a wonderful balance like Marita and Alberto or would it grow old and stale like a half filled mug of warm beer?

What a fool he was to even dream of such things. He was brown and she was white. Though she never threw this in his face, others would throw it in hers. They would say he wanted her for her money and property. They would ask her how she could stand to be with him, a man who could barely read and did menial labor to survive. He would never be able to support her half as well as she was supporting herself.

Still, he would invite her to the *Fiesta Of The Dead*, using Marita's family as cover for his heart's true desires. That was a pretense he could continue forever. But living with the pain of being so close to someone he so desperately desired, would bring his heart both suffering and happiness at the same time. What kind of fool welcomes this kind of sorrow? Yet in some unknown way, he was certain she would always be a part of his life.

Chapter 12

At the center of the field eight small boys gathered in a tight circle. They chattered among themselves, ignoring the crowd collected around them.

Each wore an identical outfit: a long-sleeved white shirt with matching pants, a straw sombrero trimmed in brightly colored ribbons, and a miniature serape thrown across one shoulder. Though it was early November, most were barefoot in the loose dust. In one hand they held a walking cane, in the other the mask of a wrinkled old face.

"What are they doing?" Brenna asked Marita.

"It is the Dance of the Old Men, a tradition at our Fiesta of the Dead." Brenna nodded in acknowledgement. The air was turning chilly as the autumn sun began to drop behind the hills. She took the black shawl draped over her shoulders and lifted it to cover her head. To an unknown eye, it would be hard to distinguish her as a *gringa* among the Mexican women.

Manuel returned from the street vendor with an armful of warm, soft burritos. He handed one each to Marita and Brenna before scattering them among his nieces and nephews. "Have they started?" he inquired, taking a great bite of the remaining burrito he held in his hand.

"No," Marita answered, "but they should start soon. See, they gather in the circle."

"This is my favorite dance," Manuel said. He sat next to Brenna on one of the hay bales encompassing the field. "The little boys dress up as old men and make fun of all the grumpy old timers in the village."

The mariachi music filled the twilight hour and the costumed children began to stir. First they held the masks to their faces and began hobbling around on the canes. Some were laughing. Others seemed nervous and forgot to use their canes as they performed. Then they fell into a long line linking themselves with the canes. The line whipped past the crowd at the speed of youth, not the crippling walk of old age. Young children watching in awe would soon be old enough to take their place in the dance, not unlike life itself. The adults, entertained by their antics, played a part in the ritual that had taken place since time began.

"They have worked very hard on this dance," Brenna commented.

"For many months they have practiced," Marita replied. "Many times their older brothers have been their teachers."

The boys turned to face the crowd. They removed their masks and bowed gallantly while the crowd cheered for their efforts.

Immediately the torches surrounding the fiesta were lit, casting a yellow glow on the camp. A peddler passed with confections shaped like human skulls and leg bones. Manuel quickly cornered her, selecting three sweets for the two women and himself. He handed a skull to his sister and one to Brenna. Brenna smiled at Manuel, wondering what to do with the trinket. When she saw Manuel eat his, she nibbled at the jawbone of the skull he'd given her. It was sweet, like a divinity and she enjoyed its taste but was repulsed by the skull itself.

"Where is Alberto?" Brenna questioned, daintily licking her fingertips. "Is he not here somewhere?"

"He is home," Marita said with a short, curt tone.

"He doesn't feel good," Manuel added. "His head hurts like a burro kicked it."

"As it should," Marita concluded.

"He started his fiesta last night," Manuel explained. He motioned like he was drinking from a bottle. "Too much." He seemed amused by Alberto's suffering while Marita appeared thankful for it.

Another dance was beginning. Four adults dressed in black walked out to the court. They wore white mop heads as wigs. Their faces were painted white with deep black holes for the eyes and ghoul-like outlines for their noses and mouths. On the front of their black costumes they had carefully outlined the bones of a skeleton.

The skeleton dancers motioned for the children to follow. The children came from every corner holding hands while following the dancers. In the black of the night their innocent, smiling faces were illuminated with the glow of the burning torches. The fact that they danced with ghouls and monsters didn't seem to bother them. There was no fear in their hearts and they danced through the crowd, prancing in front of Brenna.

They were so young and fresh, with all of life ahead of them. Their ebony hair vanished into the night until all Brenna could distinguish were rows of glistening, white teeth and uninhibited laughter. The dancers ridiculed her aching heart, saying, "See, I am here, enjoying life. And where is your Michael? What have you done to him?"

Brenna darted from her seat, disappearing into the crowd before Manuel and Marita could follow. Both stood to look for her but could not distinguish her familiar face among the other people, shadowed by nightfall.

Brenna anticipated that they would try to follow her. *They mustn't see my crying,* she thought. *They will think I'm ungrateful.* She slowed her pace to a more natural step but then she heard her name.

It was Manuel's voice. If she ignored it, he might go away, uncertain that it was her. He called again and she quickened her pace, but in a moment he was upon her. His big hands reached out, grabbing her by the shoulders from behind, and in that instant he halted her steps.

"You can't be out here by yourself," he said, turning her to face him. She dropped her head, but he questioned her again. "Brenna?" It was almost a plea.

In the moonlight she saw his eyes rest on the tears streaking her face. He said nothing but pressed her against his chest like a child would protect his favorite teddy bear. "What is it? What have we done to hurt you?" Still she couldn't speak. He sat her down on a street bench waiting for her to answer. She removed a handkerchief from her skirt pocket, wiping her face.

"The...chil...children," she stammered. "The ones dancing with those demons. They're all so happy, so pleased. I started thinking of my Michael. It's all too much."

"But Michael doesn't dance with demons," he replied gently, "he dances with the angels."

His kindness only reached deeper into her chest, pulling at her heart. She stood to flee again, but he held her fast. "It is all right," he said, and because it seemed convenient, kissed the top of her head.

In a state of shock, she quit crying, holding her breath, afraid to move. The kisses continued down her forehead, across her closed eyes, over her wet cheeks, and down to her trembling lips. She fully understood what was happening. Abruptly, so did he.

He froze. "Brenna, I'm so sorry. God, I didn't mean to —"

She interrupted. "No, it's all right, really." She took the back of her hands and again wiped at her wet face, now cold and chilled in the fall air. "Why don't you walk me home?"

They said very little on the way home. He directed her through the potholes in the road, around the snarling street dogs and occasional drunks. They walked past the Copper Queen Hotel where several couples sat in the moonlight on the front porch of the grand hotel and eventually they came to the doorstep of her home.

"Thank you," she said and then offered him her hand to shake. He returned the grip with both of his hands enveloping hers. She gave his hand a reassuring squeeze and his eyes met hers with an apologetic smile. She walked through the front door and watched through the lace curtains as he waited for the latch to click in the lock. When he saw that she was safe within the confines of her home, he turned and walked away.

* * * *

Brenna rose early the next day. Would Marita know what had happened last night? It was hard to imagine that Manuel would tell her such things. She would certainly not tell Marita for fear that the Mexican woman would be disgraced by her brother's boldness.

Yet his kisses were not about aggression, they were filled with compassion and kindness, not lustful like James, but tender, almost childlike. Thinking about him filled her with anxiety and excitement. She had not felt so alive in years.

Monday morning would be awkward. She would pretend it had never happened and see how he would react. It would be scandalous for her to allow him to court her. It would likely never come to that. She put her hand over her ears hoping to quiet the voices in her head. It was impossible not to think about it. *Oh, why am I worrying over nothing?*

At that moment, Sara came climbing down the staircase. "Why you little minx!" Brenna charged. "Did you climb out of your crib again?" Sara met her with a severe gaze, sure she was in trouble. She started to recoil, when she heard her mother's voice again. "Come, let's have some hot porridge before you dress for Mass." Brenna scooped up the toddler, ready to whisk her off to the kitchen. "Eric," she called up the staircase, "time to dress for church."

"I ain't goin'," Eric called down. And then to himself he mumbled, "There's no such thing as God, anyway."

Chapter 13

The autumn sun spilled through the streaked glass pane, warming the wool blankets on Eric's bed. He lay on the bed, fingers clasped behind his head, gazing at the patterns in the punched tin ceiling. What were they called? Octagons? Pentagons? His teacher said he was stupid and may flunk reading. No matter. He didn't need school or education. He didn't need nothin' or no one.

He had no intention of going to church ever again. If God really loved him, he wouldn't have taken his brother. Nor would he have such a stupid mother to let his brother get killed. It didn't matter much when Pa disappeared. But Michael, he was okay. Why couldn't it have been his stupid little sister instead of Michael?

He sniffed under his armpit. He could use a bath, but he'd wait until his mother yelled at him. That way he could get a rise out of her. As soon as she left with Sara, he'd dress and leave for the day. His mother's footsteps on the stairs echoed through the upstairs hall. Quickly he turned on his side, pretending to be asleep.

"Eric!" Brenna screamed. "Get out of bed and dress for church." Her quick pace brought her across the room to his bed. She swept her hand in front of him, lifting the covers off his body. To her dismay and his, she saw he was naked from the waist down.

"Oh my," she gasped. "And where would your bottoms be?"

"Don't wear no bottoms. Gets too hot with all these blankets."

"It's I don't wear any bottoms," she corrected, "and I would much rather you use less blankets and more clothing. Now make yourself decent and come to church to ask for forgiveness."

She exited the room as quickly as she arrived. This was going to slow him down a bit, but he could still lose her at Saint Pats. He'd play along until they got to church and she started yappin' with the priest and others, and then he'd manage to disappear. She never paid no attention to him anyway.

It took about thirty minutes to walk to church with Sara tagging along. Just as he figured, the minute they walked up the steps, she began talking with the parishioners. Eric hung back slightly. He was easily lost in the crowd of adults. The minute Sara broke away from her mother's grasp, she'd go chasing after her and then he'd escape.

"Eric! Eric!"

He could hear her calling after him as he darted down the first alley off the church. No doubt she had wanted to introduce him to one of her dumb friends, an old lady or maybe the priest. She was still trying to get him to make his communion, but with all that had been happening the last year she'd been distracted and hadn't said much about it lately. Still, she managed to remind him he was going to hell if he didn't, and he figured he was headed that direction anyway.

Eric slowed his pace to a quick walk. He swung down to pick up a large stick, dragging it along the fences that lined the alley. Coming to the exit, he saw the opportunity to have a little fun and turned several trash cans over, spilling their reeking contents. Several dogs started barking when the tin cans fell and he raced out the exit and down the next street, hoping no one had seen him, but not really caring if they had. He had yet to meet any adult who could catch him once he started running.

In a few more minutes he'd be to the place where Harry hung out. He'd usually be sitting on the fence near the graveyard with a couple of others of his kind. Sometimes they'd be sharing a smoke or even a drink if someone had been able to get a bottle. They were a tough gang and Eric admired their guts. He wasn't quite like them; he was considered the rich kid. Not as rich as the ones in Warren, but not as poor as the ones in Brewery Gulch.

Harry caught sight of Eric making his way to the meeting place. "Well, look who's comin'," said Harry in his thick street tongue. "Just get outta church, altar boy?" The other boys snickered.

"Aw shut up, Harry," Eric snapped back and gave him a shove. "Gimme a puff." He grabbed the cigarette from the other boy's fingers and took a long drag, capturing the smoke in his lungs. The smoke gnawed at his throat until he choked for air.

"You need a little practice, kid," Harry said, patting him on the back. "Oh yeah, this here is Jake. His mother just moved into town last week. She's a workin' woman, if you know what I mean." He gave Eric a nasty smirk from under the brim of the wool cap he was wearing.

"You don't have to make it public knowledge, Harry." Jake dropped his head, eyes fixed to the ground. For a moment Eric thought Jake might get mad and slug Harry, but instead, Harry's tone softened.

"Sorry, Jake. I know it must make you feel bad. Say, you ever see her doin' it?"

"Naw. She usually knows when they're comin' and kicks me out of the house. She's got one up there this mornin'."

"Really?" Harry's eyes sparkled. "On a Sunday morning? No kidding!" He shook his head. He jumped down from the fence and expelled a large wad of spit. "Hey, you think we could get a peek?"

Jake looked up from the ground he'd been staring at. Eric understood Jake's shame. He also knew, given the opportunity, Jake would shame his mother to get back at how she was embarrassing him.

"Well, I guess it'd be okay," Jake answered. "But it'll cost you a pack of smokes."

"Deal," said Harry. Eric had seen Harry steal cigarettes from his father before. It would be no skin off Harry's backside to get the cigarettes for Jake. "Come on," said Harry. "Let's go!"

The trio ran through town, finally coming upon steep stairs that twisted around the back of a two-story flat. The white washed wood was splintered and in need of new paint.

Jake stopped them at the foot of the stairs, motioning for quiet. It was obvious he'd had some experience in his silent intrusions. At the top of the stairs he peered between two boards with a large gap separating them. There was a short pause and then Jake came clamoring down the stairs.

"We're too late," he announced. "Bed's already made and he's gone. Musta been a fast one. Come on, let's go inside anyway. I'm cold."

The three boys raced up the stairs, opening the back door that led down a dark, narrow hall. Eric stole a look into the bedroom as he passed the open doorway and sure enough, a lavender quilt neatly covered the bed in the sparsely furnished room. They continued to the kitchen where they found Jake's mom.

She sat at a small wooden table still wearing her flannel night coat. She was a very young, very pretty woman, counting a large sum of cash. Looking up from her accounting, she was pleasantly surprised to see the boys.

"Hello, Jake darling. Where've you been this morning? Are these your new friends?"

"Mom, this is Harry and Eric," Jake said politely.

"Hello boys. I'm glad Jake is making some new friends. You're welcome here anytime."

She was so pretty; Eric could hardly keep his eyes off her. Her hair was chestnut brown, hanging long and full over her shoulders. Her eyes reminded him of the color of the sky on a clear spring day. She had face paint on too, making her lips full and pink. She even smelled good. She sure didn't look like no whore.

"Look, Jake. Mr. Baxter paid me in advance for his laundry." She pointed at a large pile of white shirts draped over a ladder-back chair. "He paid me real well too. Here, you boys each take a nickel and go buy some candies." The street urchins, unusually well-mannered and obedient, took the coins and departed. No one said a word until they reached the bottom of the stairs.

"I like your Ma, Jake," Eric said. "She's real nice."

"She's good looking too," Harry contributed.

"She didn't' say where she really got the money," Jake replied. "She always covers up, like I don't know what's really goin' on. We never stay in one town very long. As soon as the women start findin' out what she's doin', they run us out of town. She's always afraid someone's going to try to take me away from her so we up and leave when things get too hot. Soon as I can I'm leavin' her. I'm going to California. I want to see the ocean."

Harry put his arm around Jake's shoulder. "Yeah, well at least I don't owe you no cigarettes." He seemed bored with Jake's pain. "Let's get some candy."

It was warm inside the Calumet. A couple of men wandered through the mercantile, one buying tobacco, the other looking at a blue enamel coffee pot. Harry whispered something to Jake and Jake grabbed Eric by the arm. The older boy was quite strong, nearly pulling Eric off his feet.

"Over here," he said to Eric, dragging him toward the counter. "Let's go see what kinda candy we can buy." Eric looked back over his shoulder to see Harry walking behind the aisle across the room. Jack redirected Eric's attention to the storekeeper, who was helping them to the candies. They pooled their money to buy several jawbreakers and a pack of gum. When they turned to leave, Harry had already left the store.

They met him on the corner. "How'd you do?" Jake asked.

"Did good." Harry reached into his pockets. "Got a deck of cards, set a dice and a fan. You get my candy?"

"Yep," Jake replied. "Got some gum too."

"Here, Eric. You can have the dice. You want the cards, Jake?"

"Rather have the fan for my Ma," Jake said.

"Sure thing." Harry handed the silky painted fan over to Jake. We make a good team." He paused and stuffed a stick of gum in his mouth. "We're a regular gang, that's what we are. Let's finish the candy and go see if we can steal some money from the Mexicans."

They wandered the streets like a flock of vultures, true opportunists, looking for whatever they could steal. This was all new to Eric, but it was evident that Jake and Harry had been at it a while.

"Look over there," Jake said. He pointed toward an old drunk, lying face down in the alley behind a row of cantinas. He still wore his sombrero. "Let's see if he's dead or just drunk," Jake suggested.

As they approached the motionless man, the air collected with a fierce odor.

"Whoa, this one is ripe," Eric said, holding his nose. "He must be dead."

"We gotta turn him over," Harry said. Each boy gingerly pinched at the drunk's clothing and hoisted him over, face up. He was still clinging to his bottle, now broken into pieces. His hand was covered with crusted blood and brown glass fragments. Eric surmised that he must have crushed it on his way down to the ground.

"He's still breathin," Jake said. "Jesus, he pissed all over himself."

"He had to have shit his pants too, to smell this bad," Eric said. "Must be all those *frijoles* those Mexicans eat." The other two boys started laughing at Eric's off-colored humor. Harry began going through the man's coat pockets. "Anything good, Harry?" Jack asked.

"Found a knife," he replied, while still exploring. "Look, here's his wallet."

"Let's get out of here," Eric said. He was getting nervous. The man let out a deep groan.

"Wait a minute, let's pants him," Harry said.

"No, Harry. Let's go," Eric repeated.

Harry reached across the man's belly and began to unbuckle his leather belt. He yanked it out of the loops and cast it aside. Then he pulled off his boots. "Grab a pant leg, Jake, help me."

They pulled on the man's grimy Levis until they slipped over his bony hips. His long white underwear, stained yellow and brown, clung to his butt cheeks. They dragged the pants down the alley, past several saloons, before depositing them in a trash can. The drunk, seemingly oblivious to the disturbance, rolled over on his side, curled in a fetal position. There, he fell back asleep. The boys, still laughing, turned the corner and disappeared, leaving the man to discover his situation at a later time.

Eric looked up at the sun. It had to be late afternoon. He felt dirty and tired. He wanted to wash his hands with strong soap and sit in a hot tub of water. His imagination told him vermin were gnawing at his skin and scalp and he began to scratch himself. His stomach rumbled with hunger and he could not get the smell of the street and its wet gutters out of his nostrils. This part of town was good for finding trouble, but he didn't want to live like this. He was always going to have money in his pocket one way or another.

"I'll see ya, fellas," he said. "I'm heading home."

"It's early, Eric. We too much for ya? Can't you take it?"

"Naw, that's not it. I was out late last night," he lied. "Snuck out."

"Yeah, well we'll see you around," Jake called out.

Eric didn't want to confront his mother when he got home. His clothes were nearly as dirty as the drunk's and he just didn't want to deal with her belly achin'. He opened the front door and leaped up the stairs to get some clean clothes and a towel. On his way to the bathroom, she popped out of the kitchen, spying him.

"Eric, where have you been?" Her shrill voice could make my teeth rattle, he told himself. "Were you at church today?"

Eric ignored her and continued to walk to the bathroom. "I'm gonna take a bath, Ma. I need one, I'm starting to smell." He shut the door behind him, hearing only silence. He was amused by his mother's reaction and it was almost as good as getting a rise out of her. He knew what she was thinking. Eric offering to take a bath? On a Sunday afternoon? Where has he been and what has he gotten into? She would never ask and he would never tell.

Tonight he didn't have any patience to eat with the boarders and his mom. He'd eat supper in the kitchen by himself. All he wanted was to escape to his room. In his room, he answered to no one but himself. In his room, he could allow himself to feel the grief and loneliness.

Sleep came quickly that night and he did not awaken until the next morning when he heard the screams.

Chapter 14

"Marita, calm down. I can't understand you. Is it one of the children? Alberto, what is she saying?" Marita was babbling in both Spanish and English. It was like conversing with someone who was riding a carousel as she ran circles around the kitchen. Brenna grabbed Marita, steered her to a chair and sat her down. "Now, tell me…slowly, and in English…what's happened."

Marita swallowed hard, grasping for the right words. "They have Manuel. They say he murdered a white man. How can they say that? He can't even wring a rooster's neck without feeling sorry for him."

Holding Marita's hand, Brenna sank into the chair next to her and tried to steady the distraught woman. She looked across the table to where Alberto had taken a seat. "Alberto, how did this happen? Tell me everything you know."

Alberto took a deep breath. "Well, Manuel, he says last night he was down on Main Street playing cards. I've told him before not to go down there to gamble. Because we are different, they don't trust us. Well, Manuel was sitting at a table with two, maybe three white men and another Mexican, a miner. This Mexican was losing a lot of money and getting very angry. After a while, they threw him out. Manuel, he wasn't doing so good either, *verdad*? The game began to break up after that, but Manuel decided to stay for one more drink. He leaves the Orient Saloon and heads for home when he trips over something, you know, soft in the alley. He feels down there in the dark and sees it is a man, full of blood. The man is still alive so he drags him into the light for a better look. He has a bad belly cut so Manuel takes out his knife to cut the man's clothes away to get a better look at the wound. But the man wakes up, sees a Mexican with a knife standing over him, and starts yelling and screaming.

Everyone comes running out of the bar and there's Manuel standing over the man with a knife and two bloody hands. Then the man dies and Manuel was arrested."

"Does Manuel always carry a knife?" Brenna asked.

"You know the knife he carries," Marita said softly. "It is the one you bought him in Tombstone."

The kitchen was oppressively silent except for the dripping water in the icebox pan. "I can't think about this now," Brenna said, her mouth pinched in a worried frown. The boarders would be up soon and expecting breakfast. After we feed the men we'll go down to the jail and see what we can do."

Methodically she went about her tasks. Marita was viciously beating the eggs while Alberto sipped at his black coffee. Brenna removed a box of cornflakes from the cabinet and walked to the dining room to lay out bowls and pitchers of milk and cream. She would not be eating breakfast today. A wave of nausea overtook her and she ran to the toilet, coughing up a mouthful of bitter coffee and yellow bile. Brenna put a hand on the sink to brace herself. *Why did this have to happen? Why now? I'm not supposed to be happy,* Brenna thought. *For some reason God wants me to suffer through life.* She pressed a hand to her churning stomach and pondered Manuel's chances of a fair trial. One thing was certain: the sheriff was definitely a white man's lawman. Even if Manuel was innocent, and she was sure he was, it would take hell's fury and the best lawyer to be had to win his freedom.

* * * *

Brenna sent Marita on ahead, with some breakfast for Manuel. Once all the men had been fed and given their lunches, she rushed upstairs to change into something that made her appear more formidable than a boarding house homemaker. She pinned her hair up in a severe bun and dressed in her gray traveling suit with a somber black and gray hat. She walked to town, and not knowing what to expect, stood outside the jail for a few moments, gathering herself. Chin up and shoulders back, she opened the door.

"Mornin', ma'am, may I help you?" A burly man stood up from the desk where he'd been finishing his breakfast. He smoothed out his red beard and pulled the napkin out of the neck of his yellowed shirt. The room was tiny and bright. Brenna wondered if all jails were built out of bricks to thwart escapes.

"I'm here to see Mr. Rodriguez," Brenna replied.

"I figured as much," he responded, shuffling across the floor. "Seein' as how he's our only prisoner. I think his kin's back there with him now." He opened the door leading back to the cells. "But you ain't no kin, I can see that." He waited for her reply but Brenna had already decided she would not give him the satisfaction. The deputy had no reason to know she was Manuel's employer. He stopped at the cell where Marita and Manuel were waiting. "I'll go get you a chair." Manuel sat on the edge of his cot, head in his hands. Brenna remembered the softness of those strong hands. The deputy returned with a chair, one chair for the white woman. "Now not too long, ma'am," he said. Brenna waited until he had left and shut the door before speaking to Manuel. Instead, when he raised his head and looked at her, she gasped and then wanted to cry. Large purple bruises marked his face where he had been beaten. Knowing Manuel, he would have tried to fight off the men who had subdued him.

He stood up from the cot and turned to face the corner of the cell. He folded his arms defensively across his chest. "Go away, Mrs. McEvoy," he said. "This is not your problem."

"Manuel, stop talking like that," Brenna chastised. "You've always been there to help me when I needed someone. You'd never—"

He cut her off. "This is different. This is murder!"

"Manuel, did you kill this man?"

He spun around and glared at her through his puffy eyelids. "If you have to ask that, then you do not belong here."

"Manuel!" Marita scolded. "How can you talk to her that way?"

"No, Marita." Brenna placed a restraining hand on her arm, before she could say any more. Although she wanted to admonish Manuel herself, for turning her away when he needed her most, she understood where his anger came from. Still, his rejection hurt. The last time she had seen him, he'd held her in his arms. Now, he treated her no better than a stranger. He'd even called her Mrs.

McEvoy. "If he does not want me here, I'll go." With a dull ache tugging at her heart, she called for the deputy.

Marita followed her out of the jail, hurrying to catch up with her. "Manuel did not mean what he said. You will help, no? I do not know what to do."

"Of course I'll help." She stopped on the sidewalk and embraced Marita. She didn't care who saw them or what they thought.

"Madre de Dios. I cannot believe this has happened." Mindful of their unseemly show of familiarity on the street, Marita eased out of Brenna's arms, careful not to let her think she was rebuffing her as Manuel had. "I am so sorry Manuel spoke to you with so much unkindness." She peered at Brenna through watery eyes. "I do not understand his anger at you."

"Oh Marita, I don't think he's angry with me. He's a proud man. I think he's ashamed to have me see him this way, in jail and charged with murder. But whether he wants me to or not, I'll do everything I can to help him. Now, come on," she said, taking hold of Marita's hand and practically dragging her down the sidewalk. "The first thing I need to do is get him a good lawyer."

* * * *

The whole process went remarkably fast. Manuel was tried before a white jury and found guilty of second degree murder. The jury judged him on the relevance of the knife and the poker game, evidence enough to convict a Mexican. Nothing she'd done for him had helped, not the pricey lawyer she'd hired for him, not what she had said on the witness stand. Fortunately, the judge showed leniency as no one had actually witnessed the stabbing. Instead of sentencing him to hang until dead, Manuel would spend the rest of his life in prison at the new state penitentiary in Florence, north of Bisbee.

Marita's sobs and those of Manuel's nieces and nephews echoed through the cavernous room as the lawmen led Manuel out of the courtroom and out of their lives. She marveled at how quickly one's life could change. The most painful part of it all for her was the guilt she felt in having given Manuel the very knife that had led, at least in part, to his conviction. She regretted having ever laid eyes on the cursed thing.

For a fleeting moment she was terrified. Then, an innate calmness stole over her. Despite it all, the anger, the hurt and frustration, she knew she could continue on without Manuel, just as she had without her father and without James. No man yet had proven indispensable to her existence. Survival was the only choice she had open to her, and she'd be damned if she'd disgrace Manuel by failing now.

Chapter 15

Brenna had to read the letter three times before she finally understood. It was a very kind letter, something she was not used to associating with her father. Without her knowledge, Marita had asked her son, Enrique, to write to Brenna's father, letting him know that Michael and James were dead. Apparently she felt obligated to inform him of his grandson's passing, or for some reason, sensed Brenna's inability to cope. James was likely to have been an afterthought, for Brenna knew Marita had never liked the way he treated her. Whatever the reason, father was now offering to marry her off again.

She would not have given it a second thought had she not lost Manuel. Each day she scraped up just enough courage to complete the day's tasks. Money continued to come in on a regular basis. Sara and Eric seemed to be thriving. Her heath remained constant and Marita, with Ana in tow, continued to show up for work each and every day. Usually one of the miners helped out with repairs around the house. Still, a void remained in her life and she lacked the companionship that she had become accustomed to: someone to share in her life, however boring and pitiful it was.

The letter said her proposed suitor was a wealthy man who had made his money in the market. He had never married, being too busy with his investments to court a woman. The newspaper clipping from the *San Diego Tribune* showed a handsome man, stout, with a mustache and beard. He appeared to be in his mid-forties and for the life of her Brenna could not understand how her simple father would know a man like this Edward Donohue.

Inside the letter was money for a train ticket to California. Mr. Donahue was staying at the grand Hotel Del Coronado, and if Brenna agreed, her father would introduce them.

Marrying a man like this could change her life. Undoubtedly he would want to live in a big city. For the children's sake alone, it would be a tempting opportunity. Maybe a change would bring her better luck. But could she leave Marita and this life behind? Was she strong enough to start all over again?

There and then she knew she had to try and win Mr. Donohue's attentions, regardless of whether she liked him or not. It never seemed to make any difference anyway. And it was like all the old women would say, "You can learn to love him." She had never learned to love any man and certainly didn't care to now. But before she left for San Diego, she had an important task to complete. She would arm herself with all the feminine persuasion she could master, however distasteful it was.

Carefully Brenna penned the letter, guarding her anonymity. From the desk drawer she removed a white envelope, stuffed the letter and one dollar in the pocket and sealed it with a good amount of spit. It was nine p.m. and if she didn't hurry, her plans would be ruined and possibly her reputation.

Upstairs in her room she draped her head and face with a heavy, black scarf. Over the scarf she pinned a hat and finished by tucking the scarf in to the high collar of her navy blouse. She threw a gray cape over shoulders and, with the letter in hand, made her way to Brewery Gulch.

It was fortunate that it was a work night. The Gulch was calm this evening as she headed for the tenderloin district of town. The cool evening air was drying the sweat underneath her hat as she avoided the looks of curious men. In the shadows she waited.

There were always street children out and about. It was just a matter of waiting for one to appear. She listened for their high voices and after an eternity of ten minutes, two boys came down the alley. They were in the midst of some childhood squabble, shoving one another as they progressed toward Brenna.

"Boys," she called out of the darkness. The children looked up to see the strange woman. "Can either of you read?" They looked curiously at one another.

"I can't," said the littlest child, kicking the stones in the dirt.

"I can," boasted the older boy. "Teacher says I'm one a her best readers." Brenna bent down to talk to the smallest boy.

"Do you know me?" she asked.

"Don't know, ma'am. Caint see your face."

"Take this letter to the saloon girl inside." She directed him to the building behind him. "She's the pretty one with the yellow hair."

"You mean Miss Rainy?" he asked.

"Course she means Rainy, stupid." The older boy smacked him on the chest. "You think she's talkin' about that old cow Lola, do ya?"

"When you drop it off, tell her there's a dollar for you inside the envelope. She'll open it for you. If the envelope is open when she receives it, you'll get nothing."

"What do I do?" the older boy asked.

"Nothing," Brenna said. "I needed someone who couldn't read. I'm sorry." Disappointment reached across his face.

"See ya, Willie," called the youngster as he raced up the back stairs to make his delivery.

Brenna hurried back to the house. She had little more than an hour to prepare to receive her guest. She tip-toed through the parlor, sneaking past the boarding house rooms. Most of the men had to be in by now. There were various pitches of snoring and heavy breathing coming from each room and she felt safe in assuming that there would be no more disturbances tonight.

She darkened the entire house, checking to see that the back door was unlocked. Upstairs in her room, she would wait for her visitor's arrival.

Brenna had dozed off in the rocker. When the downstairs door opened, she was instantly awake. The squeak of the hinges was notable and a gentle closing followed. Footsteps approached until the glass doorknob jiggled and the door cracked open. A tuft of blonde hair was the first thing Brenna saw, soon followed by a curious, young face.

"Ma'am?" she asked. "Did I do everything right?"

"So far," Brenna reassured her. "Please come in and close the door behind you."

She was a beautiful, young girl. Only traces of face paint remained on her white skin and she had dressed in a conservative print frock. No one would know, sans her reputation and customers, that she was a popular prostitute.

"What is it exactly, that you're wanting, ma'am?" Rainy seated herself on the bed without asking permission. "I mean, I suspected by the handwriting that you were a woman, but I ain't never done anything like that before. I mean I heard things. I supposed I'd be willing to learn if you wanted me to and if the price was right."

Brenna could feel the blood rushing to her face. She had been afraid that this would happen. She thought Rainy might assume she was soliciting sexual favors for a man, but never for herself. Jesus, Mary and Joseph, she'd never known such a thing, but then, she didn't know much of anything when it came to intimacy.

Brenna turned away from Rainy, concealing her embarrassment. She fidgeted with the perfume bottles on her dressing table before composing herself.

"Please, call me Brenna," she started. "You might as well know my real name as you could find out anyway, knowing where I live. I just didn't know any other way to do this." Slightly more composed, she turned to face the young woman. "You see, Rainy, I asked you here for advice. I'll pay you for your time. It's just that you know so much more than I do and I'm willing to listen to what you have to say."

Rainy released a little sigh, relieved of her assumed obligation. Then her posture straightened and she placed a hand to her bosom pointing at herself. "Me? You want advice from me?" she asked.

Brenna sat down on the bed next to the young girl. "I need feminine advice," she said. "I need to know how to seduce a man and keep him coming back." The slightest smile came across Rainy's face and her impish blue eyes brightened.

"Brenna," she said, "you ask the questions and I will explain... everything."

Now they were two, young women plotting against every man in their world. They had until dawn to formulate their attack, and Brenna was sure it would take hours to get past her ignorance.

"So how do I get his attention?" Brenna began.

"Do what the flowers do to attract the bees," Rainy said. "Make yourself real pretty and soft and put on perfume. You can rub glycerin on your skin. Why sometimes I put a few drops of perfume in the glycerin before I use it. Rub it everywhere!" she squealed. "Then, if you're some place private, let your hair down, maybe just a few tendrils in the back. Wear something that is flattering, but show a little of that soft skin. But now don't go dressing like I do at the saloon."

"But what do I do after I get their attention?"

"Why, you just let nature take its course. A man has to feel like he's in control. What they don't know is it's us doing the controlling. We know what they're thinking and what they really want. They don't have an inkling as to what is going on. Those egos of theirs tell them that they're the best lovers in the world. Look here."

Rainy stood up and pulled Brenna to her feet. "You be the man," she said. "Don't mind me touchin' you." Rainy paused and looked Brenna square in the face. "Honey, why you are stiff as a frozen sheet. You have any brandy around here to warm you up? You need to relax and have some fun with this."

"I have some good liquor downstairs. I think I need a drink." Brenna slipped her heels off and crept down the stairs, returning with two long stemmed glasses and a bottle of dark liquor.

Rainy took the bottle from her hand and poured a shot for each of them. She held her glass up. "To women," she toasted.

Brenna took a deep breath and in one gulp the liquor spilled down her throat. Her eyes widened and she brought up a delicate cough. Rainy giggled and stepped toward her. "I want to show you what you can do. This is how I handle Lester. He's kinda my manager." Rainy pressed her body close to Brenna. She rested her head between Brenna's shoulder and chest. "Lester," she cooed. "You know I always feel so safe with you. You make me feel so good." She took Brenna's hand and led her to the edge of the bed where they both sat down. If Brenna hadn't been so terrified, she would have laughed. She took another deep breath. Rainy gently pushed her down to lay flat on the bed. Without saying a word, Rainy brushed several stray hairs from Brenna's face. Her hands continued to wander over Brenna's chest working slowly past her waist and moving down her abdomen. When Brenna was sure she couldn't let this go any further, Rainy was out of character and grinning like a boy that had tied his first shoe.

"That's about all the coaxin' they're gonna need," she said.

Again, Brenna took a deep breath. She looked at Rainy.

"And what do I do once they get started?"

"That's the easy part. Let them do what they want. That's the best way to keep 'em coming back. A few reassuring moans and kind words don't hurt."

"Moans? I don't understand."

"Not like you were hurtin', honey," she clarified. "Like you were eatin' an ice cream cone on a hot summer day."

"I see," Brenna said. "And what if I don't like what he's doing?"

"That's a hard choice to make. About the only thing I don't put up with is pain. Anyone tries to slap or hit me, they're out the door and Lester is after them. But see, you have choices that I don't. If they don't come back, I don't eat."

Rainy softened. "Brenna, don't cheapen yourself. Remember it's you in control, not them. You got someone special in mind?"

"I don't know yet," Brenna said. "There's a man, a wealthy man, I'm to be introduced to."

"Ah, now that's the best kind. I think I could put up with almost anything if he had money." She dropped her head. "But nice men, they don't want me for long. I got to get out of this business or I'm gonna end up working the border at Naco."

"I was thinking about that," Brenna said. "You know it's only a matter of time before they run you girls out of town. The mine's pushing for family men now, no more tramp miners."

"I know. They say the men come to us and lose their money gambling and whoring. Then they get drunk and go back to the mines. Sometimes they don't' show up for work and sometimes there are accidents. Somehow, even though it's their choice, I always get blamed for their stupidity."

"How about another glass of brandy?" Brenna asked. "I'm enjoying our little talk." This time Brenna poured a generous glass for each of them and handed one to Rainy.

"You know, Rainy, I was thinking. Have you ever waited tables?"

"No, doesn't seem like something I couldn't learn, but who in this town would hire the likes of me?"

"Have you ever heard of the Harvey Girls?"

"Sure, you're talking about those waitresses that wear the black and white uniforms, nice ladies that wait the trains."

"If you got in as a Harvey Girl, you wouldn't have to work in this town. Why they'd send you anywhere the rail cars wandered. I hear they're in need of women in our territory. There's a Harvey place in Winslow and at the Grand Canyon. Both of those towns are up north. They'd give you room and board and keep you honest."

"That would be nice," Rainy said in a dreamy voice. "You know, I wasn't always like this."

Brenna sipped her brandy. "What's your Christian name?"

"Lorraina," she said. "Lorraina Jean Mayfield. My little sister and I came down from the state of Washington. My stepfather, he used to do things to me, things that wasn't right. He'd make excuses to get me alone, maybe take me berry picking in the woods. Men don't pick berries. That's always been women's work. But he'd make me go out there with him. He started touching me. Then it just got worse and worse 'til he was treating me the same as my Ma. I'd drop hints about it to Ma, but I never did have the heart to tell her. When he started in on my sister, Louise, that was it. Next night we packed our belongings and stole what money we could, heading as far south as we could. I told her I'd have to find work to support us, but at least I'd get paid for what I'd been doing for years. She used to call me Rainy, cause when she was little she couldn't say Lorraina." Rainy finished her brandy in one fast gulp. Without hesitation, Brenna filled it up again.

"Where's Louise now?" Brenna asked

"She met up with a young man in north California. He was a farmer's son and seemed like a nice fella. She was awful young to marry, only fourteen. I wouldn't have approved unless I thought he'd take good care of her. That family never knew about me and how I was working. Now she's got two kids of her own and the ranch is doing real well."

"That is quite a story. And I must say I'm sorry to hear it. Listen, Rainy, uh, Lorraina."

Brenna pulled a wad of green cash out of the dresser drawer and counted off several bills, handing them to Lorraina. "This is what we'll do. You take some of this cash and have Mr. Fly make you a portrait. I hear he's in town for the next two weeks and you know he's one of the best photographers around. Mind you, look as innocent as you can. I'll write a letter to Mr. Harvey answering his advertisement and include the photograph. I'll tell him you're my housekeeper and use this address. If he likes you, you're on your way."

"Why would you do that for me?"

"No woman asks for the kind of life you've had and you're right. If you don't get a new start soon, you will end up in Mexico. The mine is determined to clean up this town and isn't worried about a few casualties. Besides, someone helped me out once when I was in a desperate situation. I'm just carrying on the kindness."

Brenna looked up. Soon it would be daylight. "You must leave now, Lorraina. I can't take a chance with anyone seeing you here."
Rainy nodded obediently. With the light of day the wall went up between their two worlds. Brenna walked Rainy to the back door, pausing to watch a tiny bat darting around the street lamp. That's me, Brenna thought. So brave in the safety of the darkness, and a coward in the dawn of light.

Chapter 16

Compared to Bisbee, San Diego might well have been Paris. It was a city brimming with sophisticated dress shops, and exotic restaurants that laced the air with wonderful and unusual smells. People of all races, even Chinamen, freely walked in the streets. The damp salt air was a constant reminder of the presence of an ocean that spanned the surface of the earth all the way to another continent.

Father's home stood atop a crest overlooking the original community of San Diego. Mission Hill was one of several new communities designed to replace downtown San Diego which, in Father's words, "was a bawdy sin pit."

Inside the tidy white bungalow, three bedrooms and a bath took up one entire side of the house. Although the kitchen was cramped, a large living room and walled patio provided ample room on those rare summer evenings when the humidity and heat became uncomfortable.

Widow O'Meara had made a good life for Pa in the time since they had left Bisbee. Brenna recalled her resentment for Katherine, now feeling childish and naïve. At the time she didn't understand the need for companionship, and could only feel jealously toward her new stepmother. Beyond this was the knowledge that her father was abandoning her for his own needs. Now she could see that he was only doing what he thought best for both of them. There was no malice in what he had done, but still she found it difficult to forgive him.

Brenna learned that Edward Donahue had come to know her father through his job at the bank. Money breeds intimacy, and soon Pa and Edward became friends. Marita's letter had weighed heavily on Pa's mind when the subject of Edward's restlessness surfaced.

The two men, both of a practical nature, took control of the situation, plotting Brenna's future.

When a familiar knock came to Brenna's bedroom door, a flood of memories returned. It had been nearly ten years since Brenna had heard that crack on the wood, her father's request to enter her life again. She allowed him to come in, but poised as a flighty sparrow, he hovered near the doorway.

"I'm glad you could come, Brenna. You're looking well. Tell me, have you heard from your sister, Virginia?"

"No, not for years," Brenna answered. For a moment, Brenna found it difficult to remember her face. "Last I heard she was in San Francisco. What do you hear?"

"I've heard from her several times, usually when she needs something." He exhaled a great sigh. "I guess she'll never change. Brenna, about Michael and James-"

"It's all right, Father," she interrupted. "I'm doing all right now."

"You've become a strong woman. Your mother would be proud." She wanted to tell him about Manuel. How it was his strength that made her strong. How Marita treated her like a sister. And now, how she may be letting both of them down. But to turn away a compliment from a man that had never expressed approval, she would have to be an idiot. Instead, she showed her pleasure in a demure smile and changed the subject.

"When am I to meet Mr. Donohue?"

"He's already been in town for two days. He's meeting with some brokers on Coronado. He said he would send an automobile out to pick you up tomorrow, and the two of you can meet and have dinner at the hotel. Does that meet with your approval?"

"Of course. Whatever the two of you have scheduled will be fine." She was starting to feel small and unworthy. It was that same notion that she was being auctioned off.

"I'm really tired now, Pa. If you'll excuse me, I'd like to rest." He nodded to acknowledge her request and in his usual style, left without another word.

* * * *

Brenna woke to the sounds of horns in the harbor. Thick, low clouds enveloped the open skies, parting in random patterns to admit rays of sunlight. Fog hung heavy in the air but soon vanished as the morning warmed to afternoon.

Katherine had planned a picnic at the beach. Sara and Eric were enchanted with the rolling waters and the mysteries the ocean held.

"Look at your little one," Katherine said. Brenna watched Sara stop to pick up a large white half shell. Her tawny hand reached out to the treasure, when an approaching wave caught her off guard. She screamed with shock when the icy fingers of the ocean grasped her ankles. The sand raced out from underneath her feet while she struggled to balance. Gentler waves retracted and the ordeal passed, but it certainly wasn't too late to cry. Brenna answered her wails with a comforting embrace. It was possibly the first time the child had ever been inclined to need her mother.

Eric was mesmerized by the curling waves. At first he was content to build a sand castle with Katherine's boys but then seemed bored with their childhood games. He stood alone on the shoreline, a solitary silhouette outlined against the vast blue waters. Sometimes Brenna wondered how well he was adjusting since Michael's death. He had developed his own circle of friends which Brenna never saw. She suspected that most were from Brewery Gulch, the children of immigrant Cousin Jacks, Italians, Poles and the like. Not a very well-bred group, but Brenna did not want to be too quick to judge. Just once it would be nice to meet some of them.

Amidst the protests of the children, it was time to return home. Secretly, she too wished the day could have lasted forever. There had been little time to reflect since Michael's death and the loss of Manuel. Soon she would be facing another confrontation.

At home, Brenna washed and changed into a silvery gray, chiffon suit for her dinner engagement. Katherine helped her dress for the long awaited encounter. "Are you excited?" she asked.

"I'm very nervous," Brenna said. "I don't know what to think of this man yet."

"You know, we could have gone shopping at one of the dress shops in town. They have some lovely dresses for special occasions."

"I'm sure this will do." By her frugal nature, Brenna thought it was impractical to buy a new dress for a man she'd never met. "Katherine, what if I don't like this man? How will I tell my father that I'm not interested in Mr. Donohue's intentions?"

"Don't worry about that now. And if it comes to that, you let me handle your father," Katherine finished pinning up Brenna's hair. "Perfect," she pronounced, handing Brenna her wide brim hat.

The car arrived promptly at five-fifteen in the afternoon. Sara and Eric watched her leave. Getting into the automobile, she had a funny feeling she would never see them again. She had never known the insecurity of being in an unfamiliar place, hundreds of miles from home.

A ferry passage was waiting for her when she arrived at the dock. Mr. Donohue had a keen sense for details and seemed to have taken care of her quite well. Perhaps she could get used to this kind of attention. Or, maybe, she would come to hate it.

One forceful swell after another rocked the boat from side to side. The sun slipped into the ocean and the water changed from a royal blue to a threatening black. There seemed to be so much uncertainty with this restless ocean. The desert, as foreboding as it was, was predictable.

A driver from the hotel was present to meet Brenna, delivering her to the grand lady herself. The Hotel Del Coronado had acquired an enviable reputation since opening twenty years ago. Painted virgin white and capped with a red tile roof, the Del was easily recognized.

Brenna was standing in line waiting for a clerk when, without warning, an orchestra of violins and string instruments began playing at the top of the staircase. Drifting down to a crowd of onlookers, music filled the room like mist. Never had she seen so much splendor and opulence. The crowd, dressed in evening attire, applauded the musicians that continued to play as they descended the stairs. Awed by the display, she had not been paying attention when the desk clerk spoke to her.

"Madam?" he repeated, waiting for her acknowledgement. He was an arrogant little man who made her feel unwelcomed. She identified herself and her purpose. "Mr. Donohue wishes to be notified upon your arrival. There is a ladies' lavatory to the left and down the hall should you wish to freshen up. Mr. Donohue will meet you in the sitting area directly behind you."

Brenna turned around to find a small grouping of maroon chairs and a matching couch. No one sat there resembling Edward Donohue, so she made her way to the lavatory.

She felt slightly nauseated and the cool water she splashed on her face was soothing to her hot skin. How she wished this was all concluded. Life in Bisbee seemed so much more comfortable than the business of courting. Remembering Manuel at this time only served to make her lonelier in this crowd of strangers.

She dampened her hands at the faucet, brushing up the stray hairs unleashed from her bun. Reaching for the pearls draped over her bosom, she made an effort to straighten them although there was really nothing to straighten. She pinched her cheeks and bit her lips bringing the blood to the surface of her skin. *Oh well,* she thought, *better to get on with this.*

She immediately recognized him, standing near the small couch. He was talking to a man and woman, dressed even more beautifully than any others she had seen before. He appeared older than his photograph. Brenna took a deep breath before approaching him, trying her best to remain composed and sophisticated. He sighted her before she reached him and excused himself from his acquaintances to welcome her.

"Mr. Donohue?" she asked.

"Yes, yes," he responded, returning her handshake.

"It is a pleasure to make your acquaintance, sir." The conversation was stilted and pretentious, but Brenna remained firm with a genteel expression plastered to her face. She felt like an actor in a Greek drama, wearing a mask to shield all her uncertainties.

"I trust you had a pleasant journey?"

"Yes, you attended to every detail."

He offered her his arm. "We have a table reserved in the dining room if you would care to accompany me."

She felt very regal perched upon the arm of such a wealthy, influential man. Brenna could feel heads turning to watch as they crossed the room. Their table was secluded, set in a shadowed corner of the room. It was the choice of either a hermit, or a man who cherished his privacy.

Edward quickly took control, ordering for both of them. He did take the time to question Brenna's taste preferences, but had he ordered poison hemlock, she would have agreed to his choice. More than anything, she wanted to please this man. At first she refused wine with dinner, so as not to appear like a harlot, but when he seemed disappointed she agreed to join him. Before the meal had ended she had almost acquired a taste for the fruity drink.

Dinner was a feast for the eyes and stomach with each dish prepared for its own presentation. She imagined a flurry of cooking staff whirling about the kitchen, checking each plate arrangement for the correct garnish and spots of dribbled gravy. After dinner, Thomas, the waiter, came with a little brush and silver pan to collect all the crumbs on the table. Brenna nearly broke into open laughter, thinking how ridiculous all this attention was, but caught herself before her ordinary expectations could give her away.

It was getting late when the flaming dessert emerged from the kitchen. It was stunning and to Brenna's relief, Thomas extinguished the flames before serving them. The brandied bread pudding was sweet and warm and filled her with an irresistible sense of well-being. Perhaps it was really the wine, but no matter, she relaxed after the burden of eating was behind her.

Immediately after dinner, Edward directed her to the gardens facing the sea. The air was cool and the breezes rushed past her head, blurring the sounds of the beating ocean. A beautiful ivory moon looked down upon them, following them down the path that trailed through the fragrant flowers. It wasn't long before Edward suggested they return to his suite for a nightcap.

Oh no, Brenna thought, *here we go. Let's see what you're made of*, she told herself. He was waiting for her response. She remembered Rainy's words, "Give them what they want."

"Yes, of course," she said and then realized she was shaking.

"Are you all right?" Edward asked.

"Yes, just a bit chilled."

"Well, my dear," said a fatherly voice, "let's not waste any time getting you inside."

There was a gentle creak in the floor boards as they made their way down the hall. It was very quiet and Edward motioned with his finger across his lips, a wicked smile suggesting they needed to remain silent. His key clicked in the lock and he allowed her to enter his room.

Brenna placed her handbag and jacket on a table near the door. He crossed the room, pulling back the heavy, blue drapes that covered the window. As money seemed no matter to this man, he had a room with a view of the ocean. The same moon that had followed them outside, cast a sparkling light on the turning waters.

"How beautiful!" Brenna exclaimed. "You must have a spectacular view in the morning." She waited for a reply and there was none. Instead she felt the grasp of two harsh hands around her waist. She was pivoted around, thrown off balance and then he was kissing her. It was an angry kiss, hard on her lips and pressing against her with such force that her lips were aching against her teeth. He smelled of liquor and tasted like a stale cigar. She managed to break free.

Again, Rainy spoke to her. How desperately she wanted this to work. She straightened her clothes and smiled at Edward, hoping to try again. "Edward," she said, "you needn't hold on to me so tight. I'm not going anywhere."

He stepped forward again, still saying nothing. Closer he came, until they stood toe-to-toe. She relaxed a little while his hands caressed her neck, fingering the collar of her blouse. The hands continued to wander like a moth flitting from one blossom to the next. He paused at the lace edging the front panel of her blouse. Then wasting no time, he was unbuttoning her bodice.

"No," she said. It was more of a plea than a request. But Donohue was not a patient man. In a fraction of a second, he grabbed the delicate fabric, effortlessly ripping the blouse down the front.

In Brenna's eyes it happened in slow motion. Her body swayed slightly forward with his force as she searched his face for whatever it was that made him do this. She was through trying to please him and now feared for her safety. Her hand cracked across his face and she bolted to the other side of the room, putting a sofa between the two of them.

Donahue, however, was not accustomed to not getting his way. "You little tart," he rumbled, rubbing his stinging face. "Is this how I'm repaid for an exquisite evening?"

"Repaid?" Brenna cried. "Mr. Donohue, I am not the livestock you trade across the board. I had thought your intentions were honorable and that marriage may have been possible, but you are an animal and I want nothing to do with you."

"Marriage?" he balked. Then he laughed. "Who said anything about marriage? Do you think I would take a working woman such as yourself for a wife?"

"I don't understand," Brenna stammered. "My father said you were lonely and interested in companionship."

"Of course," he bellowed like an old ram. "I would welcome a young woman's affections when I am in town, but as for marriage, that was never a consideration."

"So I was to be a kept woman? Is that what your plan was?" She had been edging her way toward the door, preparing to exit. He turned to face the same window she had been assaulted at.

"Your father has misunderstood," he said to the ocean. In silence, she slipped her jacket over her torn top and retrieved her purse. With the other hand she grabbed a goblet from the table.

"And so have you, sir." She flung the glass at him, barely missing his thick neck. It bounced off his back and crashed to the floor. He was aghast by her disrespect and she could see it on his face. Her hands were sweating and slipping on the doorknob, but she managed to make her escape while he crossed the room to confront her.

She raced down the hall but knew he wouldn't let her have the upper hand. Three doors down, she cowered in the doorway of another room. She could hear his labored breathing forcing air through his stuffy nose. Could he hear her breathing? For a moment she held her breath. Chances are he would not want to cause a scene and was probably worried she would make one. Really, what did she have to lose, the common woman that she was? Gently the door closed and all was quiet.

Confident that he wasn't going to pursue her, she buttoned her jacket. It would cover her torn blouse and once she touched up her hair no one would be the wiser. She slipped down the stairs, but could feel her legs shaking with each step she took. If she lost her balance and fell, people would come forward and she didn't know if she could keep up the façade at that point. The desk clerk eyed her suspiciously as she crossed the lobby and headed for the restroom. No woman would be walking alone this time of the night.

She remained in the bathroom a long time. No one entered except the cleaning staff. To Brenna's relief, they ignored her. She looked at the pocket watch stashed in her purse. It was two in the morning. If there was a late ferry, she had surely missed it. There wasn't enough money for a room and if she didn't get out of the ladies' room soon, the staff would report her.

"When does the morning ferry leave?" she asked the wary clerk.

"Just a moment, Madam. I'll have to check the schedule." He glanced back at her seemingly annoyed. What if he decided to call security and have her thrown from the hotel? She felt as if her mind had run away without her.

Quickly she disappeared before the clerk returned. In two more hours, it would be daybreak. She could hide in the flower garden until it was light, and then make her way to the dock. She had enough money with her for a ferry and cab. She just had to be calm and patient.

While she waited, she thought about her father. If she told him what had really happened, he could lose his job at the bank. It would be best to dismiss the incident and hopefully Donohue would too. She was nothing to him and was counting on that to save her father's reputation.

A delicate pink rose was blooming in the garden. Its presence called to mind the time she had given a winter rose to Manuel. She drew the rose forward to smell its sweet fragrance, but thorns tore at her fingertip and she retracted. By the moonlight she could see that the top of her finger was bleeding. She was offended that something so precious had caused her pain.

She eyed her bleeding finger, thinking of the red-tipped ocotillos that bloomed every spring. She didn't belong here, and the rose only served to remind her how far she was from home. What a fool she had been to believe she could seduce a man. Like a hurt animal, she licked her wound until the bleeding stopped, and then found a bench to rest on as she waited for daylight's return.

Chapter 17

The sun was well into the morning sky when Brenna returned to her father's home. She dragged her tired body up the shallow steps leading to the front porch. The children were playing under Katherine's watchful eyes. "Brenna, are you all right?" she asked.

"I'm fine," Brenna reassured her. "It just didn't work out." The look on Katherine's face said she'd concluded what Donohue's real intentions had been, but she was polite enough not to press the matter. It was shameful enough that Brenna had been out all night. "I'm going to take a bath and begin packing. I'll be leaving on the next train."

When Brenna brushed by Katherine, she reached out with her hand. "I'm so sorry," she said. "I had hoped it would work out well for you." Brenna looked deep into Katherine's eyes, pooling with tears. Her actions were sincere and for the first time Brenna realized that Katherine had shared the same emptiness; known the same despair. Katherine, if anyone, could understand.

In the tub Brenna finally allowed herself to cry. The gurgling waters splashing into the basin muffled her sobs.

No one could hear her or see her tear-streaked face and swollen eyes. She decided then and there she didn't need a man in her life. Men had done nothing but hurt her. From this moment forward, she was determined to make it on her own.

The train ride to Bisbee was not nearly as long as the ride to San Diego. The tracks were the same, identical in measured miles, yet the anticipation of returning home made the hours race. How happy she would be to see Marita again. She would tell her everything. Marita had a way of making her open up and it would be good to express her hatred for that wretched man.

In the last hours of the day she caught a glimpse of a dust devil. It swirled across the desert, picking up a red cloud of dirt. When the greasewood joined in the dance, the spinning cloud collided with a bunching of mesquite trees, and it melted like a passing spirit.

A small herd of grazing deer raced away from the tracks, startled by the sharp whistle of the train. The children snuggled next to her, ignoring the disruption. She continued to watch the sunset and within minutes the sky filled with a pink hue, sending red rays upward to touch the hanging clouds. A faint scent of creosote lingered in the evening air like expensive perfume on a fancy lady.

Brenna was overcome with a feeling of serenity. This was home. Not the rambling ocean, the changing shore line, the constant crash of the frothy waves beating the shore. The desert would remain as it had for thousands of years, a constant marker in a fast-changing world. Some things in life simply could not be changed and others... they were sure to be challenged.

* * * *

Like a vine in summer, Bisbee had grown in the short time that Brenna was away. A new motion picture theater had opened up and the banker said the population had climbed to 15,000. Now that Arizona had become a state, Bisbee was certain to remain one of the leading western cities. There was great disappointment when Phoenix was made the capital city, but as long as the Copper Queen kept producing, prosperity was sure to follow.

Still, there was an increasing sense of resentment among the miners. Listening to the conversations around the boarding house table, grumbling rose regularly. Investors and mining magnets clawed relentlessly at the land, manipulating whoever and whatever to satisfy their greed. Any working miner had a fifty-fifty chance of sustaining an injury.

"Durn near got it today," Frank said. The rattling dishes and clanging silverware halted, as the miners silenced to hear his tale. They were fully aware it could be any one of them at any time. "I was ridin' those carts and not paying attention. This big ol' jagged rock hangin' from the ceilin' came up on me. Shoot, if Sam hadn't a shoved my head clear into my drawers, I wouldn't have no head now."

"Wouldn't a mattered," one of the miners retorted. "Don't seem to be doing you any good anyhow." Frank threw a biscuit at the comic who promptly caught it and bit into it like a starving animal.

"Something's got to be done," said John. His eyes were downcast and filled with contempt. He was more educated than the rest of the boarders and spent a good deal of his free time following political news. "I understand the Wobblies could be coming to our town," he announced, "and they need to."

"What do you mean by Wobblies?" Leroy asked.

"Union men," Hugo replied with a mouthful of potatoes. He swallowed hard. "But that could mean big trouble if the bosses get wind of it."

"Don't be kidding yourself," John said. "They already know about the Wobblies. Why I bet they've already had meetings to figure out how they're going to keep them out of town."

"What are they afraid of?" Jacob asked.

"Higher wages, safer working conditions, fair jobs. Ever notice how the Mexicans and Darkies get the worse jobs? That's no accident. No offense, Marita."

"None taken, *Señor*, and you are right. Alberto has been working the same, hot, miserable job for ten years. He knows his job better than his white boss but his skin is the wrong color. We would go back to Mexico, but the Revolution is so bad I fear for my family."

"Well I don't know about Wobblies and revolutions," Jacob said, returning to his food. "I just wanna keep my head."

The back door slammed with a single bang. "That will be *Señor* Pinto," Marita said. "And he will be wanting his supper." Each woman collected a handful of dirty dishes and walked to the kitchen. Pinto was sitting at the table, nearly motionless. He failed to chatter in his usual way. His nonsense often annoyed Marita, but it was obvious that something was bothering him.

"Pinto," Marita asked, "how are you feeling tonight?" Pinto said nothing. "Pinto?" she repeated. "*Señora*, there is something wrong with Pinto. He will not speak to me."

Brenna put her dishtowel down and sat across from Pinto. "Pinto, is there something wrong?" She watched him push his food around the plate, take a forkful of stewed tomatoes, and force them down his throat. He raised his face and Brenna could see the white of his eyes discolored with redness, his eyelids swollen like a wet sponge. He wiped his mouth on his sleeve, making the same motion on his eyes.

"My mule up and died today." He took a large, dingy handkerchief from his back pocket and made a trumpet-like noise with his nose. "Ate my whole bag a self-risen' flour. Then the fool went down to the stream, had her fill and bloated to death."

From across the room Brenna could see Marita's eyes widen like two big tortillas. Marita wanted to laugh, but even she couldn't be that heartless.

"Oh, Pinto, I'm so sorry," Brenna replied.

"That mule was the only friend I had."

Brenna tried to comfort him. "Pinto, don't you think of us as your friends?"

"You're the best friend a man could have, Mrs. Mac. I trust you more than anyone. But I'm gonna miss that nasty, old mule."

"What did you do with her?" Marita asked.

"Wasn't nothin' I could do. Found her under a nearby tree. Couldn't move her, haven't got no strength any more. I just covered her with brush and some river rock. Took me most the day. Damn fool mule. Lord, I hope she didn't suffer none. Sure will be lonely without her."

"Any time you're lonely you're welcome to come here for a visit," Brenna offered. "You know I'll always need your help in the garden."

"No one's ever needed me for nothing," Pinto said. "Except for that old mule."

"Well, we need your help and we need it now," Marita commanded. "Two women here, working alone. First we lose one man, then another. It's about time you started doing something to earn your meals."

"She's right," Brenna added. "With Manuel gone I need everyone's help."

"Don't mean to be a freeloader, ma'am, I'll be here first thing tomorrow mornin'." Pinto looked down at the scraps on his plate. "Marita, you got anymore of this good food? Reckon I didn't get much to eat today."

Marita looked at Brenna and winked. His mule may have been dead, but his appetite certainly wasn't.

* * * *

Marita came in the next morning cursing in Spanish. "Where am I going to put them all?" she asked herself in English. "That damn Poncho Villa. He wants to free all the Mexicans, but instead he terrorizes the people. Every month I get more nieces and nephews and cousins under my roof. They tell me now, he may invade Naco."

"Naco!" Brenna exclaimed. "Why that's just down the road."

"*Si.*" Her voice rose. "The man is loco. He is taking on the United States of America."

"Well, pity him," Brenna replied. "The United States will destroy him. And besides, I have better things to worry about."

"Oh, and please tell me what would be more important than a war with Mexico?"

"Justice for your baby brother. I'm going to get Manuel out of jail," she said matter-of-factly. "I don't know about you, but I'm finding life pretty difficult without him." For the first time in her life Marita was without words.

Brenna knew Manuel would not want to see her, but it was important for her to have his permission to put her plan into effect.

* * * *

It was a Sunday afternoon when Brenna, Marita and Alberto showed up at the prison with dozens of other families to visit their loved ones. After greeting his sister, Manuel turned on her, ignoring Brenna like a cat would ignore its owner.

"Why have you brought Mrs. Mac? Are you crazy?"

"Where are your manners, Manuel?" Marita demanded. "Did you forget what it's like to be civilized?"

"I am sorry, Mrs. Mac. I really don't mean to be angry with you. A woman like you should not be in a place like this."

"And neither should you. Let's find a quiet corner where the four of us can talk." Brenna and Marita led them to an isolated table where they could share lunch. Alberto put his arm around Manuel's shoulder as they journeyed across a dry, grassy field.

"So, are you ready for the priesthood, *hombre*?" Manuel looked at him, puzzled.

"Why do you say that?"

"Well, let me see. I would expect that you have not had a nice, soft woman lie by your side in some time. Since you are already celibate, should I bring the Bible next time I come?"

"Yes, bring it so I can throw it at you. I see you are still a smart-assed little fucker."

"Ees that gangster language, Manuel? You were always so polite. Now look at you."

He lowered his voice placing his bushy mustache close to Manuel's ear. "You should listen to what the *Señora* has to say. A white woman with some money may be able to get you out of here."

"But that's just it, man. I don't want some Whitey bailing me out of trouble. Why should it be that way? Why can't they believe me?"

Brenna had heard the entire conversation. Not only was he still trying to protect her, but Manuel resented the advantages her white skin provided. He was a stubborn man and this wouldn't be easy.

"No! Absolutely not! I won't have you doing this, Mrs. Mac."

"Manuel, you fool, be reasonable," Marita begged. "It's not good for you to be locked up here. You're so thin and tired-looking."

"Manuel," Brenna cautioned, "I'm doing this with or without your blessing. I need you at the boarding house and your family misses you. This may be deceitful but I know you didn't murder Floyd Johnson. There's no reason for you to pay for something you didn't do. The justice system has deceived you. We're just returning the favor."

Manuel watched the trio walk away. Back in the prison yard, Crazy Chinga was tending to his chili peppers and tomatoes. Manuel joined him, pulling a few stray weeds from the garden. Chinga gave Manuel a rotten-tooth grin, pointing out a weed Manuel had overlooked. Manuel was the only prisoner Chinga trusted near his garden. Just last week he had beaten one inmate with his digging stick when the inmate tried to steal a tomato. Chinga and Manuel had an understanding and each would trade one act of kindness for another. Chinga handed him a firm, red tomato in pay for the meager weeds he had pulled.

In a few weeks the prison was to tear down Chinga's shack and garden. New buildings would replace his little home. Chinga was sure to die when they destroyed his garden and maybe that's what they wanted, to be rid of the mindless, old man.

Manuel did not want such a fate. Pride or not, he had to let Brenna rescue him. But when he did get out, if he got out, no white man would ever do this to him again.

Chapter 18

It was easy to recognize the Fred Harvey insignia in the upper left corner of the envelope. Brenna cast aside the remaining mail, fingering the mysterious letter. It had arrived much quicker than she had anticipated. She had heard that references were sometimes requested from the mayor or minister in town, and she had not indulged in either formality before sending the letter out. She wasted no more time and tore open the letter.

The letter stated that a job was waiting for Rainy at the Grand Canyon with an enclosed train ticket to get her there. Never again would that girl have to compromise her self respect to survive. She could use her own wits and intelligence to buy her life back and as far as Brenna was concerned, this was her way of getting back at all the rotten men in the world: one less female victim in circulation.

If only she could see Rainy's face when she got the letter. But that would not be possible. If she could not be seen with Rainy she would arrange a signal to be assured that the letter was received. She removed a large envelope from her desk and placed the letter inside with her own note.

When you receive this, hang a red bandanna in your bedroom window. I come to town next Tuesday. I'll look for it to acknowledge you have received your ticket. Wishing you the best.

Your Friend
* * * *

When the day came for Rainy's departure, Brenna watched from a distance as the young woman boarded the train. She looked so fresh and innocent, unmarked from last night's troubles. It was

Lorraina, not Rainy, who delicately lifted the hem of her skirt to climb the steps to the car. It may have been Brenna's imagination, but she seemed to stand a little taller than the woman she had once been. Even the porter seemed fooled by her new identity, respectfully nodding his head while offering his hand to the new passenger.

Lord God, had she done the right thing, sending this woman off on her own? She would be a stranger to everyone, as they would be to her. Yet how many of us would ever get a second chance for a new life; to live twice in one lifetime? Lorraina would be just fine.

The train began to pull out of the station, groaning and complaining like an arthritic old man. Brenna was surprised to see a slender, white arm flail a red bandanna from the window of the last car. The bandanna caught the wind in its sail and released, soaring through the air, and then dropping from the sky like a fallen angel, no longer bound by her sins.

****

From the train station Brenna began her walk to St. Patrick's for a visit with Father Lawrence. It was a cool spring morning and pleasant enough, but still the walk was long and tiring. A noisy motor car loaded with passengers left the station and lumbered past Brenna, leaving a coat of fine dirt on her clothes and hat. She reached for her lace handkerchief which did little to filter the dust flying through the air.

It would be nice to have such a convenience and it certainly was a time saver, but could she ever learn to control a motor car? She could barely drive a buggy. Luckily she flagged down the town trolley and made it to the church in good time.

The school yard was crawling with uniformed children, and in the middle of the crowd stood Father Lawrence. Brenna was getting nervous. Her proposition had to be firm and unyielding. She had to bargain with this man, his church, and his God, without instilling guilt. If it went well, all parties could benefit. Most importantly, Manuel would be free.

Father Lawrence was quick to honor her request for a personal conference. Brenna watched the youngsters yanking on his black

Cossack, thinking he was probably relieved to be excused from the playground follies.

His office was library quiet. One wall was lined with books of theology and volumes of what man presumed God's words meant. How could there be any real truth with an innocent man in jail? Brenna would quickly challenge this notion.

"Father Lawrence, when a man or a woman gives a confession and you hear their sins, no matter what sins they've committed, you are to forgive them, isn't that correct?"

His eyes darted around the room as he searched his mind for an honest, but non-committing answer. His hands were folded, providing him the expected pious look. Whatever angels that were present and guarding him were well armed and standing nearby.

"Jesus died so that we could be relieved of our sins," he began. "I, in turn, have been granted the right to absolve man from those sins."

"And it is written that when a man confesses," Brenna continued, "he is always forgiven for the sin he has committed and is protected by the church and God."

"I'm not sure I understand your question."

"He would not be exposed for what he did."

"Well, yes, he would confess in confidence. Brenna, what is it? Is something troubling you?"

"If you were to find out a man had been wronged, what would you do?"

Again he thought carefully about what his response would be. This time he turned the question on her.

"What would you expect me to do?"

"As an honest man, a man of God and a member of the community, I would hope you would try to right it. Wouldn't that be the thing to do, Father Lawrence?"

"Yes, Brenna." He smiled. "I would never want an innocent man to suffer. But what is this all about?"

She did not respond to his question. "Oh my, it's getting late. I must be getting back to the children." She thanked him for the visit and abruptly changed the subject.

"You'll have to stop by to see me sometime, Father. I understand the school is in need of some new textbooks. Perhaps I can see about making a donation for their purchase."

He stammered a bit, just then, as if all of the questions had some connection to her generosity.

"Oh yes, the children are in great need of language books. I could drop by sometime this week."

"Yes, why not work up an estimate for me as to what the school will need. You know, I've always felt it was important that we all work together in our community."

Father Lawrence eagerly agreed to her request and they exchanged polite goodbyes. Brenna was no fisherman of men, but if she was correct, Father Lawrence had just been baited and hooked.

* * * *

"Shut up, Sara. Quit your cryin' and do what you're told!"

"She ain't gonna do it, Eric. I want my ten cents back." "Yea, you can't make her do it," Jake chimed in.

"I can make her do whatever I want and she better if she knows what's good for her. Sara, pull down your bloomers or I'm gonna smack you." Eric reached for the child's clothing but she resisted and fell into the dirt. The sobbing continued while she remained helpless, sitting on the cold floor of the garden shed.

"Sara? Eric? Where are you?"

"Jesus, it's your mom," Harry said. "You said she'd be gone all morning. I'm getting outta here."

"I'm gonna get you for this, Sara," Eric threatened. "You tell her and I'll beat you." He wasn't about to be caught with Sara and took off trailing after the other boys. Just as the dust settled, Brenna came around the corner, finding Sara in the shed.

"Sara! I can't leave you alone for a minute. Just look at your pretty dress all full of dirt. Can't you ever stay out of trouble?" She grabbed the child by the arm and dragged her to an upright position. Her black high-top shoes were dusty as she tried to grab a foothold. Several times she fell as Brenna continued to pull her toward the house. Once inside, she sat her on the counter, removing each piece of clothing as she cleaned the little girl up.

The only sound in the kitchen was the gasping of a little girl as she tried to stifle the spasms in her chest. Now and then a shiver ran through her body, chilled by the cold wash cloth her mother used to bathe her. Her face was clean and dry and her tears had stopped falling. She remained motionless, yet her eyes never left her mother's face. Brenna seemed completely unaware of how her daughter watched her. Unless one looked very closely, it was nearly impossible to notice her clenched teeth and the anger in her bloodshot, blue eyes.

Cleaning up Sara had wasted nearly the whole afternoon and still she had not talked to Marita. It wasn't hard to locate her. She followed the smell of tobacco smoke around to the side of the house. Marita was sitting on a stump of wood, legs spread wide for balance, the brown paper cigarette pinched between her fingers.

"Marita, who are you hiding from?" Marita looked up, startled to have been discovered.

"Sorry, *Señora*. I guess it is a habit to hide."

"You know you shouldn't be smoking. It's not very ladylike."

Marita took a long drag.

"At my age, *Señora*, I don't worry about being a lady. I worry that Alberto will kill me if he finds me smoking." She chuckled and ground the butt into the dirt adding to the collection of cigarettes that had accumulated.

"Come inside, Marita. We have to talk about your brother. I don't want anyone to overhear us out here." Marita obediently followed her inside. Brenna moved about the kitchen checking windows and doorways. She looked into the sitting parlor, making sure it was empty. No one must know about this except a few members of the Higuera family. Surely they would not betray each other and had come to know the importance of anonymity in their struggle to survive.

Brenna sat down at the kitchen table. "You have a nephew," she began, "that has just moved in with you, correct?"

"*Sí,* Carlos is still looking for work. That freeloader." "No, no. I do not want him circulating around town.

You must tell him to stop immediately."

"What? Arc you loco? We need the money. I have many mouths to feed."

"Marita, you do not understand. Carlos will be the one to get Manuel out of jail. I will take care of Carlos and get him out of your house and settled in the United States. But for Manuel's sake, you must follow my instructions. Now, how is his English?"

"He has learned a lot since he's been here. It is improving."

"Good. Have the children tutor him every night. He must sound like he's been here for a year or so."

"Will you not tell me what is going on?"

"At this point, the less you know the better. Just tell Carlos his worries are over. I will pay him handsomely for his help. He should know that there is a good deal of risk involved in this. I suspect having left Mexico, he is used to taking chances. I need someone who can lie and make people believe him. Bring him to me in two weeks and we will see how he is doing."

* * * *

Brenna followed the voices upstairs where she found Marita and Ana comforting Sara.

"No *hija*," Marita cooed, "I am sure she will come home."

"No," Sara said and sobbed. "Eric killed my kitty. He told me so."

"Sara!" Brenna cut in. "You don't believe that tale. Why would Eric kill your kitten?"

Sara lowered her voice to barely a whisper. "He hates me. Someday he'll kill me too."

"How can you say such a thing about your brother?" Brenna asked.

"It's true," Ana interjected. "I heard him tell her so."

"Now listen," Brenna said. She shuffled the girls out of the bedroom and toward the staircase. "I'm sure Eric was just being playful. Why don't you both go outside and look for Snowball. She'll come home."

Ana gave a soulful look to Marita who could only shrug her shoulders at her daughter's pained expression.

* * * *

Downstairs, Eric crouched in a corner of the yard. In a tin can he had collected several kinds of insects, mostly spiders. One by one he removed a victim from the can, holding it close to the match. He seemed to take a keen interest in watching the creatures squirm in agony until they burst into a tiny flame.

The girls watched in horror, shocked by both the cruelty of Eric's behavior and the vast collection of insects he had acquired. He dangled a large beetle in front of Sara's face, chasing her around the yard.

"I'm not afraid of you, Eric," Ana warned. "You stay away from Sara. I got brothers and cousins that can beat you up." Ana had placed herself between Eric and Sara, extending her arms over her fragile friend. Eric seemed amused by Ana's feisty nature. He almost liked her.

"Shut up, you little Spic," he replied. He grabbed her two braids from behind her ears, pulling straight up. "I oughta hang you by your tails." Ana flung her round little arms at Eric, releasing herself from his grasp. Eric countered, putting his hands around her throat. "I should choke you the same way I killed Sara's stupid cat; turn your neck 'til it snaps. Then I'll throw you in a trash can." Sara began to whimper.

"Let go of her, Eric, let go! I'm gonna go tell."

"Hey, *hombre*, if you hurt my leetle *amiga*, kick I will your ass." Eric looked up to see a tall Mexican man standing behind him. He dropped his hands like lead weights.

"No, Carlos." Ana corrected his poor English. "It's not *kick I will your ass*; it's *I will kick your ass*!"

Everyone turned to look at Ana, sure that the devil had spoken through her sweet mouth. Ana cupped her hand over her mouth, eyes wide; she was shocked by her own words.

"I didn't mean it, Carlos. Don't tell Mama."

Carlos was smiling. "No *niña*, I will not tell. But be careful. She will make you drink chili peppers if you speak it again."

"Eat chili peppers," Eric corrected. Carlos glared at the boy.

"*Si, si*, you keep gone of her or..." He motioned with his finger across his neck. "Like a cheeken."

"Ah, horse feathers," Eric retorted and turned to walk away.

"I no like heem," Carlos said with a raised eyebrow.

"He is not good. Who is he?"

"Eric," Ana replied. "Mrs. McEvoy's boy."

"Oh, she is who I must see. Take me to her." The girls led Carlos up the back steps to the kitchen.

"Ah, it is my handsome nephew," Marita said. Carlos dutifully walked to his aunt's side, placing a gentle kiss on her cheek. He seemed to know how to charm women, both young and old.

"And it is my beautiful aunt," he replied. "Working very hard."

"As you should," Marita responded, not looking up from her cooking.

"But *Tia,* I work. I am here to see Mrs. McEvoy."

"*Bueno.* Maybe you will be ready to start earning your keep. Mrs. McEvoy is in the sitting room doing her sewing. You go talk to her." Carlos removed his hat and smoothed his center part. Next he twisted his handlebar mustache and wiped off his dusty boots with his pant legs. He looked to his aunt for her blessing. She gave a nod of approval, grabbed his hand and took him past the swinging door to where Brenna was sitting.

"*Señora,* this is my nephew, Carlos Montoya. He has been studying very hard, just as you asked. Would you like to speak with him?"

Marita left the two conspirators together. She wondered how long it would be before Manuel could come home again.

Chapter 19

Dusk was falling as Carlos crossed the street, making his way to the white man's church. It was a magnificent red brick building, tall and impressive; very different from the adobe church he had known in Mexico. Large sheets of colored glass filled the window panes making Carlos feel insignificant in God's presence. He paused before entering the arched doorway. How would God feel about what he was about to do? Surely he could not damn him to hell for trying to save another man's life or judge him for trying to save his own.

He did not look the same as he did a week ago. His hair was very short and he had shaved his mustache. *Hijola*, that had been hard. Even worse was the lousy looking theatrical mustache he had pasted to his upper lip. *Señora* McEvoy had bought him American clothes and shiny leather shoes to prepare him for his new identity.

But tonight, he still looked like the Mexican national he was. He wore his torn straw hat and ragged leather vest. To protect him from the cold night air, he covered himself with a long overcoat. Most important, tucked inside the pocket of the overcoat was a one way ticket to Texas, a place called El Paso.

Mrs. McEvoy put up six months' rent for him to stay at a boarding house while he learned to fix motor cars. In a few months he would have a life of his own, never again having to choose between going hungry and stealing for food. This was a wonderful country. Who would have believed that Americans could be so generous?

Scanning the room, he selected a pew at least twenty feet from the other parishioners. He counted six others in church, mostly women, heads draped in black lace mantillas that would obstruct most of their side vision. The church was beginning to darken, lit only by candles for worship. A small door creaked open and an old woman holding a Rosary stepped out. The confessional for Father Lawrence was empty.

His steps were quick and he wasted no time in entering the black closet. A small holy candle was all that illuminated the confessional. The fragrance of mildly spiced incense hung in the air. Carlos felt like he was running out of oxygen but now was not the time to lose his nerve. He fell down on the kneeler before him, taking a quick glance at the brass crucifix hanging on the wall in front of him. There was a rattle and a flash of light. The small door opened that separated sinners from the priest on the other side of the wall. Only a thin cotton curtain separated their two souls. Carlos spoke first, crossing himself.

"Bless me, Father, for I have sinned. My last confession—" He stopped. He couldn't remember his last confession. Probably when he made his Holy Communion as a child. It was time to start lying. "My last confession was a very long time ago, maybe two or three years."

"And why have you waited so long to confess your sins, my son?"

"Father, I have done something terrible," he replied. "I can no longer live with this guilt."

There was silence on the other side of the curtain. The priest waited patiently for the sinner to continue. "It was some time ago. I became angry with a man here in town. I had been gambling and drinking, you know? It was not good. I was kicked out of the saloon, but I didn't feel well so I sat down in the alley to rest. Then, that very man comes out of the saloon. I knew he had the money I lost gambling. I went to get it back. I didn't mean to hurt him. He struggled and I cut him. I ran like hell—oh, sorry, Father. I ran and hid. Later, I heard another man had been jailed for what I had done. I hid for a long time. Father, I can't go to jail, but that man, he should not be in jail for what I did."

Carlos heard a huge sigh come from the man on the other side. His mortal-like qualities were interfering with his God-like duties.

148

Had he believed the tale? Would he suddenly pull back the curtain to expose him?

"Why have you not gone to your own church to confess this?" Carlos could tell the priest was annoyed, being burdened with this dilemma.

"I have no church, Father. And besides, if I went to the Mexican church who would believe our *padre*? And what if I was recognized? You've got to help me, Father."

"What is it you would like me to do?"

"Tell me I am forgiven. Save me from Hell."

"This man you stabbed, did he die?"

"Yes. They said he died in the street."

Father Lawrence spoke slowly with a grave tone to his voice. "You have taken the life of another man for your own greed and selfishness. Perhaps there is no greater sin in the world. God will forgive you, but you must forgive yourself. It sounds as if you have suffered a great deal of anguish for what you have done. For your penance, take the equal sum of money you have stolen and give it to the poor. Say the Rosary every night for the next six months and ask God's forgiveness while you pray."

"Father, will you help that man in jail? They took him to Florence."

"And his name?"

"I do not know. All I can tell you is that his first name is Manuel."

"I will see what I can do. Bow your head for God's blessing."

Carlos heard the Latin words rolling off the priest's tongue. It seemed like an unusually long blessing and maybe he needed one. He removed the switchblade from his pocket, marked with his own blood, and laid it on the floor. Quietly, he escaped while the priest continued his invocation.

"Now try to live out the rest of your days as a good Catholic, will you promise me that?" But there was no answer to Father Lawrence's request. "Are you still there?" Silence replied.

Father Lawrence came out of his hiding place, glancing around the church. No one was there. He knocked on the door of the adjacent confessional and cautiously entered where the man had been. The box was vacant with the exception of a knife, covered with what he believed was dried human blood.

Carlos ran like a wild dog, tearing through the blackened streets. Nearing the train station, he heard voices. He slowed to a normal gait to avoid attention. Anyone seeing a Mexican running through the dark streets was sure to get suspicious. The train was due to arrive within the next five minutes, but most likely would be late. He decided to wait outside where the street lamps were dim.

Instead, the train arrived early. Carlos hung back until the other passengers had stepped off the train. Ticket in hand, he boarded with his borrowed suitcase and found a comfortable seat.

Several hours passed before the train pulled into a station where he could begin his new identity. He entered the men's toilet room, locking the door behind him in the first empty stall. Without hesitation, he ripped off the sticky mustache glued to his face. Glad to be rid of it, he was tempted to flush it down the toilet, but instead continued as he had been instructed. Next, he removed his vest, pants and boots, quickly trading them for a new gray suit and a pair of calfskin shoes. Last, he discarded his hat for a new gray fedora. All that belonged to Carlos Montoya was wrapped in brown paper, and when no one was looking, he stashed it in the bottom of the trash bin. Antonio Abrego left the station in his new American clothes, destined for a new beginning.

When the train whistled, Antonio boarded and returned to his seat at the back of the car. He took out the black rosary his mother had given him on his communion day, kissed the crucifix and crossed himself. He would say it once, tonight, just for good luck. And because he still felt bad for lying to that priest.

* * * *

Father Lawrence sat at his desk, head in his hands. Morning prayers had yet to reveal a solution to the confession he had heard last night. Where was he to begin? It would be so easy to just forget the so-called innocent man in jail and go about the business of organizing the new school and church. But thinking about that option made him uncomfortable. What if he, himself, as an ordinary man, were locked up for something he had not done? His whole reason for living would hinge on the perseverance of another human being. Who was he to make that decision? No, at the very least he must engage in a little research to determine what had really happened.

The murderer, no doubt, was either on his way to Mexico or was already living there. All he had to go on was a bloody knife. Perhaps a stop at the library would help him locate the information he needed.

"Yes, Father, I'm sure we have something for you. We go back many years. Do you know what year it is you're looking for?" The wiry librarian reminded him of a nervous canary. She seemed eager for the challenge ahead of her.

"It was a murder involving a white man and a Mexican. Don't know whether it was uptown or in Brewery Gulch. Murderer's first name was Manuel."

"Well, let's go back four years and work our way forward," she suggested. "At the very least we know the event was over a year ago. Something like that should have been front page news and easy to spot. I'll just set you down here and you can get started."

An hour had passed and still Father Lawrence had found nothing. *Oh, why is God testing me so?* he lamented. Removing his wire-rimmed glasses, he rubbed his weary eyes, all the time thinking he needed to return to the church.

The eager librarian popped around the corner, note in hand, with a bright look on her face. "Father Lawrence, I took the liberty of contacting the newspaper office and look what I found." She bent over the table where the priest was seated, proudly reading the headline. "*Murder on Main, Mexican Murders White Man.*"

"Does it say what the Mexican's name was?" the Father asked.
"Right here, Father," she pointed with her bony finger, "Manuel Rodriguez who lived on Chihuahua Hill."

"You have been most helpful. May I borrow this copy?"

She drew close to the priest and spoke in a whisper. "Normally, reference material doesn't leave the library. But if we can't trust you, who can we trust? You go ahead and take it, but please bring it directly back to me tomorrow morning."

"Yes, I'll be extremely careful, and thank you again."

Father Lawrence tucked the precious paper under his arm and left the library. At least the day hadn't been a total loss. He would have to prepare his staff for his departure this week. It seemed that he was going to be making a trip to Florence.

* * * *

Brenna's visit to Father Lawrence assured her that her plan was falling into place. She could hardly contain herself when she heard the news.

"Yes, my dear," Father Lawrence responded, "I got your donation several days ago and I apologize for not contacting you, but I'm preparing for a trip and have been quite busy."

"A vacation, Father?"

"Oh no, strictly business. I need to drop by Florence to visit a man..." The priest's voice dropped off and his mind seemed to wander somewhere else. Seconds passed that seemed like hours, before Brenna could get his attention again.

"Father, are you all right?"

"Yes, yes, I'm fine," he replied. He had been set up as sure as Judas set up Jesus. It all clicked when he stared into her face. Tricked by a woman. Look at her, with the face of a cherub.

"Well, I can see you're terribly busy and I should let you go about your business. Hope the donation will cover the cost of the books. If not, let me know."

She had been pleasant, downright innocent. What if he'd been mistaken and it was just coincidence? But her questions at their meeting had been so pertinent. If he backed out there could be serious repercussions. What if there really was an innocent man in jail? He couldn't quit now if he wanted to. He hadn't slept well in days and this had to come to a conclusion. Perhaps he would know better if he met the man. Maybe his heart and God would lead him to the right decision.

* * * *

"You see, sir, after having spoken to this gentle, young man, I am convinced that what I heard in the confessional is the truth. The man you hold in jail, by the name of Manuel Rodriguez, is not the murderer you believe him to be."

The warden sat behind his desk, piled sloppily with papers and dirty coffee mugs. "Well, you're right in that respect, Father. Rodríguez has been a model prisoner. But a knife with blood, and not much at that, with a confession to a priest, is not a lot to go on. On the other hand, I'm not sure that the evidence they used to put Rodríguez in here was entirely conclusive. But then, that's not mine to say. Tell you what. You leave the knife and a written statement with your signature. I'll put it before them big shots and we will see what happens. At least you'll know you tried."

Not a bad fellow, Father Lawrence thought, as he made his way from the prison. *But Lord, what a fate for these wretched men.* He hated to see anyone caged like an animal; isolated and alone. Rodriguez certainly didn't belong in this crowd.

But now his fate was in God's hands.

Chapter 20

Manuel's palms were sweating as he approached the McEvoy's back door. He had experienced more beatings in prison than he ever expected to endure in his lifetime, and he wondered if any of the scars would fade with time. He wanted to forget that part of his life, and all the bitter men at the prison whose empty lives meant nothing to anyone. His life, on the other hand, meant something to Mrs. Mac. How would he ever thank her for saving his life?

When Brenna heard the footsteps on the back porch and the knock on the screen door, she raced across the kitchen. It was unmistakable, the sound of Manuel's boots on the wooden deck; his knuckles banging against the door. If she lived a thousand years, she would always recognize those special sounds.

Forgetting her place, she threw her arms around Manuel's neck, and he returned her embrace like one would greet a family member after many years in absence. Her eyes puddled with tears and through her blurred vision, she was sure she saw the same in Manuel's eyes. "You're really here," she said, still holding his hands. "What did they say when they released you?"

"The committee said the evidence wasn't enough to prove that I had committed the crime. Based on the priest's testimony and the other knife he had given them, they decided I wasn't worth holding onto."

"So you're a free man," Brenna said. "Does Marita know you're home yet?"

Manuel smiled. "Yes, she wanted me to surprise you. We've been celebrating since I got home yesterday. I brought some tequila and limes to celebrate with you. Will you have a drink with me to toast my freedom?"

Brenna was a little surprised, but felt daring. She was getting good at taking risks. "I don't know how to drink tequila, but I'm willing to learn."

"Ah, I won't get you drunk," he promised. "But it would be bad luck for me not to toast such a wonderful woman." He opened the paper sack and brought out a bottle of the liquid gold and two tiny shot glasses shaped like beer mugs. Four limes rolled out of the bag. He cut them into small wedges and placed them on a plate.

"Sit here, at the table," Brenna directed. "The boarders have all been fed and the children are ready for bed. We can talk for a while."

"So what was it like?" Brenna continued. "Those men in there with you, were they mean to you?"

His eyes continued to focus on the shot glasses, avoiding her face. "I had a few run-ins with some inmates who wouldn't stay clear of me. It was whites against black against brown. It's just like the real world. I think everyone in there was angry, including me. We took it out on each other."

"Were you hurt?"

"A couple of times. Once I needed some stitches, but it doesn't matter now." He finally looked up at her. "I healed. I learned to keep to myself."

"It must have been lonely," Brenna said. "All those men, yet no one you could trust."

"I should have trusted you more," he admitted. "I hope you understand it was hard for me to take help from a white woman when the reason I was jailed was because of a white man. I was bitter and took it out on you. I am so sorry."

"I have learned not to think in terms of color," she replied. "You and Marita, Alberto and the children, you're my family. And quit calling me Mrs. Mac."

"Okay, Brenna. Now this is how you drink tequila. Watch what I do." He filled both shot glasses with the tequila, placing them in the middle of the table. The limes were placed on a plate. Without taking his gaze off her, he licked the top of his hand near the thumb. Then he sprinkled salt on the wet spot. Her brows furrowed.

"What's all that for?" she asked.

"When my cousins taught me, they said it was to make bad tequila go down easier. Now watch. You lick." He took a swipe at the salt with his tongue, grabbed a shot glass, put it to his lips and threw back his head. The tequila disappeared in one gulp. He reached for a lime wedge and bit into it, wiping away the juice that ran down his chin. "You lick, drink and bite. That's it."

"What does it taste like?"

"Did you ever drink any of your father's Irish whiskey? Well, it doesn't taste like that."

She laughed out loud. It was a laugh he had waited years to hear again. He had dreamed of her laugh, lived only for that moment when the past would be behind them and they could look to the future. He could see she was enjoying herself, so he continued with the demonstration.

"Your turn."

Brenna looked at him hesitantly and repeated his instructions. "You lick and sprinkle." She put down the shaker. "You lick again," she grabbed for a mug, "drink," she mumbled with salt on her tongue, opened her mouth and tossed back her head, but when her head came down her eyes were wide and watering, "and bite!" she screamed. "Oh, my Lord, oh is it supposed to burn like this? I believe I'm on fire! But you know, it feels really good going down, warms you up a bit."

"You would make a good Mexican," he said. "And I mean that as a compliment."

"Let's do another," Brenna suggested, "now that I know what I am doing."

There was one more and then another. She was getting silly, saying the most outrageous things. Manuel worried that he had taken this too far. Just like a woman to get herself drunk like this. He hadn't met one yet that could hold her liquor.

"Teach me to drive, Manuel." She proclaimed this while releasing a tiny burp.

"Teach you to drive? You don't even have a motor car."

"Then I'll buy one. I have the money."

"You shouldn't talk like that. People will try to take advantage of you if you talk like that."

"Don't be ridiculous," she slurred. "Let's do 'nother."

"No, no, I don't think so. You've had enough tequila lessons for one night." Just then a lime rolled off the table and hit the floor.

"I'll get it," Brenna volunteered. She pushed back her chair and reached for the lime. Manuel tried to stop her but before he could get there, she tumbled out of the chair and onto the linoleum. She lay there giggling, unable to control her laughter. "Everything is moving," she said.

"Come on, let's get you back in your chair before you hurt yourself."

"Too late," she said, rubbing her behind.

He stood her up, but her knees buckled and she fell into him. He slid her onto the table. At least she was still sitting up on her own. "You're going to hate me in the morning," Manuel said.

"No I won't," she replied. "I love you, Manuel. I really do."

He looked deep into her eyes to see if it was her heart or the tequila talking. He could take the opportunity to tell her the same. Maybe she wouldn't remember and he would feel better for telling her.

"I love you too, Brenna," he replied and bent over to kiss her, but at that precise moment, she passed out.

"*Madre de Dios*, just my luck." He threw her over his shoulder, trying to locate a safe place to deposit her. He thought about putting her on the couch, but what would the boarders think when they found her there tomorrow morning? If she got sick and threw up she could choke to death, and he wasn't ready to lose her again. No, he had to take her upstairs to her own bed. There, he would watch her through the night and slip out before Marita came in the morning. If Marita found out what he'd done, she'd beat him with a broom. He grabbed the bottle of tequila and toted her up the stairs.

Manuel pulled back the bed covers and laid her down, supporting her head with a pillow. She groaned a little when he slipped off her shoes. That was a good sign. She wasn't totally unconscious, just pickled. God, if anyone caught him doing this he'd go straight back to jail. He was beginning to sweat. Was it the tequila or fear?

Then he stopped, working hard to bring his eyes into focus. He took a swig of tequila from the nearly empty bottle. She lay before him, blissfully at peace. He wanted to touch her. It would be like flame and ice, both at the same time. His breathing was deep and deliberate and this time he questioned if it was the tequila or desire. For a long time he stood there, starring at what he knew he would never have. He could have it now, if he wanted to, but how could he soil it and make it ugly? Manuel took a cleansing breath, knowing he had to remove himself from these thoughts. Tonight, no matter what his heart said, he was not her lover. His head told him he was her nurse and had to help her through the night.

First he had to take her clothes off. For this, he would need more tequila. He wiped his mouth on his sleeve, put down the bottle and with the gentlest touch, peeked underneath her skirt. Good, there was something there. It was some kind of frilly underwear; he'd see it on his sister's wash line. Manuel tugged at the buttons on her blouse, pausing to still the shaking in his hands. He hadn't been this scared since his last beating in prison.

Brenna came to briefly, as he sat her up and pulled her forward to remove the shirt. "Shh, everything is fine," he reassured her.

"Uh-huh," she agreed, and fell back into bed.

"I am halfway there," Manuel said to himself. Now how do I get this skirt off?" To his surprise, she answered.

"Bu-un."

"Bu-un?" he repeated.

She was gone again, drifting off to sleep. He pulled back the covers and searched the waist of the skirt, discovering a short row of buttons on the side. "Ah, *si,* buttons. I got you, Mrs. Mac." With that he slipped off the skirt, carefully folding it and laying it on the dresser.

All that was left were her black cotton stockings. That would involve putting his hands up her slip and tequila or not, there wasn't a Chinaman's chance that he would do that. No sir, enough was enough. He pulled the covers up under her chin and tenderly tucked in the sides to warm her.

His work finished, he pulled up a chair and glanced at the mantle clock. Marita would arrive early this morning and as soon as he heard her downstairs, he would have to jump out the window. For now he would finish his tequila and hold his vigil.

* * * *

"*Señora?* Are you home?" It was Marita's voice, calling from downstairs. Manuel rubbed his hands over his face several times, trying to wake up. He scrambled for the side window. It was further down than he thought. If he hung himself out the window it would not be so great a fall. He would have gotten completely away, had it not been for that old bucket.

He caught the tip of the metal can on the top of his shoe making a terrible racket as he went down. The empty tequila bottle he had clamped in his mouth dropped to the ground and shattered. Several dogs started barking, announcing his clumsiness. Manuel could hear Marita in Brenna's room.

"Who is out there?" she called. Manuel sprung to his feet, brushing the dirt from his pants and straightening his clothes. He wasn't going to make a getaway now; his sister was too sharp for that. Seconds later her head poked out the window.

"Manuel! It is you. Where are you coming from? Have you been out all night?"

"Shhh, woman. Can't you see I can't take any of your belly aching this morning? I need some coffee. Put a pot on so I can clear my head."

"It is already brewing, you bum. Your first night home and this is what you do." Her head disappeared like a jack-in-the-box. She was finished scolding.

Manuel smiled. That had gone very well. And he didn't even have to lie. Quietly, he walked around back and let himself in. His favorite coffee mug was still in the cupboard where he had left it. A few ragged lime wedges lay crumpled in the sink. Like a cat swatting a mouse, he batted at the fruit and hid the remains in the trash.

"The *Señora* is still sleeping," she said to Manuel. "That is not like her. I wonder if she is sick."

"She did seem a little tired last night. I stopped by and thanked her before I went down to the Gulch to celebrate."

"Well, you have done enough celebrating." She handed Manuel his coffee. "Sober up and then get home. Alberto has good news for you. One of his coworkers in the smelter was taken ill or had an accident or something. He thinks he can get you in right away. How can you get so lucky, *verdad*? Out of jail one day, working the next day."

Chapter 21

When the door chimes rang, Marita scurried past Brenna to answer the front door. Then the familiar scolding began.

"Manuel! What do you mean by this nonsense? What are you doing coming to the front door?"

"Madam," he said with sarcasm, "I understand you have a room to rent." Manuel pushed his way past Marita, carrying a battered suitcase.

"What are you talking about?" Marita asked. "You have a home with your family."

"Don't be offended my sister, but it is time for me to get a place of my own. You are crowded enough as it is. I've been working for several months in that sweat shop and I've saved enough money for board. Besides, I will still be in your home. Don't forget, you are part owner of the boarding house."

Brenna was delighted that Manuel would even consider moving into her home. She rose from her desk.

"Manuel, would you like to see the vacant room?" she asked.

"I will trust you Brenna. For now, I would just like to move in."

"Aiieee!" Marita threw her hands up in the air. "Well, if you will not listen to reason I suppose the least I can do is help you unpack." She grabbed his suitcase. "Is this all you own?"

"Almost. Francisco is bringing a trunk over later today. He's going to borrow a truck from work."

Brenna watched them disappear around the corner with Marita still berating Manuel for his decision. She didn't see him again until supper time when he wandered into the kitchen. "Get out of here," Brenna said, pointing to the door with a long-handled wooden spoon. "You don't belong in here anymore, least not at mealtime. You eat in the dining room with the other miners."

"But in here, I get to taste," Manuel whined.

"This time you taste in the dining room," his sister said and pushed him out the door.

* * * *

"Mmm, mighty fine dinner, Mrs. Mac," Leroy stuttered. "You've outdone yourself."

Brenna felt her face flame with the attention, afraid that Manuel would know it was all for him. She mustn't cook like this every night, but now and then she could spoil him. She poured him an extra cup of coffee, making the round of the table.

There had been no discussion between the two of them about her previous tequila lessons. She assumed he had been the one who had put her to bed and halfway undressed her. Her confidence wavered just thinking about that and the stupor she was in at the time he was removing her clothes. As far as she knew, nothing else had happened. She would never ask him about the details of that night and she hoped he was enough of a gentleman not to ever tell her.

"There's a meeting tonight, Manuel." John sipped at his steaming coffee. He had become what some would interpret as a traitor, a full-fledged Wobbly, recruiting as many men as he could to support his cause for miners' rights. "You're welcome to join us and help fight for the working man."

"I don't know much about these politics," Manuel apologized. "But I don't have any plans tonight. It might be good for me to attend a meeting or two since I am working at the smelter."

After dinner Marita pulled Manuel into the kitchen for another sisterly talk. Her voice was low and secretive. "Manuel, Alberto is already involved with these Wobblies and I am worried for both of you. You could lose your job or worse. Most of the time it's hard to tell who's on what side. What if the mine finds out you are going to those meetings? Then what? You stay away from those troublemakers."

Manuel's face contorted with anger. "Why must we always be afraid of them?" He waved his hands in the direction of the Copper Queen. "Those big men, with their big companies and their big lies.

You should be proud of your husband for standing up for what he believes in and fighting for better working conditions."

Marita cradled her head in her hands, covering her ears. "I cannot talk to you anymore. You have all these fancy ideas of what you'll never have. Including the *Señora."* She turned to walk away but Manuel grabbed her by the forearm and forced her out the back door. Once outside, he released her.

"What do you mean by that comment?"

Marita exhaled a big sigh, already seeming to regret her hasty criticism.

"You are my baby brother and I would never hurt you. You know I have never said anything about her but I see the way you look at her. I'm not sure it is so good that you are living here."

"Is it that obvious?"

"*Si.* I don't know if the other miners have noticed. They are men and don't see these things. But you watch yourself. Remember your place."

"I'm going for a walk," he said.

"No, you are going to that meeting," she replied, correcting his lie. "Just be careful."

Brenna watched Manuel walk down the alley heading for the meeting at the Y.M.C.A. She stepped away from the upstairs window and waited until Marita had returned to the kitchen before she switched on the bedroom light. Neither of them must ever know that she had heard their conversation.

* * * *

Brenna had finished setting the dining room table, preparing for the morning meal. She glanced at the grandfather clock in the parlor. It was almost midnight and the men still had not returned home. She wasn't sure how long she stood there in her night robe, chewing anxiously on her upper lip. It took the low din of approaching voices and footsteps on the porch to bring her back to herself. Hurrying into the kitchen, she hid behind the closed door, determined to find out what had happened at the meeting. There was a struggle with the door as it opened. She could hear heavy breathing and sensed tension in the voices.

"In here, bring him this way," John directed. Brenna peaked out the swinging door. Manuel and Alberto carried in Michael, battered and bruised. Their clothes were torn and dirty, marked by blood and sweat.

"You beat the shit out of that one guy," Manuel said to Alberto. "God, man, I thought you were going to kill him." Michael let out a cry as they continued to drag him down the hall.

"He shouldn't have started the God damn fight," Alberto said. "There was no reason theese had to happen. I was only protecting us."

Brenna had heard enough. She burst out of the kitchen hurrying toward Michael, pushing the dazed miners aside.

"They jumped us after the meeting," Manuel said. "We were just walking home and they decided we needed to learn who was buttering our bread, least that's what they said."

"They said we weren't Americans and never would be," Alberto murmured. "Mike, he did not like that and he went after the big one. Guess he was a little too much for the little Englishman."

"He needs medical attention," Brenna said. "He's got some broken ribs for sure, but I can't tell if he's bleeding inside. We've got to get a doctor and quick."

"What are we going to do, take him to the company hospital?" John asked. "They're sure to finish him off there."

"You've got to trust someone, John," Brenna said. "I have an acquaintance who works at the hospital. Maybe I can get him to come by and look at him."

* * * *

One by one Dr. Carson examined each man, sending him off to his room. Some got stitches, others bandages, and all had broken spirits. Michael would recover but his healing would be slow and require time off work. There was no guarantee his job would be waiting for him when he recovered.

"I'm afraid this kind of thing will only escalate," Dr. Carson told Brenna. He was a kind, old gentleman, sincerely concerned for the health of others. It made no matter to the doctor as to whose side was right or wrong. He just didn't like mending bodies broken by other men. "I fear something terrible is going to happen before this is all over." He handed Brenna a bottle of laudanum. "See that Mr. Hollands gets a teaspoon of this every four hours. And be prepared for the worst."

Within a month's time, Michael was on his way to a full recovery. Marita and Brenna were excellent nurses, force-feeding the skinny man chicken soup and giving him extra portions of meat, potatoes, and sweets to build up his strength and fatten him up.

Michael returned to work quickly, but as a broken man fearing retaliation for speaking out against management, he chose to keep a low profile. While his bones healed, his anger and that of his friends and cohorts did not. It hung in the air like laundry on washday, clearly visible for everyone to see. There was no indication that either side would deign to back down anytime soon.

"Mrs. Mac?" John's voice called. "May we go somewhere private? I'd like to discuss something with you. I need your help." This put Brenna on edge, but she obliged the man. John hardly ever asked for anything. She led him from the parlor into the kitchen where they could be alone.

"Mrs. Mac, I'm scared." The air was dry and cool yet beads of perspiration shined above his lip and forehead. "I'm scared someone's after me with what I've been doing. You were right, saying I needed someone to trust. You're the only person I do trust, a miner's angel I'd say. The other men said they'd trust you more than any bank. Here." His hands shook as he gave her a thick leather wallet filled with cash. Obviously ill at ease, he turned back to the kitchen door and peered into the parlor, checking to make sure there were no uninvited visitors listening in.

He returned to where she stood. "Put that in your pocket," he told her. "I've got several thousand dollars in it."

Without taking her eyes off his face she quickly squirreled the money away in her skirt pocket. "My goodness, John. Where did you get all this money?"

"I been puttin' money aside for a long time now, building up a little savings. Would you look after it for me? Please. If something should happen to me, say I'm hurt bad, or I go to jail, I'll know my money will be in safekeeping with you until I can come for it."

"John, are you sure you want to do this? Have you been threatened?"

"Shoot, I get threatened every day."

"And the sheriff, have you told him?"

John laughed. "All due respect, ma'am, but you know the sheriff works for the mines. If I disappear under mysterious circumstances, I'd be doing him a favor."

"I'll take care of your money, John. But let me write you a receipt." They walked to her desk in the parlor, the money bag still concealed. She drew out a paper and pen from the top drawer, scratching out the guarantee that someday he could collect his money. "How much did you say was here, John?"

"Three thousand dollars." She completed the note.

"I'll count it myself upstairs, to make sure we agree." She handed him the note. "Let's get some sleep now, John. You can rest easy that I will protect your savings."

* * * *

It was the miners who first informed Brenna the United States was at war with Germany, its allied powers from Eastern Europe, and the Ottoman Empire. Word had spread fast among the men, some walking straight off their mine shifts to enter the fight on foreign lands. Many had yet to let go of their emotional ties to their homelands. They fought, not only for America, but for their motherlands that had spawned generations of their families.

"What's going to happen to us?" Brenna asked Marita. "Will all our men leave the mine to join the war effort?"

"I think it will all work out," Marita said, trying to comfort her. "This war may take their minds off of the troubles at home. Maybe they will see life as it really is and learn to be grateful for what God has given them here."

In no time at all, copper prices skyrocketed. Mines were operating around the clock to meet the demands of warfare. Men were tired and angry; unsatisfied. Like a crystal soap bubble— fragile, tense and ready to break—the time came when men and machines, both overworked for monetary gain, erupted in disaster.

The mine whistle was heard across the whole town, the voice of death ringing through every home. Women all over town immediately looked to where their men were—at home or at work. It didn't take Brenna long to figure out that Manuel and Alberto were working the current shift.

Marita came flying down the stairs, still grasping fresh linens in her arms. "*Señora, Señora!* The mine! The whistle!" Her voice quieted. "There has been an accident," she said solemnly. Brenna could see she was already crying. Tears flowed freely down her cheeks but she didn't utter another word.

The entire town emptied as everyone headed for the mine. It would be a long walk for Brenna and Marita, but if they were lucky they might be able to hitch a ride in someone's car or truck. By the time they reached the mine, a large crowd, mostly female, had already gathered in front of the gaping entrance to the mine. To Brenna it looked like the mouth of some great carnivorous monster. Anyone with any authority was there to face the families. Word passed among them that the accident, an explosion, had taken place in the smelter.

Marita's knees buckled when she heard. Brenna reached for her, catching her by the arm, just before she collapsed. Now she wished Manuel would have found employment somewhere other than at Alberto's side. She didn't want to consider the possibility, but there was the chance that they had already lost both of them.

Brenna would not allow herself to cry. In the first place, all they were hearing were rumors, spreading among the anguished crowd. Most importantly, she had to stay strong for Marita. She refused to imagine that anything could happen to the man who loved her. The only man that had ever loved her. Maybe if she didn't think it, it wouldn't be so. She clung to that small hope for a miracle as the minutes ticked by.

A harried company official finally stepped up on a small platform to speak to the crowd. Standing at the back, Brenna could not make out what he was saying. From the middle of the swarm a woman turned back to speak.

"It's true, it's true!" she shouted. "The accident was in the smelter."

With that, there was a collective sigh of relief among a portion of the on-lookers. The crowd shifted, some leaving and others pushing their way to the front. Brenna held on to Marita, moving her forward like a sheepdog herding a weak lamb.

Brenna stopped a man in a suit holding a clipboard.

"How do we find out who was injured?" she asked.

"Were they in the smelter?"

"Yes, they were," Brenna responded. "Do you have a list of the men who were injured?"

The man didn't even look up from his clipboard. "Injured are being taken over to the hospital," came the curt reply. "Go over to the office, over there," he said and pointed. "Drivers are leaving every few minutes to take family members to the hospital. You family?" he asked.

"Yes," Brenna said. "And the dead? Are there any dead?"

"Yes ma'am." His tone had softened. "So far there's only been one dead. A white man. They took him over to the funeral home."

This time Brenna couldn't help herself. Tears flowed freely. "Did you hear that, Marita? A white man died, God rest his soul. I'm sure they're fine. Let's go over to the hospital."

The suited man gave Brenna a quizzical look. Brenna saw him raise his eyebrows, all that was needed to push her over the edge. She turned to face him.

"That's right," she mocked. She raised her voice for all to hear. "Hard to believe a young, white woman would care about two Mexican men, isn't it? They're disposable, aren't they? Always a ready supply of hungry Mexicans available to fill in for any white men that are killed." Marita, in fear of her boldness, began pulling her away from the man. Brenna's voice continued to magnify. "Do you know what? They bleed just like you. They have families, lives, and feelings. She was nearly six feet from the man and still she continued. "They are loved by people like us!"

The crowd was starting to back away, afraid of her outburst when Marita clasped her hand over Brenna's mouth. "You have said enough," she replied gently, and directed her to where the motor cars were waiting. "Come, let us go."

By the time they arrived at the hospital, most of the injured were already there and being treated. Men lay on gurneys in the hallway, while still more were being settled into beds. There was the smell of sweat, metallic blood, and antiseptic in the packed corridor. Brenna spied one man who was alert and at ease. A clean bandage was tied around his forehead. Brenna noticed a small trickle of blood dripping down his temple.

"How are you doing?" Brenna asked as she approached the stranger.

"Do I know you, ma'am?"

"No, I don't think so."

"Oh, that's good," he said with a smile. "For a minute, I thought I'd lost my memory."

"Can you tell me what happened?"

"Well, that's one I'll never forget," he said. "We were all going about our business when this boiler started hissing. Been doing that for some time now, but the shift boss said there wasn't any time to look at it, and it was still working good. All of a sudden the pressure started going higher and higher, like it'd gone crazy or something. Men started running around screaming, 'It's gonna blow! She's gonna blow!' But it was too late. There was metal and boiling water flying everywhere. Shift boss died trying to stop it. He shoulda paid attention sooner. Now it's someone else's problem."

"What happened to your head?" Brenna asked.

"Oh, they say I got hit in the head with something that was flyin' around. I don't remember much after it blew 'cause I got knocked out. I feel lucky it didn't split my head open."

"Manuel and Alberto, two Mexican men, do you know them? Have you seen them?"

"Sure did. Alberto had a huge slab of metal slam him in the back. He's got some burns and back pain, but he was talkin' when they pulled him out. Mostly in Mexican. Manuel's the new guy, right? Haven't seen him come in."

"Thank you very much," Brenna replied. She took hold of his calloused hand. "I do hope you feel better very soon."

"Thank you, ma'am."

Brenna's knees began to quiver as she walked away. Strength was draining from her body. There were no seats to be found, but she leaned against the wall where Marita was sitting. "There now, you see, we just have to find Alberto." Her voice was cracking. "Maybe Manuel wasn't even hurt bad enough to go to the hospital. Why he could be at the boarding house right now." As a big tear rolled down her cheek, splattering her dark blouse, she swatted at it like it was an annoying fly.

"I will go this way to look," Marita said, heading back the way they'd come in, while Brenna wandered down the hall in the other direction. In each room she looked for a familiar face. In one small room, a doctor and nurse hovered over a table where a man lay motionless. Shiny surgical equipment was neatly arranged on a nearby cart.

"Did they find it?" she heard the doctor ask.

"Someone shoved it in this dirty glove," the nurse replied. The nurse delicately removed something small and red from inside a work glove, holding it between her thumb and forefinger.

"It's not likely it will reattach," the doctor said, eyeing the object. He took it from her hand and examined it. In order for this to heal, it needs excellent blood flow." He paused. "Guess we won't lose any ground by trying. Someone help me scrub," he commanded, "and get this thing cleaned up the best you can." As the doctor went to the sink to wash up, Brenna saw Manuel lying on the table. She ran to him, one hand clasped to her mouth, the other touching Manuel. He was warm and alive, but still he did not move.

"Madam, you can't be in here," a nurse scolded. She began to push her out the door, but Brenna begged to stay.

"Wait," the doctor barked. "Are you family?"

"Yes," Brenna said. To this Manuel's eyes opened. She could see he was trying to focus on her face, but he recognized her voice. Without a doubt, he knew she was there for him. "What happened to him?"

"This man is going to be fine," the doctor said as the nurse slipped on his newly washed gloves. "His life is not in danger. He suffered some burns during the explosion. We're going to sew his scalp back down, and that should be fine. But he's lost part of his right ear, and we're going to try and reattach that. It's probably not going to work, but we'll try. I have to tell you, I'm concerned he may have some hearing loss."

Brenna wanted to tell him that he had heard her voice. She was sure of it. "He's not moving," she whimpered, more concerned about that than his hearing.

"My dear, we have given him something for his pain and it made him sleepy. I must get to work now. We'll let you know when you can see him." He then asked his nurse, "Will you show this young lady where she can wait."

Brenna collapsed into the vacant chair she was led to in the hallway and sat there staring blankly into space. She didn't hear Marita when she called to her and didn't see her waving her arms in the air to get her attention.

"I have found him," Marita said after coming to stand beside Brenna. "Alberto is awake, a little sore..." Marita suddenly frowned. "What is wrong, *Señora?*" she said softly. "Oh, no. Is it Manuel?"

Brenna finally looked up at her. "I found him," Brenna replied. "He is alive, not in very bad shape, but the doctor thinks he may be deaf." She stood and grabbed Marita's hands. "I don't believe the doctor, Marita. I know he heard my voice."

"*Dios Mio*," Marita prayed as she wrung her hands. "Not my little brother. This can't be happening. He is so young to lose his hearing. Where is he? I want to see him."

"They're sewing him up. Part of his scalp was torn and a piece of his ear was blown off."

"Will he be scarred? Is he not my handsome Manuel anymore?"

"It won't matter, Marita," Brenna replied. "He will still be Manuel. I have to hope this will not change him. He already carries so much pain in his heart."

It was near dark when Brenna returned home. She positioned herself on the front porch using the post to support her weary body. The day that could never end had finally concluded. A full moon cast a healing light on the little town. She watched the stars burst out of darkness, one by one, a spot of glitter decorating the sky. Without any warning, she burst into tears releasing the emotions she had suppressed all day. Remaining strong was not a necessity now, and in the stillness of the cool, spring night, she could stop pretending.

In the distance a nightbird sang. His sweet song rose above the other night sounds, clear and precise. Her sobbing tapered to sniffles as she focused on his melody.

She was always drawn to the nightbird's song. She pictured his gray feathered throat swelling with each note. He called to a mate, hoping to attract the finest female that would help him create life. Without a partner, life simply could not continue. It was survival in its most primitive form, and even though a time would come when he no longer was a part of life, another would be there to take his place. And so it would continue with the weakest succumbing to the strongest, all reminding her of what she was still missing in her life.

For a long time she listened to the nightbird's hypnotic song, letting it clear her mind of the day's agony. Only when sleep was imminent did she retire to her room. As she dozed off, she could still hear the nightbird's song through her open window, calling for a mate to share his life.

Chapter 22

Before Manuel was released from the hospital, Marita's worst fear was realized. Her beloved little brother had adapted to the physical scars, but the emotional scars clung to him like a second skin. Although his hearing returned, he could no longer cope with sudden, loud noises. The drop of a pan, the slam of a door, or the backfiring of a motor car would leave him with an expression of fear and confusion and finally embarrassment. He said little about the accident, spending much of his free time alone, but sometimes Brenna would catch him unconsciously brushing back the black hair on the injured side of his head, fingers searching for the hard, raised ridges of scar tissue and the piece of his ear that was no longer a part of him.

Anger would swell inside of him like a kettle of boiling jelly. Something that once was sweet and pleasant, would heat into a frothing pot, hot enough to take the hide off any fool who got too close. His circle became the men who fought with him and joined him at the meetings that separated them from the rest of the miners.

* * * *

It was a summer morning following a steamy, angry night. One of a string of dog days that can test a man's patience. Sweat drips off your brow, making your face itch as it trails down your cheek. Your clothes stick to your back and you have to pinch them off your body just to keep from smothering and going mad. Still, you scrape out your day's pay. The best thing to do is just walk away, but you know you can't.

They broke into the homes where men slept and said the men were troublemakers who never should have left their jobs. Striking, even if it was for the sake of safety and better working conditions, threatened the security of the United States and disregarded the war effort.

During the early morning hours the day was still cool and their justice seemed right. It made no difference that men were being taken from their families, that there would be bellies left empty and dreams shattered. Why should it matter that these men had broken no law?

The pounding on the front door made the downstairs chandelier rattle like a diamondback. Brenna stumbled downstairs, but not before the other door, the one to the boarding house wing, was kicked in. Men whose faces were painted with hatred, rifles and pistols in hand, stood before her. She very nearly wet her drawers. Sara and Eric cowered on the stairs near the top of the floor, peering through the banisters.

"My God, what is the meaning of this? What do you want, and why have you broken into my home?"

One man stepped forward from the circle and walked across the parlor to the front door, unlocking the latch. "I apologize, ma'am," the stranger said. "We don't mean no harm to you and your family. We're just here to collect some men and help them get out of town. Jackson, where's your list?"

"Let's see, we got John Sanders, Manuel Rodriguez and Michael Hollands. Let's go, boys." They pushed their way down the hall, opening each door, checking the identity of the man in the bed.
"You have no right to do this," Brenna cried, beginning to recognize some familiar faces among the mob. Had she seen them on Main? Were these some of the shop owners in town? "Leave my boarders alone and go home."

"Sorry, ma'am. We do have a right to be here to apprehend these men. Been deputized by Sheriff Wheeler to get these strikers on a train and out of town so the rest of us can go back to work."

Some of the boarders began to wake, struggling to get out of bed. "Stop this!" Brenna shouted, throwing herself between Michael and one of the intruders. "He's not well." Another man spoke up.

"Hal, help Mrs. McEvoy find a seat and see that she stays there."

A large, red-faced man pulled her by the arm all the way into the parlor. He motioned for her to sit and remained standing over her with his rifle. The boarders emerged from their rooms. They had been allowed to dress, but that was all. The ring leader marched the men past Brenna toward the front door. For a brief moment she made eye contact with Manuel, and then he was gone. Leroy ran past her in hot pursuit, and Brenna bolted from her seat following them out the door. "Th, th, this ain't right, deputy." Leroy stopped them at the front door. One side of his suspenders held his pants on his hip bones. He was shirtless and unshaven and at the time looked menacing.

"Get outta my way, Leroy," the deputy threatened. "You keep your nose out of this mess or I'll throw you in with the rest of these traitors." He shoved Leroy out of the doorway.

Brenna struggled to see over her remaining boarders. Finally, she just pushed past them and ran out onto the porch. "Manuel, look for me! John, Mike, I'll bring you some food and money! Please, just look for me." Then she turned loose on the withdrawing deputies. "You scum!" she shouted, running down the steps, scanning the flower bed for Sara's mud balls, baked firm in the July sun and hardened like adobe marbles. There they were, ten of them lined up in front of her roses. She scooped up a handful and hurled one into the crowd of men, hitting one on the side of the head. He let out a yowl, rubbing where the ball had hit him.

"What'd she hit you with, Jackson?"

"Hell if I know, but damn it smarts."

"What God-given authority do you have to treat these men like cattle?" Brenna shouted, throwing another mud ball. It missed hitting Jackson's associate, so she hurled another one, finally striking Jackson's cohort in the small of his back. "You're next, fat boy!" Brenna screamed, and three mud balls pelted them all at once. One man turned around. "Oh Christ," he sputtered. "Now she's got a brick." They all took off running, shoving their captives out of the gate before Brenna could launch her next weapon.

Leroy walked up to her while she was staring dejectedly after Manuel, John and Michael. "Mrs. Mac," he said, "I do believe they could use your skills overseas with the war effort."

But Brenna didn't hear him. Rage coursed through her like an electric current. "Leroy," she said, "watch the children for me. I'm going to dress and take the men some food and money to tide them over."

She scarcely noticed her two petrified children still sitting on the stairs as she passed them. Whatever she grabbed from the closet she threw on, deciding as she dressed that last night's leftover roast would make good sandwiches. She hurried down to the kitchen to make eight sandwiches, using up all the bread in the house. They were wrapped in waxed paper and thrown into a saved shoebox. By this time she realized Leroy was fixing the children a breakfast of fried eggs, bacon and biscuits. Grateful, she thanked him while tying a length of string around the makeshift lunch box. Then she was out the door.

Water. She'd forgotten water. She hurried back to the garden shed to retrieve James's old canteen. It was the only one she had. They'd have to share.

She raced down the alley, cutting across side streets. Crowds were gathering and heading toward the center of town. She joined them, ending up in front of the post office. There, the captive men, what appeared to be well over a thousand, were being detained in the blazing heat.

Hundreds of men had gathered around them. The Loyalists stood armed, guarding the strikers and their sympathizers while others added more men to the collection. The crowd swelled, while women circled like a pack of coyotes, hungrily looking for their lost mates. There were tears from the women while a few of the trapped men laughed in defiance of their captors. Expressions of fear marked some faces, but most were sullen and quiet, wondering what would happen next and who would take care of their families.

Brenna searched the crowd for nearly an hour before she caught sight of Manuel. She forced her way through the ring of Loyalists surrounding the captives. Reaching over several men, she handed the box to Manuel.

"Food," she shouted above the roar. "And some money. It was all I could scrape together. I was afraid I wouldn't see you again. Please, share with the others." And then she was swept away.

"You can't be here, woman," an armed man yelled. "Get yourself out of her before you get hurt." He grabbed her by the waist and shoved her toward the back of the crowd. She was passed like a sack of dirty laundry from one Loyalist to another until she stood on the outside once again.

She made her way to the opposite side of the street, looking for her other two boarders. Without warning a signal sounded, and the men began pushing forward. She stood in front of a Loyalist, trying to slow his gait.

"Where are you taking them?" The man kept marching, trying to ignore her. "Stop." She pushed against his chest.

"Tell me where you're taking them."

"Get out of my way, lady. I got a job to do." The pace of the group quickened and Brenna stumbled. "Gotta get these men to Warren to pick up a train."

"What do you mean? You can't just herd these men out of town, forcing them to abandon their families and homes."

The sun was climbing in the cloudless sky, and sweat was dripping down the man's neck, soaking his white shirt. His eyes burned from the salty sweat that had found its way past his forehead and there was the matter of his incredible thirst. He took a hold of Brenna like a snake biting into a small mouse. At the edge of the crowd, using all his force, he cast her away from the line of marching men. She fell to the ground, breaking her fall with the palms of her hands.

"Stay out of the way or you'll really get hurt," he growled. He turned from her like she was a discarded rag and continued his march.

Men stepped around her but no one stopped to help her rise from the cloud of dust. It was clear they saw her as a sympathizer and perhaps she had been lucky not to have been hurt worse. She picked the gravel out of her hand, silent tears running down her face. Defeated, she returned home.

"You done all you could." Leroy comforted her with a timid pat on the back. But doubts rose within her, and she wondered what would happen to her boarders. Between the war and the mines, she was sure to go broke. It was nearly one in the afternoon when Marita finally came in, still shaking and crying. Brenna didn't have to guess that Alberto had been captured and marched out of town with the others.

"When they got them to Warren, they started shouting at them," Marita explained. She had followed Alberto to the lines of marching men from Main where they fed into the group from Brewery Gulch. "They told them they had a choice to make: return to work to support their country and families or go out in cattle cars. *Señora,* the cars were full of shit from those damn cows. They made those men stand in shit.

"Alberto started thinking of the children and decided to go back to work. I know they will treat him bad now, worse than before. They say the train is headed somewhere in New Mexico and that these men can never come back here."

She had lost Manuel again and this time she didn't even know where he was. "Did you see Manuel?" she asked. "I left him with some food and money."

"No, I could not find him. Alberto said he never saw him. There were many men who were forced onto the train."

Brenna took Marita's hand in hers. She reached up to Marita's brown face, wiping the wetness from her cheeks. Her voice was quiet and calm. "Manuel has been taken from us before and then returned. But I don't believe we will ever see him in Bisbee again. His anger is fresh and raw. But we will wait. Someday, when he is ready, maybe he will come home. We'll just look up and he'll be here. In the meantime, if they learn to take care of one another, they'll see their way through this."

* * * *

When a week's time had passed and the men had not returned, Brenna and Marita decided to empty the rooms and store their belongings until they came home. All were credited two weeks board. Sheets were washed, clothing boxed, belongings labeled and put away. In a short time it was as if they had never existed.

Foremost on Brenna's mind was finding a hiding place for John's money. Had he known this was going to happen? Brenna suspected he had informers about town and had made plans to be prepared for the kidnapping.

Between all the miners, past and present, a large sum of money had accumulated. They would come home after payday and ask her to hold onto some of their cash so they would have something leftover after a visit to the Gulch. Others besides John had asked her to hold their nest egg in case they ever needed money in a hurry. She had it hidden in various places: sewn into hems, underneath dresser drawers, in hat boxes at the back of the armoire; she had even considered cutting a floorboard. But this would never do in the long run. She had to buy a safe for these precious possessions. Brenna recalled how important her cash had been when she was near destitute after James' disappearance. These men would need that money to begin a new life and it was the least she could do to help them build a bridge to a new beginning.

Her Sears Catalog offered several fine safes. She selected one of the smallest to insure it would fit inside her closet. It came with a tumbler lock and two inch walls and weighed over 100 pounds.

The past may have had its share of turmoil, but this was one way to protect the future.

* * * *

"Mrs. McEvoy, got a delivery for you today." The Postmaster handed her several envelopes and pointed to a large crate in the corner of the post office. "Heavy as all get out so you're going to need help getting it home." Brenna was reluctant to say just what was in the crate even though she knew curiosity was aching at Cecil's insides.

"Anyone coming up my way, Cecil?" She signed for the crate.

"Oh, I suppose I could wrestle something up. May take a couple of days."

"That would be wonderful. Eric can help me get it up to the house if you can find a wagon and someone to drop it off."

"Any word from your boarders, Mrs. McEvoy?"

"No, Cecil. Not one letter. It's like they disappeared in a dust devil and were wiped off the face of the earth."

"Lord, that was a sorry sight to see those men shipped out. I hear they're asking for passports for anyone coming from the east. Don't even want them coming back to town. But you have to ask, where would we all be without the mines?"

"Oh really, Cecil. Does that give them the right to take advantage of the working man?"

"No, ma'am, can't say that it does or should. It's just the way things are sometimes."

There was sadness to his voice, like he was forced to walk a narrow road, being prodded along, careful to stay centered so as not to ruffle someone's feathers on either side. Most town folks had found themselves in the same position as Cecil, torn between feeling sympathy for the rights of the working man and guilty for not supporting the war effort, first and foremost. Either way, you couldn't win.

* * * *

"What's in this, Ma?" Eric groaned as he stopped to rest on the stairs. They had arranged a pulley and a length of boards over the stairs, pulling and pushing as they went. "It's a secret," she replied.

"Oh come on, Ma," Eric begged. He was intrigued with the mysterious box that had been delivered. "Tell me what it is."

"You'll see soon enough." Just inside the bedroom door Brenna stopped to open the crate. Eric peered inside.

"It's another box," he complained.

"Looks can deceive," she cautioned. She used a crowbar to pry off one side. Out rolled the safe. It was wrapped tightly in burlap protecting the black paint. When she removed the covering her name was revealed in large gold letters.

"Jesus!" Eric exclaimed.

"Eric," Brenna scolded.

"Okay, Jesus, Mary and Joseph, why'd you get a safe?"

"I need it. For important papers. Things that I don't want to misplace." She stood and rolled it across the room and into the closet. "Now, all I have to do is memorize the combination to the lock and no one can get in it but me."

"No one?"

"Oh, I suppose a locksmith could get into it if he had to. But that won't be necessary as long as I am around. Now run along so I can put all my papers away."

From around the room, Brenna began collecting her guarded treasures. When she finished there was room left to store her jewelry in one of the small drawers. Next she made two identical lists with the miners' names and how much money they had left with her. One she placed in the safe and the other was hidden underneath the insole of an old pair of shoes. It was a tremendous relief to know that the lives of nearly half a dozen people were now more secure.

Chapter 23

The end of World War I brought old friends back together. The sight became commonplace, a familiar face, somewhat aged now, had returned home. Stepping down from the train, they appeared a bit blurry-eyed as they stood there, filling their souls with the comforting sights and sounds of a home that had been a world away just a short time ago. There were those who didn't return home, of course. The men who did were usually the hardy ones, those who maintained strong bodies and quick minds. They had learned to dodge trouble, fight infections in festering wounds and decipher truth from fiction, which in the fog of war and horror could seem nearly identical.

The mining companies, on the other hand, met with their own grim reality. They had relished the demand for copper brought on by man's greed and the high demand during wartime, but now, in times of peace, they had their own battle to fight. Surplus copper forced prices to plummet and a gentle unrest continued to rumble with labor. Mines around the state opened and closed and as copper quality played out, investors questioned the profitability of paying men to rip through mountains. Instead, they explored a new method they called open pit mining. It created ugly craters that pockmarked the land, but it was a means for Bisbee to survive.

"My goodness it was busy in town today," Brenna complained. "I barely made it to the sidewalk before a Model T nearly ran me down. And his obnoxious horn. Lady or not, I wanted to remind the driver of his manners, as he had clearly forgotten them."

"I can't get used to all these new machines," Marita replied. "Yesterday, I heard this great roar in the sky and looked up to see an aeroplane overhead."

"I heard about that. Did you really see it?"

"*Si*. And I was told you could pay two-fifty to get a ride in that thing." She paused and gazed out the window, lost in her thoughts. "You must be able to see the whole world from up there. But I will wait until I get my wings in Heaven before I do any flying."

"We're turning into a couple of old hens," Brenna said.

"Got that right," Eric replied. He had walked into the dining room, collecting a red apple from the bowl in the middle of the table.

"Oh, that's right; I forgot. We're dinosaurs now, Marita. Eric turned eighteen and suddenly we don't know anything anymore."

"Children have no respect for their parents," Marita jumped in. "Why if I had talked to my mother like that, I would have been thrown on a burro and dropped off at the convent."

Eric shot back, "Mom doesn't think I'd make a good priest, huh, Ma?" He followed them into the kitchen, nuzzling close to his mother's ear. "You're still prettier than a dinosaur," he whispered.

She gave him a sideways glance. "You think you always know what to say to charm a woman," Brenna said. "But I think your efforts would be better spent on a younger woman."

"That reminds me," Eric said, "my buddy and I were thinking of taking a drive to Inner Tube Beach this weekend. I mean if we get enough rain, that mud hole should fill up for swimming. Can we take Ana and Sara with us?"

Marita gave Eric a wary look. Her distrust was plainly written on her face by the worry lines creasing her brow. "Ana should not be going out without an escort. She is still a child."

"For Christ's sake, Marita, she's fourteen years old. Sara will be with her. If you don't trust me, you can surely trust Sara."

"I think Sara would look after her," Brenna said. "Sara's always been so protective of Ana."

"You mean Ana protects Sara," Eric countered. "Ana used to tear into me like a wildcat when I teased Sara."

"Oh, I suppose it will be all right," Marita reluctantly agreed. "Maybe I have forgotten what it is like to be young. I will pack a lunch for Sunday after Mass. And I want to meet this friend of yours before you leave. If I don't like him, she doesn't go."

"You'll like him fine," Eric reassured her. "He's even more charming than me."

"And that is what worries me. Ana will do something special with her life. And I will make sure she does just that, no matter who gets in my way." Eric gave the worried mothers a mocking salute and left the room the same way a weasel would exit a chicken house.

* * * *

They stood outside the door like a groom and his best man.

"What's this Mexican momma going to do to me?"

"Aw, calm down, Lew. Are you afraid of an old woman?"

"I just don't trust Mexicans," Lewis complained. "Quit foolin' with my tie." He slapped at Eric's hand. "I had this one old woman chase me with a broom 'cause she thought I was messing with her daughter."

"Were you?"

"Yeah, but that old witch didn't have to bruise me with a broom. She should have been using it on her daughter."

Eric gave a hoarse, noisy laugh. "This Ana, I've known her since the day she was born. She just keeps getting prettier and prettier. She's ripe for the picking."

Lewis put his arm around Eric's shoulder. "Why, Eric, my good man, you're not thinking of deflowering that fair rose?"

"You're such a pompous ass, Lewis," Eric said. "That's what I like about you. Just make sure you distract my sister when I come ask Ana to take a walk with me. This trip will be my only chance to get her away from her mother. Let's go in and meet the old battle-ax."

The girls were all smiles as the boys were scrutinized by Marita. She wanted an exact location of the picnic and the time they could be expected to return.

"If you do not return on time, Ana, I will send every man in my house looking for you. Do you understand?"

"Yes, Mama," she replied. "I won't disappoint you."

"Do you understand?" she asked Eric and Lewis.

"Yes, ma'am," Lewis replied. "My father taught me how to drive."

"Well, I hope your mama taught you how to pray." She crossed her daughter on the forehead.

"Mama, stop," Ana begged. "You're embarrassing me."

Marita retreated but hovered near the doorway to watch the four teenagers drive out of sight.

"She's still watching us," Lewis cautioned. "I can see her in the rear view mirror."

"I'm sorry," Ana said. "My family is very protective." She turned to look at Eric who had put his arm over her shoulder as they sat in the back seat.

"That's okay, Ana," Eric said. "I'm used to your mother. Don't forget, I've known her longer than you have. We're going to have a great time today, girls. The fun is only beginning."

The watering hole was nearly at capacity, an unusual sight in early summer. A few couples and one or two families were scattered around the area. Out on the water, a man and woman sat in two black inner tubes, bobbing like fishing floats.

"I have never been here," Ana exclaimed. "This is wonderful. Let's find a tree and lay out the blanket. I want to go swimming before we picnic."

"That would be swell," Lewis said. "How about here, Eric?" He pointed to a large, shady spot under a cottonwood tree, surprised no one had taken it yet.

"No, how about something a little more private," Eric suggested. "Let's walk around the pond and see what's over there." He pointed to the other side and began walking ahead when Sara pulled Ana back. Eric could see that Sara was already starting trouble. He stopped and turned around. "What's wrong now, Sara?" His voice was belittling.

"I just can't see over there, Eric. It's fine right here in the open. What if there are snakes?"

Lewis leaned over to whisper in his ear, "She's got you there, buddy. You really are a snake in the grass."

"Shut your trap," Eric snapped, eliciting a laugh from Lewis.

"We'll stay right here, Eric," Sara called out, and then she faced her friend. "Tell him you want to stay here, Ana."

"Come on, Eric. This is fine. We can take a walk later."

"Smooth move, pal," Lewis said. "Did you plan it that way?"

Eric just grinned and the two boys made their way back to the cottonwood tree.

"I have to put my swimsuit on," Ana said. She was blushing. Sara took over.

"We'll go change in those bushes." She pointed to a small covering. "You go on the opposite side. Understand, Eric?"

"You need any help changing?" Lewis asked.

"No thank you." Sara giggled, and grabbed Ana's hand as they ran for the bushes.

"This couldn't be going any better," Eric said as he unzipped his pants. "This is going to be too easy."

"I don't think your sister likes me," Lewis said.

"She's man shy," Eric replied. "You just have to warm her up. Just tell me if you need any pointers."

"I think I can manage on my own," he said, pulling up his trunks. "Come on, let's give them a scare."

The boys ran over to the bushes, rattling the branches. "Oh, girls," they called.

"Go away!" Ana demanded. "We're not dressed yet."

"That's okay," Lewis said.

"Fresh!" Sara yelled.

"There you go again, Lewis. She's never going to trust you."

Lewis motioned for him to be quiet. "We're going to go ahead and test the water," he called. "Come out when you're ready."

"That's better," Eric said as they ventured back toward the pond. "She'll give in. Just give her time."

The girls emerged from the bushes looking nearly identical in their navy blue swimming dresses. Their hair was tied up and they had removed their stockings. Once in the water, the tension was lessoned. Soon the murky water was churned until it resembled a chocolate soda.

"Ana, come out here with me," Eric called.

"I can't swim," she said. "I'm afraid to go out any farther."

"I'll help you," Eric offered. "Take my hand."

Ana smiled at the young man before her, comforted by his gallant behavior. Sara watched her brother with suspicious eyes.

"How about it?" Lewis said as he offered Sara his hand. Slowly she made her way toward him and Ana followed her lead. Ana began to stretch her neck to remain above water. Suddenly her feet no longer touched the bottom.

"Stop struggling," Eric said in a velvety voice. "Relax. I'm holding on to you." He saw her look down, realizing his hands were encircling her waist. At first he thought she would push him away, but her fear of the water forced her to cling to him. Before he knew it, she had her arms around his neck, snuggling next to him. He continued his soothing mannerism, all the time aware of Sara's glare. Although she was a fair swimmer, she had refused to come out further to place herself in Ana's position. After a while, Lewis gave up and suggested they begin the picnic. Eric was completely confident that Ana was in his control.

It didn't take the boys long to bring out the liquor they had smuggled from Lewis' house. They had brought some wine for the girls which Ana had no trouble drinking.

"Ana, how could you? It tastes terrible."

"We have wine at my house, always," Ana replied. "My cousins know how to make it. Where did you get yours?"

"My father knows some men who get it for him," Lewis replied. "I think most of it comes from Mexico."

"That's where we get our hard drink," Ana said. "But the wine we can make at home."

"Sara?" Lewis offered her some whiskey.

"I'll try it," Sara said. She put the brown bottle to her lips and seemed accepting of the drink until she started to swallow. She ran to the grass spitting out what remained in her mouth. "How awful! It's bitter and it burns!"

"I'm getting warm," Ana interrupted, fanning her face. She lay down on the blanket appearing to be tired. While Sara was in the grass recovering, Eric winked at Lewis.

"Let's go on a walk, Ana. Maybe that will make you feel better." Sara returned just in time to see the two of them walking away hand in hand. Not trusting her brother, her suspicions were aroused.

"Where are you going?" Sara called.

"Come sit down with me," Lewis suggested. "They're just going for a walk."

"How long have you known my brother?" Sara said.

"Just a few months. Why?"

"Then you don't know my brother," Sara said in a dreary voice. "You don't know him like I know him."

* * * *

Eric could tell that the walk was only serving to make Ana more fatigued. Soon they would get to the covering and he could lay her down in the grass.

"I'm getting dizzy," Ana said. "This is not so good." She stumbled over a small stone that rose in the path.

"We're almost to a clearing," Eric lied. "We can sit down when we get there."

Ana continued obediently. When it seemed like they had been walking forever, Eric brought them to a stop. "This is a good place to rest," he said. He took her into a small cozy hideaway, far removed from the rest of the people at the water hole. The trees formed a canopy over a grassy patch.

"Why is it so dark in here?" she asked.

"We're in the shadows," Eric answered. He helped her sit down on the ground. "No one can see us here," he said in a low, quiet voice.

"I need to rest," Ana said. "Can we do that?" She laid back, closing her eyes. "Maybe if I can't see, I won't be so dizzy."

Eric lay next to her studying her face for a moment. Her black braids had come unwound and wavy coal-black hair spilled about her shoulders and face. He brushed back her hair and began kissing her face.

Ana's eyes opened wide, first in surprise, then in fear. No man had ever kissed her that way. She started to protest but Eric motioned for her silence by placing a finger over her lips.

"It's just a kiss, Ana. It's not going to hurt you. I promise."

He started again and this time, she didn't object. She was too dizzy to move and after a moment, relaxed and closed her eyes. The next time she awoke he was on top of her.

Before she could begin to struggle the battle was over. He was stronger than her, bigger than her and Eric was confident he could finish what he had started. She wants it too, he told himself. Even though she scratched him as he pulled at her swimming dress and cried as he covered her mouth. When he was finished with her, he fell to her side. "You still fight like a wildcat," he said, panting.

The second Ana was free of him she covered herself and ran off into the brush, heading for the pond. "Where are you going? Ana? Oh, be that way."

What did he care if she was a bad sport? Maybe he shouldn't have been so rough with her but he knew she liked him. He picked himself up and walked back to the cottonwood tree. Sara was lying on her stomach, propped on her elbows, appearing to get along fine with Lewis. But when she saw that Ana was not with Eric, her face lit with anger.

"Where is she, Eric? What have you done to her?"

"I'm tired of your lip service, Sara. Why do you always accuse me of things?" She drew close to his face.

"Because I know what you are," she replied. "Do you think I don't remember all those things you did to me when I was a little girl?"

Eric's narrow, cold eyes stared back at her, undaunted by her words.

"I'm going to go find her," Sara said. "Lewis, would you come with me?"

"Sure, let's go." He tried to make light of the situation. "You know my dad taught me how to track. I should be pretty good at this."

Eric threw himself down on the blanket, exhausted from his day of play. *When they find her, we better head back home*, he thought. Ana would never tell anyone what happened, but Marita would skin him alive if he showed up a minute late.

* * * *

Eric was switching the radio dial relentlessly. *Toot, Toot Tootsie* blared from the speaker, only serving to aggravate his anxiety. Two miners passed by the parlor on their way to the boarding rooms. "I declare," one said to the other. "I don't think there's that much racket in the mine shaft. Boy, can you turn that music box down?"

Eric looked up from his newspaper. "It's not a music box, old timer," he chided. "It's called a radio."

"I reckon I know what it is, son, but I can't say I like it any better."

Brenna walked into the room. "Find any work yet, Eric?" They weren't going to leave him alone today; he was going to get badgered to death.

"No, I didn't find a job yet," he replied. "But in case you didn't notice, I was looking for one." He threw down the paper and stormed off to his room.

How long he had slept, he didn't know. The bright light that had filled his room had faded to shadows. The days were shorter now, the evening air cool and inviting. He felt refreshed and ready to go out on the town. It was a Friday night, and the miners would be spending money and entertaining each other in the Gulch. Maybe he'd get lucky and find a card game.

It was the loud voices that woke him, and now they seemed to wail. *Someone is crying,* he thought. He opened the door and looked downstairs. Sara and his mother stood at the base of the stairway. They appeared to be arguing. Slowly, he walked down the stairs, never taking his eyes off the two. As he approached, Sara turned to face him.

"You're a pig, Eric. A low-life pig. I hate you so much. If you died today, I'd be glad to be rid of you." She walked past him, slamming the front door as she left the house.

"Why, Eric? I trusted you. We all trusted you." Still he didn't speak. "Ana is with child. She says you got her pregnant."

"How does she know it was me?" Eric defended. "You know those Mexicans. They reproduce like rabbits. How come she thinks it's me?"

"This is Ana we're talking about. Not some whore from the Gulch or Tin Town. She is only a young girl. She said you forced yourself on her."

"That's a lie. She wanted it."

"What's done is done. Now you must face up to your responsibilities."

"What responsibilities?"

"You're going to be a father."

"I'm not marrying that Mexican."

"No, Sara and I have already talked about that. It would ruin her life if you married her. But you still must take care of the baby and help support the family."

"Both of you are nuts!" He waved his arms like red flags. "I'm not taking care of her or her baby."

Brenna stood before him. She was smaller than him now and had to look up to speak to him. "You listen to me, young man. You have made a careless mistake toward another human being and your selfish actions are now affecting two other lives. Ana will finish her education. You and I will care for this child with Marita's family. In the eyes of God, you will now deal with the consequences."

Eric laughed out loud. "Nice speech, Mom. But God can go to Hell and so can that Mexican bitch. I'm not taking care of no Mexican trash."

Brenna's hand flew out, cracking Eric across the face. He pulled back to strike her, but she was all over him like a rooster on a cockroach.

"You're no son of mine!" she screamed in his face. "Get out of this house. What makes you think I'm going to take care of you if you turn away from this family? Get upstairs and pack your things. Don't return until you've made some serious changes in your pitiful life. And may God, my God, forgive you, because I never will. And your sister, your poor sister would sooner see you in hell before acknowledging you are her brother. There's the door."

She pushed him aside starting to leave the house herself, but then changed her mind. "I'll give you one hour to pack your things. I'm inspecting your bags before you leave. You're not stealing from me anymore."

He brought his bags down the stairs and laid them on the sofa, stepping out of the way. Brenna opened the suitcases, pausing at a wad of bills.

"It's my own cash," he advised her. "I do have some money of my own."

She locked both cases and walked to the door. "Do you have a coat?" she asked. Her voice wavered. "It will be getting cold at night." Tears spilled from her eyes.

"Yeah, I'll get my coat." He walked to the hall closet and removed a gray wool coat and draped it over his arm.

"Take care of yourself, Eric." She blinked her tears away. "I've done all I can, you know. I tried my best, but it was always a struggle raising you without a man in the house. Now, you've grown from a child to a man, and I don't approve of the man standing before me."

He smirked at her and didn't even bother saying good-bye as he walked out into the night and toward a new life. He wondered what the weather was like in Los Angeles. Maybe he would pay a visit to his Aunt Ginny, provided he could find her and that Kike husband of hers.

Chapter 24

"Did you see the expression on the men's faces when Ginny pranced into the parlor?" Marita took the cup and saucer from Brenna's hand, pouring the steaming water over the tea bag. "I hope she didn't expect us to recognize her. It's been over twenty years since your sister walked out that door."

"I just wish she would have written first," Brenna complained. "I would have liked to have been more prepared for company, but then Ginny always did enjoy making an entrance." She stopped and looked at Marita. "Listen to me bad-mouthing my own sister. It's been decades since we've seen each other. Maybe she's changed."

Marita didn't stop. "Not by the way she looks. That wild print dress and dangling beads. Why her calves were showing. Her hair's bobbed so short there's hardly nothing there. And I bet she has to take her face paint off with a knife. *Señor* Leroy nearly choked on his oatmeal when she paraded through the door. And what does she want?" Marita continued. "She'd never show her face unless she wants something."

"Let's try not to judge so quickly. I mean, maybe that's how they dress in Los Angeles. All the movie stars are living there now. Take her the tea. She's had a long trip. Later we can find out what's going on."

When Marita and Brenna entered the dining room a round of laughter broke out from the table as Virginia finished telling her tale to the miners.

"Why, Ginny," Brenna exclaimed, "I had no idea you were so entertaining."

Virginia responded by pulling out a pack of cigarettes from her red cloth purse. She tapped the pack against her hand, laden with pewter and diamond jewelry. "Honey, living on the coast of California is a completely different experience than living in Bisbee. I could tell you tales you wouldn't dare to imagine. Why just last week my neighbor caught her husband with…well, maybe I shouldn't tell that one just now."

"Well, Father seems to enjoy living in San Diego."

"How is the dear old man these days?" She blew a puff of smoke into the air. "Jeepers, I haven't seen him since he disowned me." She let out a short, sassy laugh.

Marita was agitating like a cutworm on an ant hill. "*Señores*, you will be late for your shift." They were mesmerized by Virginia's spell but Marita was determined to undermine her credibility. Brenna could see by Marita's expression that she had designs on Virginia and would not let up until she had discovered what she was up to.

"Oh, she's right, boys." Harris shot a glance at his pocket watch. "We'd better move it. Say, Leroy, how about a ride in that new truck of yours?"

Brenna watched the men exit the side door, stopping to collect their lunch pails from Marita before entering their underground world. Once they had left, Virginia spoke up.

"How do you do it, big sister?" she asked. "How can you stand serving all these grimy men day and night? It certainly isn't the kind of life I'd want to lead."

"You and I were never much alike, Ginny," Brenna replied, swirling her sugar spoon in her coffee. She looked up at her sister. "I feel very lucky to have managed at all. It wasn't easy after James disappeared."

"And how did you manage?"

"With good friends and a lot of luck. We discovered James had a sizeable savings account in Tombstone. I used that cash to build on the rooms. Marita and her brother, Manuel, helped with the construction until I could get on my feet. Marita's family has an interest in this house."

Virginia lowered her voice to a whisper, motioning toward the kitchen where Marita was finishing the breakfast dishes. "You mean that Mexican owns part of your home?"

"Ginny, listen to what I'm saying. Without that family, I would have been destitute. I wouldn't have been able to survive without them."

"Well, Bren, all I can say is Mama must be rollin' in her grave knowing you're socializing with their kind."

"And what about you, marrying a Jew?"

"Aw, you know I was never a good Catholic girl."

"Yes, I can vouch for that."

"Say, Sis, where's your daughter? I know she doesn't know who I am, but still, I'd like to meet her."

"Sara's still in school. She gets out around three today. And Eric…"

"Listen, Bren," she interrupted. "That's what I need to talk to you about. You know your son, Eric. He came to see us."

Brenna's heart began to race. "Eric? You saw my Eric?"

"Yeah. He came to stay with us, but honestly, Brenna, we just couldn't take care of him. He wouldn't work, and we didn't know what to do with him. So then Morris, he suggested he join one of the armed services. I mean, I thought it was pure genius. Morris said they train you to do stuff and you get room and board. And with the war over and everything, it just seemed like a great idea."

"And did he?"

"Yeah, sure thing. He joined the Navy right then and there. He's getting his training, and in a few weeks he says he'll be a real sailor."

"My Lord, my boy out there on that restless ocean."

"He seemed to like the water. We took him out to the beach a couple of times. It seemed to relax him."

Brenna thought back to her visit to San Diego. Had ten years really passed since then? A small boy standing on the shore watching the waves lapping at his knees. He seemed so far away at the time. And now, out to sea, dressed in a starched white uniform, taking orders from his commanding officers.

Ginny pulled a stick of gum out of her purse, crammed it into her mouth and was noisily popping it when Brenna blinked and came out of her daydream. "Well it's probably all for the best. Perhaps he'll grow up now and face his responsibilities."

"Was he in some kind of trouble?"

"So he didn't tell you what he was running away from?"

"No, just said he had to get out of Bisbee."

"He got a girl in the family way. Marita's daughter, Ana. When he refused to acknowledge the child, I kicked him out."

"Geez, Louise. I didn't know he did that. But, Bren, it was a Mexican girl."

"Ginny, he was responsible for bringing another life into this world. There's no telling what he'd do if I didn't draw the line somewhere."

"Well, I guess you know best. Never had kids of my own. I just thought you might want to know what happened to your kid and why I couldn't take care of him. Here." She handed Brenna a small creased piece of paper. "Here's an address where you can write to him."

"Thank you, Ginny. This is probably the nicest thing you've ever done for me."

"Aw, that's okay. So what's there to do in this town? I'd like to stay for a while as long as I'm here."

"We have a new movie theater. Would you like to see a movie this week?"

"I see plenty of movies. Living in Hollywood I see most of the movies before the stars do."

"We could always go shopping. Did you see Main on your way over?"

"You know, I wouldn't mind seeing the old neighborhood again."

"Wonderful. Let me get my wrap and we can walk downtown."

"Hey, Bren, you got a spare sweater for me? I didn't think to bring one."

"Run upstairs to Dad's old room. You can find a sweater in my closet."

Ginny sauntered upstairs, peeking in each room she passed. Brenna smiled to herself, accustomed to her sister's nosy nature. She was glad Ginny had come home, even if it was only for a short visit. She missed having a sister. Maybe things would change between them now that they were middle-aged.

* * * *

"Lady, come on, lady, put down the knife." Manuel had never faced a woman with a butcher knife before. Plenty of switchblades had crossed his path, but confronting an angry female who had backed him into a corner, that was a little too dangerous.

"What do you want just walking into this house? You don't belong here, sneaking in the backdoor. You get out of here. I'm warning you, I know how to use this."

Before he could answer, the kitchen door flew open, sending Ginny flying into Manuel. Manuel managed to raise his left arm just in time for the blade to pass between his body and the arched limb. The knife hung in the door frame while Ginny tried to compose herself.

"Manuel!" Brenna was dumb struck. She looked at the knife, looked to her sister, glanced at Manuel and was thoroughly confused. Nevertheless, without another word, she threw herself into Manuel's arms.

Ginny was struggling to put on her black heeled shoe that had come off in the escapade. "Would someone please tell me what is going on here?" she cried, totally befuddled.

"I tried to tell you," Manuel burst out. "But who's going to argue with a woman holding a butcher knife? What is it about the women in this house? Seems like I am always in trouble with somebody."

"Well how was I supposed to know who you were?" Ginny explained. "I mean, I'm here, minding my own business and in walks this dark, swarthy man. You know, you look a little like that actor, Gilbert Roland, but taller. Anyway, I'm trying to get a cup of tea and you waltz into my sister's house. The miners aren't even allowed in the kitchen, and —"

"You're Brenna's sister?"

"Yeah. And who the hell are you?"

"Ginny, may I introduce Manuel Rodriguez. Manuel, this is my younger sister, Virginia."

"You're the one who helped build the boarding rooms, right? Well, now that I know who you are, Mr. Rodriguez, would you like a cup of coffee or something?"

"It's Manuel. And yes, I think I need something to steady my nerves."

Brenna pulled out a chair from the kitchen table. "When did you get in?"

"Oh, just last night. It was a long drive from Texas."

"Texas? Is that where you went?"

"Yeah. Met up with an old friend of yours, Antonio Abrego." He looked up from his coffee to observe her expression. Brenna's eyes, large and wide, refused to tell him anything. Ginny joined them at the table.

"And is Antonio doing well?" she asked. Manuel was sure that Ginny knew nothing about Brenna's efforts to get him out of jail.

"Yes, he was a great deal of help to me. Got me a job at the automobile shop he worked at. I stayed there for a couple of years and then I went to work with a large cattle company. That's why I'm here."

"Here to stay?" Brenna asked. She could hardly mask her excitement.

"If things go well. I'm scouting for a new ranch. They want to expand closer to California. If I can find some good land, I'll be in charge of this operation."

"What wonderful news." Brenna reached out to touch Manuel's arm, sensing that Ginny was paying close attention. Quickly she retreated and stood to rinse her coffee cup. "You know, you never taught me how to drive," she reminded him. "Will a successful cattle man have time to do that now?"

"*Hijola.* I don't know if I trust your kind."

"Hey," Ginny chimed in, "I happen to be a very good driver."

"You can drive?" Brenna asked.

"Yeah, Morris taught me. Nothing to it."

Brenna turned to Manuel. "What do you say? Please?"

"Aw, give the girl a break, Manuel. I'll be leaving in a couple of days. You'll have plenty of time to teach her."

"You're leaving, Ginny? You didn't tell me."

"I have to get back home. Morris is whining that he's lonely. What he really means is that he doesn't have anyone to wash his shirts and make his meals."

Manuel stood. "I have to leave too, Brenna. I have a lot to do before I start looking for land."

"Where are you staying?" Brenna asked. "I may be getting a vacancy soon."

"If everything works out the way it's supposed to, I'll probably need a place on the outskirts of town. At least until we get a bunk house and office built. I'm not a city boy anymore."

"Will you come back for supper?"

"In a while. I promise. I just need to get settled in." He gave her a big hug again, brushing her cheek with his coarse hand. A quick smile followed before he stepped out into the winter air.

There was a long sigh from Brenna and an even longer piece of silence, which Ginny promptly cut wide open.

"So, Sis, do I detect something between the two of you?" Ginny's eyebrows were raised so high they disappeared under the top of her bangs.

"What do you mean?" She avoided Ginny's eyes. "He's just a good friend."

"I sense," she circled here finger in the air, "some kind of electricity, you know what I mean?"

"Nonsense. He's Mexican. I'd never intermarry. It just wouldn't be right."

"Doesn't mean you can't look and touch."

"Why to hear you talk. You are absolutely wild, Ginny. Who knows how I would have turned out if you hadn't struck out on your own?"

"Yeah, maybe lucky for you that I left when I did. I'd better go start packing. I need to go to town later today to get a ticket for tomorrow."

* * * *

"Mrs. Mac? A voice called from beyond the kitchen door.

"Harris? Is that you?" Brenna asked. They walked into the parlor where Harris fidgeted with a handful of cash.

"Need to see you for a moment, ma'am."

"Will you excuse us, Ginny?"

"Sure thing, kid." Ginny climbed the stairs, but paused near the top of the stairwell before entering her room. Several key words drifted upward. She was straining, but she could still piece together most of the conversation.

"…happy to hold this for you, Harris, if you are sure…"

"…don't trust those banks… boys tell me you're the one…"

"…a large safe, Harris. I have stored… many years now. Your money will be protected here, and I'm the only one that has the combination. I'll just need to get you a receipt. Come into the kitchen and count your money for me."

* * * *

The brass bells on the wall phone startled Brenna. She had just climbed into bed. No one called this late unless it was bad news. She raced downstairs as the bells continued to chime.

"It's a boy," Marita shouted. "He's perfect. You are a grandma now!"

"Why didn't you tell me she was in labor? I would have come right over."

"Ana is still embarrassed and also thinks you are angry with her."

"Tell her I am very happy for her, and that Sara and I will be over in the morning to see her son, my grandson."

"*Si*, I thought it was important that you know he had arrived. Tomorrow we will name him. Adios."

* * * *

"No! Ana begged. "You can't leave me. Not now, Sara. We've been together since we were babies." Ana broke down in tears. Soon the baby joined her.

"What's wrong, *niña*? What has upset you?" Marita raced to her daughter's side.

"Sara says she is leaving."

"Sara, is this true?" Brenna asked

Sara avoided her mother's eyes. It was obvious to Brenna that Sara had been planning this for some time, yet she had failed to tell her mother anything about her intent to leave.

"I have a job, Mother. I'll be taking care of two youngsters in Phoenix while I attend Normal School in Tempe. It will work out fine. I'm going to be a teacher."

All this time and she knew nothing of her daughter's future. Did she think so little of her that she didn't even care to include her in her life?

"When will this take place?" Brenna asked.

"Right after graduation. Mrs. Gallagher is sending me fare to get to Phoenix. It's a very nice family."

"I'm sure they're very nice, but I would like to talk to them sometime." Anger and hurt shot through her heart. It was like someone had a dull stick and was pressing it to her chest. Abruptly she changed the subject. "But that's not what we're here for, is it? Ana, may I hold my grandson?" *Perhaps this one was sent to replace mine*, she thought. "And his name will be?" she asked as Ana handed the child over to her.

"Roberto," Ana replied. "Roberto McEvoy." She waited for Brenna's reaction but was only met with an accepting smile. "I think a white name will give him a better chance at success. Later if he wants to go by Robert, it will sound nice with his last name, don't you think?"

"It's a lovely name, and we'll have a big baptism party for him. I don't care what the neighbors say or think."

"But we must have the baptism before Sara leaves. I want her to be the godmother."

Sara's eyes filled with tears. "You're just doing that so I have to come back to Bisbee, Ana. I know you well enough.

And who will the godfather be?"

"I would like to ask Manuel. I think he would be a wonderful godfather. But I haven't told him who the father is. Would you tell him, Mrs. McEvoy?"

"Me?" she turned to Marita. "Me?"

"We thought he would take it best coming from you."

"I can only try, but I can't promise he'll like what he hears. He was never very fond of Eric."

"Who could blame him?" Sara replied.

"He's on his way over. We thought it would help if Alberto was here too."

When Manuel walked in the women scattered like a flock of sheep running from a mountain lion. Brenna stood fixed next to the infant and Ana, allowing Manuel to fuss over the new child. While he held Roberto in his arms, Brenna announced the paternity.

"Eric? Eric did this to Ana?" Brenna could see his jaws tighten while a blue vein began protruding from his neck. She thought of her father's anger when Ginny had run away from home and how he looked as if he was going to explode at any second.

"Now Manuel, don't do anything you'll regret. Remember you're holding a beautiful child in your arms. It's the one good thing that has come out of this." She paused to monitor his emotions, drawing a little closer. "Anyway, we've always been like a family. Now you're a grand-uncle and I'm a grandmother. We can help raise him together, you and I."

Manuel expressed a sigh of acceptance. He returned his gaze to the baby that was fussing in his arms. "I want to kill Eric," he hissed through clenched teeth. "I'm sorry, Brenna, but I can't promise that I won't try to strangle him if I get the chance. But for now, I will concentrate on Roberto and his needs. And by the feel of his bottom, I would say that he needs changing."

That broke the circle of anger and allowed Ana to step in. "Manuel, I want you to be his godfather. Will you do that?"

"Who else will look after this little rooster? I will teach him how to be a good man, not like his bedeviled father."

On the way home Brenna likened herself to an empty shell. Her son was a thief, a liar and a rapist. Her daughter was mistrusting and unloving and had nothing left to share with her. A nonexistent father, two children who hated her, and no one special in her life other than a bunch of scruffy, old miners. Someday, they too would go away and nothing would be left. She had survived, but that was all she had done. For months her gloominess continued.

When the stock market crashed on Black Monday her bucket of pain was finally full.

Chapter 25

"I don't understand, Marita. Men are killing themselves because they don't have enough money to buy food and feed their families. You work all your life and for what?"

"We are lucky that most in my family have continued to find work during the Depression. But how are you set? You're down to two boarders, no?"

"I'll be okay if I keep pinching pennies. Sara and Eric are gone. Usually it's just me and the two men. Sometimes Pinto shows up for a late dinner. It's the upkeep that's the problem. Every time I turn around something on this old house needs to be fixed."

Marita untied her apron strings, folding the tattered wrap and setting it aside for tomorrow's work. "In the morning, we should can some of those tomatoes. We can't let anything in the garden go to waste." Brenna watched Marita exit the screen door, making her way down the alley, the same path she had taken for over four decades. She was slower now, her pace more deliberate. Sometimes her ankles would swell, yet she never complained. Her hair had turned from the color of blue-black to a mottled gray. The curves to her form had rounded, the price a woman pays for years of childbirth. Soon there would come a time when Marita would hang up her apron for good.

Brenna had yet to leave the kitchen when she heard stumbling on the back steps. Pinto, she thought, and just when she was sure she was done for the night.

"Help me, Mrs. Mac," he cried. "I don't know nothin' about doctorin'. Tell me what to do."

"Dear God," Brenna gasped. "What happened to him?" Pinto laid a scruffy brown dog on the kitchen table as gentle as a feather floating to the ground.

"Found him 'long side the road just before dark. Been hot as hell out there today and look what someone done. It just ain't right."

Horrified, Brenna's eyes came across a kitchen fork sticking out of the dog's neck. She reached to touch it but then withdrew, unsure of her next move. The dog, unable to lift his head, turned his eyes toward her, giving a feeble wag to his tail.

"Who could do such a thing?" she asked. "And still he trusts us. Did you try to take the fork out?"

"I was afraid. Didn't know if he'd start bleeding or choke to death."

"Well, he can't stay like this. Keep an eye on him. I'll be right back." Shortly Brenna returned with bandages and ointment. "We can't afford to call in a vet, Pinto. We're on our own, and you're going to have to help me. Now take ahold of his muzzle just in case he decides he doesn't like me after all."

Pinto moved to the other side of the table, using both hands to fit across the dog's mouth. The weary animal offered no resistance and for a moment Brenna hesitated, sure that she saw in his eyes the welcome of death. While she still had her courage, she grabbed the fork close to the tines using the other hand to hold the dog's neck in place. He whimpered as the crusted blood pulled away from flesh. Immediately blood began seeping from the wound.

"Keep holding him, Pinto. Talk to him nice so he knows we're his friends. I don't know if he still has the will to live." With a warm wet rag, Brenna dabbed at the wound. Unable to see clearly, she clipped some of the light brown hairs away from the wound. "What do you suppose he is?"

"Ma'am?"

"What breed?"

"Don't' know. Suppose he's just a mutt like me."

Brenna looked up and smiled. "He looks like a working dog. He might be a Border terrier."

"Whatever he is, he is sure a pathetic little thing."

"You can let go now, Pinto."

Pinto released his hold and immediately the dog righted himself. Brenna had covered the wound with an ointment and bandaged his neck with clean rags. Once again he looked up at her with big, watery brown eyes and wagged his tail.

"He appears right grateful, Mrs. Mac."

"I think he was lucky that you came along when you did. It doesn't appear the fork hit any vital parts. Let's give him some water and see if he can swallow."

The animal lusted after the cool water whining all the while as he drank. He seemed to know it was more important to drink than avert the pain in his throat. After several noisy minutes of lapping water, he laid down on a bed Brenna fashioned for him out of a wooden crate and an old blanket she placed by the kitchen stove. The tired animal, comforted by his surroundings, climbed into bed, turning in a circle several times before resting his weary body.

"Tomorrow I'll offer him some soft food like oatmeal or corn mush. I bet he's hungry, but we should let his throat rest tonight so some of the swelling can go down. You can visit first thing in the morning. How about you, Pinto? You must be hungry yourself."

"I surely would appreciate some supper, ma'am. Matter of fact, I was on my way here when I found him."

Brenna placed a plate of chicken and dumplings in front of him. "You carried him a long way. Why didn't you get help sooner?"

"These are hard times, Mrs. Mac. Who's gonna care about a little old dog? Once a long time ago, you took me in just like this here stray. I knew you'd open up your heart and home soon as you saw him. He probably never done nothin' wrong in his whole life, 'cept trusting the wrong people. Happens to all of us sooner or later." Brenna watched him wipe his plate clean with the last crust of bread.

"Come for breakfast tomorrow, Pinto. Maybe our patient will join you."

Content that the stray was in the best of care, Pinto grabbed his hat to cover his bald head, tipping it respectfully to Brenna as he left.

After several days both Brenna and the dog became accustomed to seeing Pinto morning and night as the kind old man came to check on his new friend. Following breakfast, Pinto and the dog would remain close to home, making small repairs to the house as Brenna requested. Both seemed content to pitch in and help take care of the home. Brenna studied them as they made their way around the garden plot.

"Haven't heard him bark yet, Pinto. I'm afraid he's lost his voice."

"Reckon that ain't all bad. He'll be a quiet companion."

"Yes, I think it's time you took him home. He seems quite well and has a tremendous appetite."

"What do you mean, Mrs. Mac? Don't you want him no more?"

"Pinto, you're mistaken. You saved his life. He's never been my dog."

"But I thought you was rather attached to him." Brenna dropped to one knee to pet the scruffy terrier. He had filled out nicely in the last week. His eyes were bright and cheerful, his coat silky and full. Pinto had removed all the fat, black ticks that had plagued him and with exception to his ordeal, he appeared to have been a healthy animal.

"I am attached to him, Pinto. But you and the dog were destined to be together. By the way, what will you name him? We can't keep calling him Dog."

"I been thinkin' on that. I could name him Lucky on account of his good luck that I found him. Or I could name him Chance, as he got his second chance. But if he were my dog I would name him Mac, after the lady that saved his life."

Brenna packed up Mac's crate and rags, walking the two companions down the brick path leading to the main road. The evening sun painted the sky a violent pinkish orange while behind the horizon creamy monsoon rain clouds formed overhead. Pinto turned to face her. "Mrs. Mac, I gotta tell you something. Been told it might not be in your best interest, but knowing you the way I do, I think you got a right to know. It's Eric, your son."

Brenna could feel the blood draining from her head. He'd finally gone and got himself killed. She could hardly find the air to continue breathing.

"I seen him in the Gulch, Mrs. Mac. Been there for a couple of weeks. Lots of folks say you're better off without him, but I thought you'd like to know."

"Eric's alive?"

"Oh, yes, Ma'am. Fact is he's put on a few pounds in the last ten years. I mighta even seen a few gray hairs on that ornery head a his."

"What's he doing in the Gulch?"

"From what I hear, he's working the books at The Palace. Sometimes I even see him pouring drinks. Things have been jumpin' in the Gulch since there ain't no more Prohibition."

Brenna tried to imagine what Eric must look like. His auburn head bent over a table full of paperwork, sitting in a dark corner of the bar with a lone spotlight illuminating his work. Perhaps the Navy had taught him to be useful. At last, he may have grown up.

"Thank you Pinto. I am very grateful that you are looking out for me."

"No, ma'am. It's me who's beholdin' to you. Me and Mac ain't gonna ever forget your kindness. Besides my Mama, there's no one that's been as good to me as you been." He called to Mac, waiting until he had faced away from Brenna to wipe his teary, old eyes.

He was nearly out of sight before Brenna called out, "Pinto! If you see Eric, tell him to come home." He waved in acknowledgement and the two new best friends made their way home.

* * * *

"Is it too late to get some breakfast at this boarding house?" Marita wheeled around to face the back door. It was a familiar voice, but one that had changed. She dropped her mop and called out to Brenna.

"*Señora*, come quick It is *Señor* Eric!" She forced open the screen door, allowing him to step inside. "I still cannot believe it is you. I thought you were floating out on some ocean."

"Not any more. It feels good to have solid ground under my feet again."

Eric surveyed the room. A few cosmetic changes had brightened up the kitchen. The same oak table rested against the far wall, but the dingy oilcloth had been changed to sunny yellow linen. White cotton curtains had replaced the sheeting that hung on the windows for years. Gray linoleum covered the wooden floors that Marita and Brenna had paced across for as long as he could remember.

"Come, come in the dining room and I will get you some food. Where is your mother?" she fussed.

The front door opened and Brenna walked in, removing garden gloves from her hands. "What is it, Marita?" she demanded. "I told you I'd be out front trimming the roses." She looked up to see her son standing before her.

"Eric." Arms open, she crossed the room to her son, embracing him to dispel all the anguish she had the last ten years. She gave him a long tender kiss on his cheek. Brenna took his hand, seating him at the dining room table. "You look well. You've taken good care of yourself."

"No, Ma, the Navy did. They saw to it that U.S. property was running in tip-top shape. While I put my time in they taught me how to keep track of their money. Then I got into the stock market. Always did like to gamble. I was doing real well until the crash. Lost about all I had and decided home was the best place to be until I got on my feet."

"Of course," Brenna assured him, patting his hand.

"Then you'll be staying in Bisbee?"

"Seems that way. I'll keep working in the Gulch until something better comes along." Marita brought in Eric's breakfast and Brenna waited until Marita left the room. "Eric, you know you have a son, don't you?"

There was a long silence. Eric could feel his mother's eyes pressing, waiting for a response.

"Yeah, old Pinto Bean made a point of telling me. I hear he's a pretty good looking kid."

"Ana has done a wonderful job raising Roberto. And Manuel and Marita have seen to it that he stays busy enough to keep him out of trouble."

"How is Ana? Has she done okay?"

"Ana is wonderful. She finished her schooling after Roberto was born and got her high school diploma. She couldn't make it to college like Marita had planned, but she's working as a department manager at the company store."

"Did she ever marry?"

"Hasn't found the right man yet. Most Mexican men aren't very happy about dating a woman whose child has a gringo name."

"Where's Sara these days?"

"Oh, we see her now and then. She's Roberto's godmother, you know. She got her teaching certificate at Normal School in Phoenix and then taught for about four years before she married a citrus farmer from a town called Glendale. She had a beautiful wedding at his ranch. We all went up for the wedding and Roberto was the ring bearer."

"Seems like I've missed quite a bit."

"Eric, you can still be part of this family. I could use a man's help with this house, maybe teach you the business. As an accountant, your skills would be very helpful. Why this could all be yours someday."

* * * *

Eric packed the last of his belongings. The small room he had rented was inspected one last time. Not that he had any respect for that wrinkled old landlord, but the Navy had ingrained habits that were hard to break. Aunt Ginny, for all her wild ways, had been right this time. Life in the Navy had been a pain in the ass, but worth the suffering. Once he learned to keep his opinions to himself, to observe, obey, listen and learn, he could sense the undercurrent. While others were sure he was part of their team, he could direct his efforts to suit his own needs.

Ginny and Morris had kept in touch, supportive in their own selfish way. At times, Eric wondered if he was their substitute child, quickly snatched from Brenna when she cast him aside.

Poor Mom. Still the bleeding heart wanting to mend all evil. She believed he had changed.

Eric stopped at the window to watch a man and a woman across the street, embracing in the shadows of their apartment. He studied their silent language: the smiles, the way they touched, the comfort they found in each other. The man whispered something in her ear and she cocked her head to one side, still smiling. Her hand ran slowly up his back and down again and then they disappeared into the darkness of their room. He shook his head, confused at what they must be feeling. Without looking back, he grabbed his bags and returned home.

"How does it feel to be back in your own room?" Brenna stood in the doorway admiring her son. She welcomed him home with a plate of cookies and a glass of cold milk.

"Milk, Mom?"

"Why I bet it's been years since you've enjoyed milk and cookies. Consider it a welcome home gift. Come on down stairs when you're ready, and I can show you my bookkeeping system."

The room was filled with the aroma of the warm cookies. He finished hanging up the last shirt. Drawn to the plate on the dresser, he took a huge bite out of the first cookie, savoring its vanilla flavor. She was right; it had been years since he'd enjoyed such a treat. He sat on the bed trying to understand. If only he could feel something for her; some sign of affection for this woman who had given him life. Instead, he just felt numb.

Her accounting methods were straightforward, almost childlike in nature.

"This is the account on the rooms," she explained. "They pay on a monthly basis; weekly if they are struggling a bit."

"Don't they get a receipt for their payment? I don't see any carbons."

"Oh, I get pretty careless about that. I don't try to take this too seriously. Maybe that's something we can work on."

Time after time, Eric spotted loopholes, places where cash could easily escape. He reminded himself that he needed to try and be honest this time, at least with his own mother. But it was like opening a box of Cracker Jacks. He just knew there was something good inside, a special reward just for him.

Chapter 26

Marita was complaining and swearing under her breath. "I have been cooking this meat all day, and it is as tough as an old burro. We are going to have to change butchers if *Señor* Jackson can't do better than this."

"But he's always been so consistent," Brenna replied. "I can't understand why the meat would suddenly be tough and dry. I have to go down to Main later this afternoon. I'll see if I can talk to Myra and find out what's going on."

Lucky break, Eric thought. He discarded the cigarette he'd been smoking under the kitchen window and short of a run, raced to Main to prevent Brenna's conversation with the butcher's wife.

"What am I supposed to tell her?" the butcher whined. He waved his hands in the air. "I don't know why I agreed to this. Mrs. McEvoy's been a loyal customer for years. Why, if times weren't so hard, I'd never done this."

"I don't give a damn about loyalty," Eric replied. "If you want a little extra cash in your pocket, you keep up your end of the deal. Throw in a few tender cuts now and then to keep them guessing. Make up some story about the cows and pigs getting the wrong feed. Yeah, that's what makes the meat tough. And make sure your wife doesn't get wind of this or everyone's going to be sorry. You understand, Jackson? Like it or not, we're in this together."

The old man dropped his eyes to his scuffed, leather shoes, shaking his head in regret. *Damn. He should be grateful I am helping him out,* Eric thought. He slammed the door with a jolt, sounding the small golden bell mounted on the frame. In a few weeks he'd advise the women to change shops, maybe try a new grocer and be rid of this frightened old man.

Ernie, down the road, would be easier to deal with. Ernie was Eric's kind of guy from his side of the tracks. He walked into the lumber yard, lit a fresh smoke and waited for Ernie to finish with a customer. After a few moments Ernie spied Eric, walked over to him, grabbed the cigarette from his mouth and hurled it to the ground.

"No smokin' in the yard," he bellowed, grinding the cigarette into the dirt. "You know what would happen here if you dropped your butt in the wrong place?" Eric didn't bother arguing with Ernie. No one argued with Ernie.

"You got that lumber in?" Eric asked.

"Naw. Expect it sometime next week. Everything still okay?"

"Sure thing," Eric replied with confidence. "I'll cut the check as soon as you deliver the goods. You cash the check, we split the difference."

"What you using this lumber for?" Ernie asked. "Is it going someplace that has to look good?"

"Some of it's going to rebuild a shed. Rest is going to replace floor boards on the back porch. Little paint and no one will know the difference."

"Well, I just wanted to make sure you knew what you was getting into. Don't want to be taking no blame for something you're doing. This lumber is usable, just isn't what I'd call grade A."

"Don't worry about it. It isn't a problem. I'll call you in about a week." Walking away, Eric looked back over his shoulder. Through the plate window, Eric could see Ernie back in his office, puffing on his big cigar. Suddenly Ernie looked up, catching Eric's eye. Eric gave a shrug. Neither one of them trusted the other, the only kind of relationship Eric understood.

The school wasn't far away. Today might be a good day to stop by, just to get a look at the boy. Maybe he'd see him during recess. Eric was amused at the way Robert's hair parted with the same cowlick that he always had to deal with. Sure enough, he was out there playing with a pigskin and a bunch of noisy boys. Eric watched Robert stoop to help one of the players from the other team. He seemed to have a lot of friends and a gentleness that reminded him of his brother Michael. My God, he hadn't thought of Michael in years.

Suddenly Roberto looked up to where several of the boys were pointing. Eric realized they were pointing at him. He left his post at the tree and quickly departed.

A burning curiosity stirred. He wanted to talk to Robert, maybe even tell him he was his father. What did his voice sound like? Was he more Mexican than white? What color were his eyes? This was a different feeling for him, something that almost ached inside. It would have been different if he had fathered a girl, but a son, knowing you had a son was hard for a man to ignore. Sooner or later they were going to meet face-to-face.

Returning home he found his mother reviewing his bookkeeping. His pulse quickened as the old fears of inadequacy rose inside. Calm down, he coached himself. Be confident.

"Everything looking good, Mom?" he asked while thumbing through the mail.

"I'm having a bit of a problem following your records, but it all seems to be in order." She removed her glasses gingerly rubbing the spot between her eyes. "That written bid from the lumber yard seemed awful high for pine boards. Did you get more than one bid before agreeing to that price?"

"I checked into a couple more suppliers, even one in Douglas, but you know the price of goods keeps going up. Everyone wants to make a buck. Seemed to make more sense to buy locally from someone we know."

"I suppose you're right. Sometimes buying cheap doesn't always mean buying smart." She smiled and picked up her glasses. "Don't forget today's Friday and we owe Marita a check." That was one place he wouldn't cut corners. That suspicious old Mexican didn't even trust herself, much less him. Everything from Marita's point of view had to appear perfectly normal.

"*Hijo*, how was school today?" Marita's voice came from the kitchen. "Come give your Grandma a hug. And who have you brought home today?" Young voices filled the space. It could have been any one of Marita's grandchildren, but instinctively, Eric knew it was Roberto. It seemed like as good a time as any to run upstairs and take a nap or hot shower. He snapped the large leather binder shut and bound up the stairs, two at a time, disappearing like a ghost passing into another dimension.

* * * *

"But that's impossible," Brenna countered. "We're overdrawn? By how much?" Eric picked up his cup and saucer following his mother's voice to the telephone in the parlor. She continued to argue with the party on the other end.

"Well I don't understand. It must be a clerical error or an accounting error on our part. I can bring the books in and we can go over this together. Yes. I'll be in this afternoon and if it is our fault, we'll make good on the deficit. Oh no. Glad that you called. Thank you."

Brenna hung up the receiver with a puzzled look on her face. "The bank just called to say we're overdrawn in our checking account. How can that be, Eric? Could we have made a mistake somewhere?"

"Oh I suppose anything is possible," he replied. "But you shouldn't be bothering yourself about problems like this. That's why you hired an accountant." He smiled as sincerely as possible and placed one hand on her shoulder. "I'll take care of it, Mom. I'll take the ledger down to the bank this afternoon. You know you can't be too careful these days. Do you really trust this banker? You've been storing cash for years for these old miners because they don't' trust the banks."

"Why I've known Mr. Donaldson since your father disappeared. He's been a very prudent banker and always honest. Just take care of the problem and take the money from savings to cover the checking account. Also tell Mr. Donaldson I need to know what the bank shows we have in savings. I don't know how much longer this depression is going to continue, but I don't want to be destitute before I find out."

Eric watched her disappear into the kitchen as he thought about a new approach. He had to change his plans if he was going to keep maintaining his regular cuts. Would she trust his word over a written statement from the bank? If she squawked, he'd have to forge a document. She was getting as distrustful as Marita. No wonder those biddies got along so well.

* * * *

"We're down to what?" Brenna's voice rang through the parlor. "How could our savings be down to twelve hundred dollars? My account has never been that low. Are you sure you got those figures right?"

Eric took a long, cleansing breath. "That's what they told me, Ma. I can give them a call and ask for a written statement on that account, but that seems like an awful lot of trouble to put the bank through, especially since the last mistake was our fault."

"You mean *your* fault, Eric. And do try to be more careful in the future. It's not hard to get a bad reputation. Please learn to double check your figures from now on. And don't bother calling the bank back. We're just going to have to sit down this week and decide where we can tighten our belts. I'm losing another boarder next week, and I'll have to get that vacancy filled fast."

Eric waited until she left the room to let his guard down. He dropped into the desk chair, rubbing his palms over his face. He hated it when she scolded him. He had always hated it. Her voice would get higher and shriller as her anger escalated until he had to fold his arms across his chest to keep from smacking her. He had never held back with any other woman. When they got out of line a good crack across the face had settled them down right away. But he just couldn't bring himself to hit his own mother. Besides, he was still in the clear and no one could prove he'd done anything wrong. He just had to be more careful.

Suggesting they postpone any further renovation to the house would give his mother a sense of relief. She knew they needed electrical repairs, but for now he would tape off the hazardous outlets until the wiring could be replaced. The lumber had already been delivered and that would keep them busy for a while. Each deception was going quite well, and it seemed as good a time as any to tell her about the boarder.

"He left without paying?" She was stunned. "Why he owed me for the whole month. I trusted Walter. When he said he'd fallen on hard times and needed to move on, he promised he'd get the cash from his family. How could he do this to me?"

She's taking it personally, Eric thought. She'd been betrayed by her friend. She always was a soft-touch. She'd mope for a few days, but she'd get over it.

* * * *

The next day, Eric returned home from his weekly drinking binge in the Gulch, carefully negotiating the front steps. He was going to have to stop drinking before he got this drunk. It was just too much of an effort to make his way back home in this condition.

"Eric." It was Brenna's voice calling out, but where was she? He turned his attention to where she was sitting on the front porch. He couldn't really focus on the image, but he was sure it was her.

"Mom?" he asked. "What are you doing sitting out here by yourself?"

"We have to talk. You're my only son but I'm going to have to ask you to leave. Again. And of course, you're fired."

Too many beers, he thought. *Can't think*. "What are you talking about?" he heard himself say. He tried to stand tall and act the part.

"I took a bus over to Lowell today and I happened to run into Walter. He's moved in with his sister, you know. Just temporarily until he can move to California. We had a little talk about his boarding bill. Seems he not only paid his bill, but he produced a receipt to prove it. Where's the money, Eric?"

"Jesus, Ma." Eric's head hurt. Her voice was starting to elevate and he just couldn't take it; not with the pounding in his brain.

"You're a complete disgrace. Rape. Drinking during the afternoon. Stealing from your own family. What's next, Eric? Murder?"

He cupped his hands over his ears trying to shut her out. When that didn't work, he opened the screen door and walked into the house, hoping to escape.

Brenna followed him in. "It's not going to work, Eric. You can't hide from me or anyone else. You're worthless! When you're sober enough to pack, get out of my house."

The kitchen door pushed open and a small dark head poked out. Roberto walked into the room carrying a glass of milk. A white mustache etched his upper lip against his light brown skin.

"What's all the yelling about, Grandma? You okay?"

"It's nothing, Roberto. Nothing you should worry yourself about." Brenna started to push the child back into the kitchen, but then the expression on her face changed. It was a wise-ass look, one Eric had seen before, but never on the face of his own mother. "Roberto," she smiled at the small boy, "it's time you met your father. We wanted to shield you from the pain of knowing who and what he is, but you're old enough now to know the truth. This is your father, dear. My son, Eric. This drunk, who has wasted his entire life, is your father."

Roberto put the glass down on the table and walked toward Eric, his forehead wrinkled as he peered up at Eric. "You're really my dad?" he asked in amazement.

Eric tried to project indifference, as always, but instead he felt a warm tear run down his cheek. "Yeah, I guess I am."

"I've seen you staring at us on the playground. Why haven't you talked to me? Why did you leave my mother? Where did you go?"

"Get away from me." Eric lashed out pushing Roberto aside. This isn't at all what he wanted. He'd never planned to be humiliated by his mother and confronted by his son.

"Come here, Roberto," Brenna urged. "He left you and your mom because he's irresponsible and reckless. It wasn't anything you or your mother did. Eric's been trouble since he was your age. Everything he gets near he sours. That's what happens when all you care about is yourself."

"That's not true," Eric shot back. Tears were rolling down his cheeks making his face appear shiny and pale, ghost-like. "I was going to be a father to him. I wanted to try. Just hadn't found the right way to tell him yet. I wanted to get some money together so I could help take care of him. That's why I took Walter's rent money."

Brenna's voice softened, but that didn't make her words any less lethal. "Don't you think it's time you at least quit lying? You've never considered anyone but yourself, and that includes your son. If you were a right-thinking man you'd have asked me for the money.

But stealing from me… you're despicable. And what about all the people you've hurt along the way? You feel nothing for any of them, do you? Including me. You are dead inside, Eric. Dead! And now you're dead to me too."

"But Ma, I—"

"Get out of my life, Eric. Get out of Roberto's life." She took the boy's hand and led him away from the father he had finally met and then lost in a matter of minutes.

Eric stumbled upstairs to his room, yanking the suitcase from the closet. "I'll make her pay," he mumbled to himself. "She made me look like a fool in front of my kid. I'll get even. I swear."

He stormed out of the bedroom making sure to slam the front door as he left the house.

* * * *

It seemed like the old apartment house was sitting there, patiently waiting for his return. Rarely was the building ever filled to capacity. This time he got a different room facing the alley. This room wasn't as run down as the last, but that wasn't much of a consolation if all he had to look at was trash and winos.

He heard a sharp rap on the door. "Hey, buddy, heard you were back. Let me in."

It was Jake, the last person he wanted to see right now. For some reason, even when they were kids, Eric felt Jake was below him, always looking to him for the next scheme. Maybe they were too much alike and that's why Eric disliked him so much. Reluctantly, he opened the door.

"Guess the old broad kicked you out. That didn't last long."

"Shut up, asshole. I left because I couldn't stomach it anymore."

"That's not the word out on the street."

"Yeah? So what is?" Eric poured two shots of whiskey, handing one to Jake. He was always good for information.

"They say you were dipping in the till."

"Well no one can prove nothing. And my mother's too noble to elaborate."

"Trouble is, if you can't clear up your name, you ain't gonna get a job here."

"Yeah, hadn't thought much on that. I doubt The Palace will take me back. Maybe it's time to get out. I got this idea. A way to make fast money and it could be a new beginning. You interested in getting in on this?"

"Yeah, I'm interested. Don't think I've ever had to scrape bottom like this. Even when my mother was whoring we had more money, and that's with me working an honest job."

"How do I know I can trust you?" Eric asked.

"I might ask the same of you."

"Fair enough. Gentleman's agreement," Eric said, offering his hand. "And I'll come hunt you down and kill you if you double cross me."

"Same here," Jake replied. "Now, pour me another shot and tell me about this big plan of yours."

"Can't do that now. I got too many details to work out. But I'll keep in touch. You keep me informed on what's happening on the streets and I'll fill you in on our progress."

"Hey, so did you hear what's going on overseas?"

"What are you talking about?"

"The Krauts, man, the Krauts. Don't you ever look at the paper? Germany invaded Poland two days ago. England and France are up to their asses in war. There's talk that it's going to pull us out of this depression. Only a matter of time until Uncle Sam drags his sorry butt into the game."

A war would mean black markets, lots of them. And all kinds of ways to make money. If things didn't work out here, there was always some other angle.

Chapter 27

Nearly six months passed before Eric got the nerve to write to Ginny. Opportunity was important, but preparation was essential. Eric read his letter once again, checking that he had made his needs perfectly clear. First, he informed Ginny and Morris that he had left his mother's home. He failed to say exactly why he'd left, only explaining there had been a disagreement regarding his accounting practices. But knowing Ginny, she'd probably be impressed by his underhandedness.

Next, he made sure they knew he was working. They must see him as being employed and successful. Embellishing, just a little, would help his cause but he still had to make it look believable.

Finally, he asked the all-important question. Were they still interested in that Nevada investment they had discussed years ago? If so, how much money would they need to get started? What was the prospect for development in Las Vegas? Was gambling still legal? The possibility of turning a quick profit had never held a guarantee, but this was the closest he'd come so far.

Ginny's response came quickly. She complained of all the poor Okies in California, and the rich social circles she could never possibly hope to enter. Morris had left her right in the middle, "taking her nowhere in a hurry," but Las Vegas had some definite possibilities for making their fortunes. This war business might slow things down a bit, but right after that, things should be popping. In the meantime they could save their money and make their plans. For the first time in his life, Eric had a future.

Tending bar was a mindless task and easily accommodated his daydreams. Access to the boarding house would be easy, but breaking into the safe would take some determination. After getting caught with his hand in the cookie jar, it was highly unlikely he could trick his mother into opening the safe.

Several times he had considered returning to the school. He could visualize Robert walking up to the fence and talking to him. This time Robert would learn he was okay, that he still could be a father to him. Maybe they'd have dinner together or share Christmas presents.

But he was no dope. Robert was better off without him, and his own mother would sooner shoot him dead than let him near that kid again. For now it was only a fantasy, but someday he'd be rollin' in dough. Then the kid would have respect for his old man and would see how wrong his grandmother had been.

He wiped down the bar counter after filling a mug for a regular. He'd been off the weed since the night his mother kicked him out. Every time thereafter, when he tried to smoke a joint, he was reminded of that night, his helplessness against her. Never again would he be in that state. Let the Mexicans and the Chinks mess with their heads, he'd stick with liquor.

Jake sat down at the bar. "Get me a brew," he demanded.

"Show me your money, pal."

"Some pal. You don't even trust me." Jake laid his cash on the counter while Eric filled his mug.

"Just get paid?" he asked.

"Yeah. But it doesn't last long. Whatever happened to your big plan to make all that money?"

"This is going to take some thinking, Jake. I've already taken the first step and contacted my associates."

"Big words for a small-time punk," Jake said and snickered.
Eric lowered his head, forcing his eyes to meet Jake's. His voice took on a low, authoritative tone. "Shut your mouth you stupid moron. If you don't have any respect for what I'm doing I'll go find someone else who does."

"Easy, Eric." Jake squirmed. "I don't mean nothing by it. I'm on your side, remember?"

"I'm not looking for an apology. I need someone I can trust to follow through. Once we're in this, we're in it to the end, you understand? No backing out."

"Fine. So what you got?"

Eric looked at his watch. "I get off in about an hour. Meet me over by that corner table, under the painting of the naked broad. I'll tell you what I'm planning so far. You might even be able to help. I remember what a hell raiser you used to be."

"Still am," Jake promised. He downed the last of his beer. "See you in awhile."

When Jake returned the place was packed. Familiar faces crowded the corners, and the smoke had thickened with the influx of drinkers. Pinto had passed out on one table during his last round. Eric pushed past the clusters of men and pulled out an empty chair at the designated table. Jake followed his lead.

"This is what I have in mind," he began. "My mother has a safe stored in her closet. I know this for certain. When I was a kid I helped her carry it upstairs. For years, she's been storing cash for her boarders. She promised them she'd look after their money in case there was a run on the banks or if they were to get hauled off during a strike. You remember when that train hauled all those men to New Mexico? I know for a fact she was storing money for several men and they never came back. Since the depression hit, I imagine she's stashed a few thousand more." Jake had not remained quiet for such a length for as long as Eric could remember. "Are you following me, Jake? You listening?"

"Never understood better," he answered. Eric studied his eyes, bright with anticipation.

"Don't you go get any ideas about pulling this off by yourself. I'll turn you in myself if you go against me."

"There you go again…"

"Never you mind. Just pay attention. Ma may even have some jewelry stashed. All I know is that there's plenty to be had. We just have to figure out how to get into the safe."

"And what about my cut?"

"You'll get a percentage of the take once we get clear. I can tell you it won't be fifty-fifty. Someday it was going to be my inheritance. Let's just say I'm taking an early withdrawal."

"Your Ma could get hurt, you know."

"I don't want that to happen. Much as I'd like to hurt her, I can't bring myself to do it. That's what I still have to work out. When I figure out the best way to handle this, we can do the job, go our separate ways and start living the good life."

There was the sound of a dull thud in the darkened corner. Eric looked down to see Pinto lying at his feet. "God damn drunk," he yelled. "Someone get this old goat outta here." Two bartenders came from behind the counter to answer his call. "Pathetic old shit bag," Eric snarled. He kicked at the old man's leather boots as he was dragged through the tables and out the door. "Someone should put him out of his misery."

Jake and Eric followed Pinto out the door, turning down the street where Eric's apartment house stood while Pinto was dumped on the street. Daylight would be coming in a couple of hours and it was time to rest. "I'll be in touch in a few weeks," Eric concluded. "In the meantime, you do some planning of your own, and figure out how to break into a safe."

Ginny's letters became progressively longer and more detailed. She turned down Eric's request that she return to Bisbee, certain she would easily be recognized, which would raise suspicion. All communications would have to remain in writing and the letters destroyed immediately after he received them.

Eric Dear,

I do not want to know how you are planning to get this loan from your mother, though I do have a good idea of what you're up to. It's none of my business, and we want to keep it that way. You say you need to get her out of the house for a while. It might do the both of you good if she came to visit me for a few weeks. If you like this idea, I'll write to her and invite her to L.A., for the holidays.

Things are continuing to look good in Las Vegas. The population is still expanding and there's talk of a large air base being constructed nearby, no doubt because of this crummy war. Still, it should be good for business. As far as I know gambling, hookers and boozing are still legal in town and as we see it, it's a great opportunity to take advantage of all kinds of men who want to part with their money.

Morris has his eye on some property on Fremont Street that might make us a good gambling house. We'll let you know if anything develops and how much cash we might be needing.

Love to you,
Aunt Ginny

Love to you? He had to laugh out loud. Aunt Ginny was incapable of loving anything besides money and the excitement it provoked. Her idea to invite his mother to California though, was a guarantee to get her out of his hair until he and Jake had emptied the safe. At this point, timing would be everything.

The seasons had changed again and although it rarely snowed in Bisbee, this particular morning had a bite to it. Eric put down his cup of coffee to wrap his shoulders in his bed quilt. "Damn, I don't think that bitch ever turns the heat on in this building." If he didn't move a little faster he was going to be late and get fired for sure. Still, it was hard to move when you were so cold and miserable, and staying in a warm bed made a lot more sense, but not any money.

The kitchen smells of food and soap hit him in the face when he walked through the back door. The crowd from church would be coming in soon for lunch. Working two jobs nearly drove him crazy, but Mr. Wayne had promised him a bookkeeping job if he proved himself trustworthy. Then he could quit his job at The Palace. He had grown sick of the smell of stale beer and urine stained toilets.

Raymond threw a crisp white apron at him and motioned for him to put it on. "So what do you think of them Japs? I feel like stringin' up the next one I run into."

"What are you talking about?" Eric's tone was bland.

"Jesus, don't you know? You must never read a paper or listen to the radio. Those slant-eyes bombed Hawaii this morning. A place called Pearl Harbor. Got our boys on a Sunday when they were resting up from Saturday night. They blew up planes, sunk battleships, we were caught completely off guard. You know what this means don't you?"

"Yeah, it means we're at war." He finished tying his apron and began collecting dishes and silverware.

"You don't seem too concerned about any of this."

"War's a pain in the ass," he replied. "A disruption."

"You know, you're not too old to be called up."

"They're not going to bother with me. I did my time in the Navy. Besides, I'm a bean counter, an accountant. What would they want with me?"

"Well, I'm enlisting." Raymond's face shined with enthusiasm, and he pretended to hold a rifle. "I want to see some action, shoot me some Japs."

Eric leaned over and whispered in Raymond's ear, "Those Japs are gonna shoot your dick off." He gave Raymond a nasty wink and left to set tables in the dining room.

* * * *

Ginny's Western Union telegram arrived later that week:

Mother has postponed travel due to war. Letter to follow. Ginny.

Aww, hell... how much longer was he going to have to wait? He couldn't stand working these stinking jobs much longer. Discouraged, he flopped into the kitchen chair, scanning the grungy little room that was his home. His eyes came to rest on his pet spider, a long-legged, light brown creature tucked into the corner over the kitchen window. He had taken a liking to the creepy fellow, even to the point of catching flies to throw into his web. Day after day the spider would wait patiently, believing that something good was going to come along, something to satisfy his cravings. And always it did.

The spider would hurry out to greet opportunity. Eric liked to watch him work, busily spinning silk around his prey; using first one leg, then the other, to turn the victim over and over, burying him in a fine wrap. In a while the insect ceased to struggle, accepting his fate. If the spider was hungry, he would immediately begin sucking the life from his catch to fill the emptiness inside. If not, the spider would return to his corner, delicately balancing across each branch of the web until he reached his haven. He would position himself like an old man lowering himself into an easy chair, and quietly wait for his next lucky break.

Eric looked again at the telegram he clutched in his hand. He could learn to wait patiently, just like the spider. In fact tonight, he might go down to Agua Prieta. There was a cheap tattoo house in Mexico where he could get a big black spider engraved on his arm. It would be his special Christmas present to himself. At the very least, getting a spider tattoo would be a nice diversion from the monotony of his life.

Above all, it would be a gentle reminder to be patient.

* * * *

It was not long before Brenna agreed to visit Ginny, leaving the safe unguarded. Ginny had faked an illness, female trouble that got Brenna out to help her. It could be months before she returned home and Eric would be far away before his mother could turn to him for blame.

"Any word yet?" Jake asked. He too, seemed calmed by the change that was about to take place. Eric could swear Jake had finally grown up and was beginning to act like a man instead of a buffoon.

"She's leaving ten days from tonight. Ginny says Marita will still be looking after the house and feeding the boarders. What we have to do now is case the house for a few days to see what time she leaves. Then, we pick a night. Are you sure you can get into this safe?"

"Once we're upstairs, we can take our time and do the job right. My buddy, Mel, says those little home and office safes are like breaking into a cereal box. We need to peel away the back layer of metal and crack open the concrete with a sledge hammer. Then all we gotta do is break through the tin metal on the inside and the job is done."

"How much noise is it gonna make?"

"Doesn't matter. Won't be anyone home to hear it. See, we do it on a Saturday night. We wait until the Mexican leaves. We wait until the last boarder leaves. Friday before is payday. You know no one's gonna be hanging around the house with a paycheck burning a hole in their pocket."

"Then that's all there is to it," Eric said. "It's all but done. Oh, one more thing. We divvy up the goods right then and there. Anything special from my family, like jewelry, I keep. We go our separate ways that night. You got your plans in order?"

"Doing that this week. I'm thinking I'm gonna head –"

"Stop, Jake." Eric put up his hand to halt his friend's speech. "I don't even want to know, and I won't tell you where I'm headed either."

"That's probably a good idea. We can't finger each other, right?"

"You got it. Can't tell what we don't know. So you'll be watching the house this week?"

"Planning to. I'm going to keep a notebook to record the time she leaves. I'll make a note on the boarders too and see if I can figure out their shifts."

Eric seemed satisfied. "Assuming everything goes well, I'll meet with you again in sixteen days, on the Friday before the job. I'll put a checklist together to make sure we've covered all the bases. That night we get ourselves packed and ready to leave. I got an old heap to get me out of town. When I get where I'm going, I'm getting a real car."

"Spending it before you get it?" Jake asked.

"I'll drink to that!" Eric said and both men raised their glasses to toast their good fortune.

* * * *

Eric glanced at his wristwatch. "It's time," he said to Jake. "You got all your gear?"

"Right here," he replied. "Threw it in this old burlap sack so no one would think anything of it."

"By the time we get there, Marita should be long gone," Eric said. "Back door will be open. Boarders will be out of the way and up to their ears in wine, women and song. We'll have the whole place to ourselves. Let's move."

The men got out of the car, meeting on the sidewalk. "It was sure good seein' you again," Jake called out. "Come visit again, anytime." He nodded to Eric, and carrying his burlap bag, turned in the opposite direction. For all anyone knew Jake was carrying a bag of trash.

Eric shoved both hands in his pocket and casually strolled toward the boarding house. One at a time they would enter the home waiting in the darkened kitchen for the other's arrival.

"That you?" Eric asked.

"Well, it ain't your granny," Jake whispered back.

"I already checked the rooms. No one's home. Let's get upstairs." Although the house was empty and no one was there to hear, the men crept as quietly as possible. When Jake hit the squeaky step, he jumped six inches.

"What the hell's wrong with you, man?"

"Little edgy, I guess," Jake replied. He shined the flashlight at Eric's face where streams of sweat glistened, running down his temples. "Well, what the hell are you sweating for?"

"I don't know. It's not like I do this for a living. Let's just get this over with."

Inside the closet they found the small safe, just as Eric had remembered. They rolled the safe out of the closet and turned it around to face the back.

Removing his tools from the sack, Jake laid the grimy pieces on Brenna's white bedspread. "Hold the flashlight over here," he commanded. He positioned Eric's hand and then handed him the wedge. "Now hold the wedge with your other hand and I'll slam it from the top."

Eric said nothing, but gave Jake a wary glance. Jake swung both arms back, hammer in hand, aiming for the wedge. Instead, he bounced off the closet door and hit the wedge at an angle, catching Eric's hand in the process.

"Quiet down," he warned Eric. "The neighbors on the next block must have heard you yell."

"You stupid ass! You could have broken my hand!"

"What the hell happened?"

"I hit the door frame. I'll be more careful."

"I'm not holding that wedge again. You find some other way to do it."

"It'll take twice as long."

"My hand's worth it. Use some other tool to break open that damn safe. "Besides, you said we got plenty of time. You said so."

Jake went back to work, trying several other tools to weaken the safe. Several times he stopped to wipe his brow and dry his perspiring hands, delaying the job even longer.

"Shhh, a car's coming. Kill the light." Eric ducked down from his post at the window. From the driveway on the side of the house came two familiar voices.

"I can't believe you are making me do this. You have to have this exact shawl, woman? None of the others will do?"

"It's Francesca's granddaughter's wedding. You expect me to go to church looking like a beggar? You're the only one in the family with an automobile. I'm too old to walk the streets at night."

"*Hijola*, you got that right."

"You are a devil," Marita replied, wagging her index finger in Manuel's face. "But I have to put up with your antics because you take such good care of me." She smiled and gave him a gentle pat to his middle.

Eric was pacing. "Jesus Christ, they're coming inside. What are we going to do?"

Jake put down his tools without a sound. "They come up here, we're gonna have to take care of them," he whispered. "We'll hide behind the door and hit them before they see our faces."

"I said no one was supposed to get hurt."

In the dark Eric could see Jakes' face. His eyes were wide, nostrils flared. His shiny face seemed to glow in the dark. His black hair made him look even more ominous.

"Listen, Eric. I'm not letting anyone identify me. I'll do what I have to do to get out of here clean. With or without the loot."

Eric gave him a look of resignation. My God, this just wasn't going right. Downstairs the kitchen door squealed as it opened.

"My mother always kept a baseball bat under her bed, just in case a boarder got fresh. See if it's still there."

Jake reached under the bed. "Got it." He walked across the room to get behind the door where Eric was standing.

"See? It's just as I told you," Marita said. "I left it on the couch before I walked out the door. Now we can go."

Upstairs, a board squeaked. "What was that?" asked Manuel.

"What? Did you hear something?"

"I thought I heard someone walking upstairs, in Brenna's room."

"It's probably just the voice of an old house," Marita said. "But no one should be up there. Maybe you should check it out. You be careful."

One step at a time, Manuel paced himself rhythmically up the stairs. When he got to the squeaky step, Jake moved the bat behind his head, gripping it with both hands. He and Eric waited like two rats cornered in a room, until Manuel had cleared the doorway. Jake pushed forward and without hesitation slammed the bat against the back of Manuel's head. He fell to the floor like a swatted fly.

"Manuel?" Marita's voice carried up the stairs. "Are you all right? Manuel?" Once again they heard the padded steps approaching. "Not the old woman," Eric protested.

"You'll kill her if you hit her that hard."

"I'll be careful. I just want to knock her out. I know what I'm doing."

"Who's up there?" Marita asked. "I hear you!"

But it was the last thing she heard. Jake's bat collided with her skull and he watched her fall alongside Manuel.

"Let's get out of here," Jake yelled. He grabbed his tools and bag. From inside a drawer he grabbed one of Brenna's nightgowns, using it to wipe the safe for prints.

"I been in jail, Eric. I ain't going back again. I did the right thing, I tell ya. I did the right thing." He pushed Eric aside and ran out of the room.

Eric glanced back at the safe. He had failed again. Uneasiness crawled across his skin as he sensed that Jake was no longer part of his plan. Eric heard the sound of breaking glass. He bolted down the stairs, bursting into the kitchen where the distinct odor of kerosene filled the room and an old broken lamp laid in a puddle on the floor. Exiting the back door, he arrived just in time to see Jake throw a lighted match through the broken window. There was a gust of air as fuel and flame met. Then the room was bright with orange fire.

"What have you done? Are you crazy? There are two people upstairs!"

Jake was running down the alley, stumbling as he looked back. "I ain't getting caught, Eric. I won't let them catch me!" Another burst of flames roared through the kitchen. There was no time now to worry about Jake. Eric ran back into the house, racing the fire and its hunger.

It was an old, old house. Built paycheck to paycheck by his grandfather; the dry timbers would be a desirable fuel for the fire. As he mounted the stairs he thought of all the times he had climbed them, slid down the banister with Michael; fought at the base of the stairs with his mother, hid behind the banister with Sara when the boarders had been taken away. Lives had been lived in this home. If he didn't hurry, lives would be taken.

The smoke hovered near the first floor. Upstairs Eric groped in the dark, finding Manuel before the fire did. "Wake up, man. Wake up!" He shook Manuel violently until he responded with a feeble moan. "Fire, Manuel, fire!" He was beginning to taste the smoke. "We have to get out. Damn it, Manuel, wake up!" Shouting in his face seemed to finally do the trick. "We have to get Marita and get out of here, do you understand?"

Manuel did not bother to answer. He nodded in agreement. Still dizzy and confused by the darkness, he grabbed for Marita's arms, turning her upright. Eric grabbed her legs and they carried her down the stairs.

"Anyone up there?" a voice called from outside. "I'm calling for the fire department. I'm a goin' now." It sounded like old Pinto Bean, but Eric couldn't be certain. It was possible he may have shown up looking for food and seen the flames. For the first time in his life, Eric was glad that the old man was still alive and sober.

It was no longer possible to breathe. The far corner of the kitchen was completely engulfed in fire. Floorboards above could be seen through the ceiling. Eric motioned for Manuel to continue dragging Marita out the kitchen door.

A strange groan came from above. The house cried out in pain as a wooden ceiling beam gave way to the weight of the overhead room. Eric released Marita's legs from his grip, looking up in time to see the terror in Manuel's eyes. All around him there was the sound of destruction, and then they disappeared. In the rubble beside him, lay the safe.

He thought he heard bells. Was it the sound of a distant fire truck? Was it the phone? He had to get out. Crawl, that's what he had to do. They had taught him to crawl in the Navy. Heat and smoke would rise. He could make it. He turned in the opposite direction, away from the collapsed ceiling in the kitchen. Tears streamed from his stinging eyes. No longer able to open them, he crept forward, hoping to find the front door. Reaching the doorknob, he used the last of his strength to fight his way out.

The cool air embraced him with loving arms. He continued to push himself, fearful of being discovered and going to jail, just like Jake had said. He scrambled down the street, cowering in the neighbor's bushes. It felt good to breathe again, but the pain was excruciating. He took short shallow breaths to fill his damaged lungs. Would Manuel squeal? God, he didn't even know if they had survived.

The car was still there. He patted at his front pant pocket, finding the keys for the ignition. In the light of the street lamp he could see that his right hand was badly burned. Just outside of town he would have to stop and clean up. He could still make it to Vegas. He'd get a job somewhere. When Ginny and Morris got the money together to build their gambling house, he could work for them.

He started the car, heading for Main, to get out of town as quickly as possible. Underneath the car seat was a bottle of whiskey. Something he'd hoped to celebrate with after acquiring his fortune. With one hand on the wheel, Eric removed the cork with his teeth, spitting it into the seat beside him. He took a long swallow, immediately coughing up half of it. It spilled on his blistered hand sending a searing pain up his arm to his shoulder.

He jerked the steering wheel back to the center of the road. It had been a dangerous road when it was a stagecoach trail and today it wasn't much better. Two hours ago, the moonless night had been to his advantage, but now it worked against him.

More whiskey might numb the pain. One third of the bottle was gone before he began to feel its effect. He lit a cigarette to take his mind off the pain. His eyes were still painful and tearing from the smoke. Had he seen it clearly and known it was a coyote, he never would have bothered to turn his wheels to avoid the animal. But it was the yellow eyes. The terror in the eyes of the wild, frightened animal was the same terror he had seen on Manuel's face. Unable to control the wheels sliding on the gravel, the old jalopy lurched to the left, tumbling over the rim of the canyon wall. Consumed in darkness, it rolled nearly thirty feet down the slope until it came to rest upside down against a large red boulder. One front wheel spun in ominous silence, like a child's top in its last dying revolutions.

The cigarette dropped from Eric's limp fingers and fell through his open window to ignite a clump of dry grass. The small flame waited patiently for the leaking gasoline to reach it. When the car exploded in a fireball, it lit the desert night like a meteor striking Earth.

Chapter 28

The crowd swirled about the room, mingling with the sounds of soft feminine voices and the clinking of china and silver. Mrs. Wesley's home was every bit as beautiful as the town had always raved. Victorian furniture dated the stately, old home, but then Mrs. Wesley still looked like a Victorian herself, flitting around the house like a butterfly while attending to her guests.

Across the room Brenna sat in a high back chair, surrounded by people she had come to know over a lifetime. These were familiar faces, people that had come and then gone, but not without touching her life. It was easy to see that she was trying to listen politely to the conversations, but her mind was distanced to a different time.

Now and then a slight smile would cross her face, but then the solemn expression returned. Gone were the days when she wore her thick, wavy hair in a tight black bun at the top of her head. It was shoulder length now, turned under with a soft curl and a touch of white at her temple. She balanced a plate of food on her lap picking at it like a small sparrow. Manuel smiled; her navy dress was stylish, yet tasteful, but then she always did hate wearing black.

Once, a long time ago, under the same darkness, he had watched her from afar and wondered how she would survive. She was still a beautiful woman. The lust he had once felt had been replaced with respect and admiration, but he knew he still loved her with all his heart. The other women he had come to know had hovered in her shadow, always secondary to what she was and that which he could never have.

"Grandma!" Roberto wriggled loose from Manuel's grip, darting to his grandmother's side. Brenna's eyes brightened, sighting his young face, preparing to receive his affection.

"I miss you," he said and gave her a hug that squeezed the air out of her.

"Easy *hombre*," Manuel warned. "You're going to break your grandmother's ribs."

"I'm not quite that frail," she reassured him. He embraced her, wishing all the time he could absorb the torment she held inside. How many more times would she have to repeat this scene?

"How is Marita?" she asked.

"It is not good," Manuel answered. "I hate to bring it up now. Haven't you been through enough in one day?"

"I am surrounded by the people who love me," she said. "Marita would have joined us for Eric's funeral had she been strong enough. Of course I want to know how my friend is." He separated her from the crowd, knowing that this would not be easy for either one of them.

"The doctor says she will not recover."

"What are you talking about?"

"The fire isn't what made Marita sick. It made her condition worse, and the doctor says she will gradually weaken until she dies."

His voice had cracked. He had wanted to remain strong for the both of them. But this was his sister he was talking about. A woman who had looked after him in his young life and now who he would have to look after through the end of her suffering.

"You mean she's dying?" Manuel could only nod his head. "Has the doctor said what it is? Why can't she breathe right?"

"The smoke and heat must have aggravated her condition. He says she has a cancer, in her lungs. Kind of like that old consumption we used to talk about. It's affecting her lungs the most right now, but it can spread throughout her body. He thinks those cigarettes she always smoked may have something to do with it."

Manuel thought he saw her waver a little, like a good breeze could blow her over. "Sit down. I told you this was too much. I'll go get you something to drink."

He returned with one of Mrs. Wesley's china coffee cups and handed it to her. "Drink this," he commanded. Brenna took a large gulp of the hot coffee, her eyes widening as she licked her lips.

"Why this is Irish coffee," she said. "And this is more whiskey than coffee."

"You looked like you needed it and I can't find any tequila." And with that, he got a small smile from her.

He left her with Sara and a small gathering of women from the neighborhood. It would be good for her to share her pain.

Food in hand, he found a small table underneath a shady mulberry tree. Pinto sat at the table, Mac by his side. As long as they were outdoors, Manuel figured he could still eat with Pinto. He was relieved to see he had left most of his beans on his plate, but God only knew how much he had already eaten.

"Sad, sad day," Pinto said as Manuel sat down. "That boy was always trouble. Look how he's gone and broke his mama's heart again."

"I never could figure that kid out," Manuel replied. "This whole mess is going to change everything."

"What you mean?" Pinto asked.

"The boarding house is sure to close. It would take more money to repair it than to tear it down and start over. Then there's my sister, dying from lung cancer. If it hadn't been for that damn fire...oh, who knows why things happen the way they do."

"You still reckon it was Eric who pulled the two of you out of the fire?"

"I don't know, Pinto." Manuel shook his head. "I was so confused. If it hadn't been for you, the house would have burned to the ground with us in it. But who was it that hit us on the head? Who started the fire? And if Eric did pull us out of the house, what was he doing there in the first place? There are so many questions that will never be answered."

"I got something to say," Pinto said. Manuel looked up from his food, playing close attention to the old man. "I ain't never told no one this. Something happened a few weeks ago. I thought it was just one a my drunken stupors or maybe even a dream. But the more I think on it, the more I'm certain it was the living truth. You trust me, Manuel?"

"I'm willing to listen to what you have to say."

"Good enough. I was over at The Palace, had my fill a whiskey and decided to sleep some of it off right then and there in the bar. While I was sleepin' I had this dream. At least I thought it was a dream, but maybe it wasn't. I'll let you decide.

"Two men were talking; there were two separate voices. They were making plans on getting into a safe and said it was full a money. One man kept insisting that no one get hurt. The other wanted to know how much he'd get. 'Bout that time I musta slid off the chair 'cause next thing I know I was bein' dragged out the door. Now, what do you make a that?"

Manuel was silent. Pinto has always acted like his mule had kicked him in the head one too many times, but one thing you could bet on, he wasn't a liar.

"This dream of yours, it happened before the fire?"

"Yes, sir."

"You mustn't tell anyone else about this, "Manuel cautioned. "If it were to get back to Mrs. McEvoy it would destroy her. Truth or not, if she thought her son had broken in and then set the house on fire, I don't know what she'd do. Pinto, I just don't know how much more disappointment one person can take. And now that Marita will be leaving us, she won't have a soul to turn to."

"That's just plain not true."

"What do you mean?"

"Well, she's got you," Pinto confirmed. "Yes, sir, I never did figure out why you and her never got hitched."

"What would a fine woman want with an old Mexican like me?"

"Why you and her always, you know, meshed." He interlaced his fingers in front of Manuel. "Any time she ever got in a bind you were there for her and she done the same for you."

"We were just good friends."

Pinto smiled, giving Manuel a devilish grin with his yellow, crooked teeth. "Now, son, you know there was more there than friendship. Everyone could see that. You walked into the room, and she lit up like the summer sun. Never saw her more happy than when she had you by her side, helping her run the house. That day the mines shipped you out on that cattle car, I thought she'd give up livin' right then and there. But all those setbacks, they just made her more determined. Yet I have to agree with you about one thing. Her losin' Marita and Eric and her home. You gotta wonder why so many bad things can happen to such a good person."

* * * *

"Not too long, Marita," the doctor cautioned. "You know how easily you tire."

"I must talk to my friend," Marita argued. Her respirations were fast and shallow. "Doctor, you can leave the room. Manuel, you stay." She struggled for her next breath.

"Everyone else get out of here so I can talk to these two."

"Look at her," Manuel said. "Giving orders from her bed."

"Sit down here, *hija*." She motioned toward Brenna. She took another deep breath, followed by a wet, coughing spasm. Manuel ran to her to pat her back, wanting so desperately to help her breathe, but she shook her head and pushed him aside.

"You cannot help me," she said. "But I can help you. Listen to what I have to say." Here she paused to takes several deep breaths. Her words were deliberate and slow as she worked in breathing with speaking. "Dying is never easy and the cancer will have its way with me. But I still have choices. Here I rest in my own bed among family and friends. I think and remember the years that have passed. Time is short now. Once I did not worry about that. But now I must finish what was started many, many years ago. What I have to tell you… this must not die with me." Brenna looked to Manuel who could only shrug, not knowing what she would say next.

"Listen carefully," she said. "For I can only say this once. Brenna, when your mother and father moved to Bisbee your mother was already expecting you, *verdad?*"

"Yes, that's what I was told."

"Did they ever tell you why they moved to Bisbee?"

"All I ever knew was that Dad was looking for a better job. I guess like everyone else, he was hoping to discover his own mine."

"Perhaps some of that is true," she replied. "But that is not entirely the reason they left California. They had many friends there. They loved the ocean. But they were both running from something."

"Running from what?"

Again Marita paused to take a breath. She placed her hand to her chest and began coughing. She reached for a white mug she kept by her bedside, spitting up blood and sputum.

"You have to stop this," Manuel begged. "You're making yourself worse."

"I helped your mother deliver you," she continued, ignoring Manuel's concerns. "We were both young women then. Hardly either of us had any experience having babies but your Mama trusted me. She was half out of her mind with pain. I was dabbing at her forehead with a cold cloth, trying to comfort her. She mumbled something about a Mexican bastard. I was so surprised. Your Mama never cursed and at first I thought she was talking about me. I didn't say anything. I knew she was suffering and I was used to *gringos* talking to me that way." She paused to take in air and then continued with her story.

"Soon, you decided to arrive. She was so tired I had to push on her belly to get you out. You came out screaming with good, strong lungs, and the first thing she wanted to know was what color you were. 'What color is the baby's skin, what color is the hair?' She didn't even ask if you were a boy or girl. When I told her you have beautiful pink skin and a head of thick black hair, she seemed to settle down. I bundled you up and handed you to her." Marita opened her mouth wide, her chest heaving with each breath.

Manuel could see her color was changing, and her face took on a gray hue. "Marita, you do not look good. You are not getting enough air; please rest."

"Shh," Marita scolded. "This has to do with you too." She returned her attention to Brenna. "Your mama took a long look at you and decided to name you Brenna. In her native tongue it meant Raven, big black birds, and you were sure to keep your black hair. I told her it might lighten, but she shook her head sadly and began crying." Marita raised herself in bed, using her elbow to push herself up. She drew close to Brenna, stopping to glance at Manuel to see if he was listening.

"It was then that she told me about your real father; the man who left the seed in her was Mexican. She had been raped and her husband, the man who raised you as his own, was so outraged and humiliated he took her and ran. And when you were born, they told everyone you were dark Irish. No one knew the difference. It was a new beginning for them. And for you."

"No!" Brenna stepped back as if she would run from the room. "How can you say that? It's a lie."

Marita was wheezing, thirsty for air. "No, *hija*, I tell you the truth. Why would I lie to you now? Brenna, you are half Mexican and half Irish." Brenna kept backing up toward the door, crying and shaking her head. Manuel could say nothing. He felt like he'd been hit with a baseball bat...again.

Marita was now sitting up in bed. "Stop, listen to me, please. I never told you this for this very reason. I don't want to hurt you. But I am leaving now." Tears ran down her sallow cheeks. "You two, you love each other. All these years you thought it wasn't right. Even I was convinced it wasn't right. But, Brenna, you are like Manuel and he is like you. When I am gone, all you will have is each other and Roberto. Don't deny yourself happiness any longer."

"No, no!" Brenna ran from the room.

"Go after her, Manuel. She should not be alone."

He closed his eyes, paused and then opened them again, trying to clear his head. "What do I say to her?" he asked his sister.
"Come closer," she said in a raspy voice. He bent toward the bed, and she reached for him.

"Say what is here," she replied, patting his chest. "Tell her what has been aching in your heart for the last thirty years."

Chapter 29

The rhythm of the squeaking porch swing pierced the air, yet Brenna found it soothing and relaxing. A cool breeze raced across the desert floor and brushed her face.

"Monsoon?" she asked.

"Awful late," he replied. "Still, I can smell the rain on the wind."

"Didn't you say you wanted to go look at that western plot of land before sunset?"

"Patience, woman. It is a beautiful night and should not be wasted."

She slid him an amused look. "Some would call sitting here holding hands a waste of time."

"I am letting my dinner settle."

"I see." She peered curiously at him. "You sure there's not something else on your mind?"

He shrugged. "Well maybe a little something."

"And what's that?"

He squeezed her hand and finally looked at her. "Now that we've taken the big leap, I just want to make sure you haven't changed your mind."

"About what?"

"About still wanting to spend the rest of your life with a one-eared, pot-bellied Mexican cowboy."

"And do you still want to spend your life with a half-breed, gray-haired Anglo?"

Manuel chuckled but quickly sobered. "You know what I regret the most?"

"What?"

"That we never had children of our own."

"It will still be a good life," Brenna assured him. "We have Roberto and Ana. With your family and their ranching experience we can't go wrong. How many cousins did you say were coming from Mexico?"

"Oh, dozens and dozens," he teased. "You better brush up on your Spanish."

"You'll have to build onto the ranch house."

"I'll put my cousins to work on that as soon as they arrive." She smiled and was quiet a while, focusing on the music of the wind-bells dancing in the delicate wind. "I only wish Marita could have seen our ranch."

"I don't think she would have taken it well, knowing the boarding house was destroyed."

"Maybe if she'd known the cash from the safe and the sale of the property went to buy the ranch, she would have accepted it well enough."

"Maybe so."

"Manuel, if those miners come back someday, I'll have to return their money."

"We'll find some way to repay them. I just think it was a burden you needed to be rid of. Let's go look at our land again."

While they walked hand-in-hand across the cracked, crusted earth, their world melted into shades of powder blue and lavender. The saguaros, with their backs to the setting sun, stood like sentries against the colored sky.

"Beautiful, isn't it?" Brenna asked.

"Beautiful but deadly." He kicked at a small tuft of wild grass with the toe of his boot. The grass roots clamped tight to the hardened caliche. "It won't be easy for cattle to survive out here. It will take a lot of land to feed them."

"Look at that big hole," Brenna exclaimed. She released Manuel's hand and walked to the edge of the black opening. The hole was so deep she couldn't see the bottom. It spanned almost eight feet in diameter. Small stones near the edge fell into the pit. She waited to hear them drop.

"Be careful," Manuel grabbed her by the arm, pulling her back. "The ground could be unstable, and I'm not ready to lose you again."

"This must be an abandoned mine. Think it's worth looking into?" Brenna asked.

"Not at the price of copper these days. The only way the mines are making money is with open pit mining. That Lavender Pit that they're going to tear into the ground will leave an ugly hole, just like this one but a lot bigger. But this is dangerous. We need to fence it off from the cattle. This land could be full of these abandoned mines. There were a lot of men looking for dreams they never found."

Manuel continued to wander around the site. "Look here." He reached underneath a nearby tree and pulled out a brown leather boot. It was brittle and cracked, destroyed by the heat and sun.

"Here's another." Brenna handed Manuel its mate. "What do you make of this?"

Manuel turned the boots over, carefully examining each one. "They don't even make these boots anymore. These have to be thirty or forty years old."

"I wonder how they got out here."

"Don't know. More importantly," he replied, tossing the boots down the abandoned mine shaft, "how did the man who wore them get out of here alive?"

"Perhaps he didn't. Perhaps his bones are buried somewhere around here."

"If so, he is long dead and of no consequence to us." He took her hand and they strolled back toward the ranch. Across the stillness of the desert, a nightbird sang, its voice strong; the melody sweet. Surely, the gentle evening breeze would carry forth its beckoning call for a mate whose answering song would signal the beginning of a new life.

ABOUT THE AUTHOR

Josephine DeFalco is a native of Arizona and has spent most of her adult life researching the rich history of the Southwest. Her writing credentials include over a decade of freelance writing, specializing in preventative health. She is a registered nurse, registered dietitian and emergency medical technician (EMT). Apart from her interest in history and health, her hobbies include gardening, food preservation and self-sufficiency. Josephine makes her home in central Arizona, nestled in the Sonoran Desert. Visit her Facebook site at Facebook.com/PioneerInPractice.

Made in the USA
Middletown, DE
28 October 2016